FADE TO SILENCE

David Bradwell

purefiction

FADE TO SILENCE

You know you've got problems when being hunted by a Serbian hitman is the least of your worries...

Balkan gangsters, corporate spies and a fugitive killer are all on the loose in London, but when a body shows up, all of the evidence points to the victim's wife.

Is it a domestic dispute, or part of a much bigger conspiracy? Fresh from suspension for alleged corruption, DCI Graham March seems far too eager to close the case.

Journalist Danny Churchill wants to find the truth - and enlists the help of his flatmate: Anna Burgin. But when reports emerge of a huge shipment of weapons heading to the UK, it soon becomes their most complex, dangerous and action-packed investigation so far.

Packed with twists, intrigue and dark humour, Fade To Silence is book 4 in the bestselling Anna Burgin series.

ABOUT THE AUTHOR

David Bradwell grew up in the north east of England but now lives in Letchworth Garden City in Hertfordshire. He has written for publications as diverse as Smash Hits and the Sunday Times and is a former winner of the PPA British Magazine Writer of the Year Award. Aside from writing, he runs a hosiery company with web sites at www.stockingshq.com and www.tightsandmore.com.

Get in touch at:
www.davidbradwell.com

FADE TO SILENCE

A Gripping British Mystery Thriller - Anna Burgin Book 4

Fade To Silence was first published in 2018 by Pure Fiction
Copyright © David Bradwell, 2018
www.davidbradwell.com

ISBN: 978-1-9997099-4-5

purefiction

The right of David Bradwell to be identified as Author of this work has been asserted by him in accordance with the Copyright, Designs and Patents Act, 1988 This is a work of fiction. Names, places, events and incidents are either the products of the author's imagination or used fictitiously. Any resemblance to actual persons, living or dead, or actual events is purely coincidental.

For Clare Davidson.

Chapter 1

VIOLENT explosions punctured the evening calm, flashing bright and loud in the London sky.

Emma Napier looked up, watching the colours, waiting for the bang.

"The perfect end to a wonderful evening," she said, leaning in to her companion, who in turn gently pulled her towards him. She turned to face him. He leaned down, brushed a strand of dark hair from her face, and kissed her tenderly on welcoming lips.

"My absolute pleasure," he said, giving her a gentle, loving squeeze.

They linked arms and started walking away, leaving behind the warm embrace of the restaurant.

"We should do this more often," she said.

"I can't always promise fireworks."

She smiled.

"We'll have to make some of our own."

He indicated a white Mercedes E Class that was waiting a few yards further down the street. Its engine was running, and a private hire licence plate was displayed just above the rear bumper.

"This is us, I think," he said.

As he approached, the driver lowered his window.

"Taxi for Julian..."

The driver nodded, then stepped out of the car and then opened the rear door for his passengers. It was an unnecessary act of courtesy, but all part of the service.

Once they were both settled in the back, Emma confirmed the address, and the car pulled away. The late evening traffic was light, and the driver expertly carved through west London's backstreets.

"So, what do you fancy for dessert?" she whispered eventually, hand resting on his tautly muscled thigh, the sparkle in her eyes betraying an unambiguous subtext.

"I look forward to you surprising me."

There was no time to discuss it further. The car pulled up outside an upmarket apartment block. Julian paid the driver, and within a few minutes, Emma was in the kitchen, pouring Baileys over ice in two crystal glasses. A few minutes after that, she led him by the hand to the bedroom.

Shortly after 3am, a security light sparked into life as a man in dark clothing approached the rear stairwell of a west London apartment block. He had a bag over one shoulder, a hat pulled down low, and leather gloves protecting his hands. The door at the bottom of the stairwell required a key, but that wasn't a problem. Instead, he waited for the light to go out, to minimise the risk of unwanted attention, and then climbed onto a small adjoining wall. From there it was a small jump across to an opening above the banister on the far side. It was a one-shot deal:

success and he could pull himself up and over, but failure risked a broken ankle, or worse.

He made the jump. It worked. He pulled himself up and then, once safely on the stairs, paused for a moment, scanning his surroundings, watching for anybody who might have noticed him. All seemed clear. The last thing he wanted was to arouse suspicion now.

Four flights of stairs led to a balcony, with a door to the apartment in which Emma and Julian were now sleeping.

So far so good. But now for the difficult part. He looked at the door. Surely it would be locked? Surely things couldn't be that straightforward? He tried the handle anyway, turned it and pushed, but the door didn't give. He bent down to look through the letterbox, being careful not to let it spring back too sharply. All inside was reassuringly dark and silent.

The backup plan was the kitchen window. There were contact sensors for an alarm system, but hopefully it hadn't been set. The window was old, and the wooden frame had buckled slightly. There would be just enough room. He took a metal ruler from his bag and inserted it into the gap, working it back and forth until it connected with the latch. Within a few moments it was released and he pulled the window open. Now he just had to climb inside, without a sound, and without being spotted by an over-attentive neighbour.

He stopped, shrinking back into the shadows. When he was convinced that nobody was watching, he pulled himself up and through the open window, being careful not to dislodge anything, hoping the counter could carry his weight. The only light was the green glow of the microwave clock, but it was enough. His eyes were quick to adjust.

He left the kitchen and found himself in a small hallway. There were four other doors. All but the one at the end were open. He headed towards it, past a spare bedroom, living room and bathroom. He put his bag down on the floor, and pressed the handle, and gently edged the door open, trying his best not to disturb the silence.

Lying in bed, Emma stirred from a deep sleep. She turned, restless, as though something was starting to trouble her subconscious mind. Maybe it was the slight change in temperature as the bedroom door started to open, letting in colder air from the hallway. Maybe it was her base survival instincts sensing that something was seriously wrong. She struggled to open her eyes, and in the split second it took her brain to process the sight in front of her, she let out a piercing scream.

She reached out for her bedside light. The merest touch of the base brought it to life. Julian woke immediately, and saw the man standing at the foot of the bed.

"Who the hell are you?" he shouted, pulling himself up in bed, instinctively putting a protective arm around Emma's naked shoulders.

"More to the point, who the hell are you?" said the man. "This is my flat, my bed. What are you doing with my wife?"

"Shit, Tom, I can explain," began Emma in a voice laced with panic.

"I think it's a bit late for explanations. How long has this been going on?"

"But you're supposed to be away."

Julian reached out to pick his discarded clothes from the floor and hurriedly started to dress under the covers.

"Yeah. And I got back early. I caught an early crossing. I tried calling you when I got back to England, but it just kept going to voicemail. So this is what you get up to while I'm away?"

"No - Jesus. Tom. It's just a one-off. Honestly. It's not what you think."

"I'm pretty sure it is what I think. You know the stupid thing? I couldn't find my door key, but I didn't want to ring the bell because I didn't want to wake you up. I didn't want you to freak out with someone at the door in the middle of the night. So then I thought about the window. And I crept in, as quietly as possible, trying not to wake you out of sheer bloody consideration. Who is he?"

"This is Julian. But ... God."

"Julian? From the Famous fucking Five? Well, he can get the hell out of my flat. And as for you, I can't deal with this."

"Tom, I am so sorry ..."

"You're sorry? It's a bit late for sorry. I'm going in the spare room. Now piss off the pair of you. We'll discuss this in the morning."

As Tom slammed the door of the spare bedroom, Julian finished dressing, then looked at Emma, who was still in bed, with her head in her hands.

"I don't know what to say," he started.

"Just go," she said.

"I had no idea."

"Please, just leave."

He stopped, seemingly torn between wanting to make a quick exit and giving Emma a reassuring hug.

"Go," said Emma, sensing the indecision.

Julian was still doing up the buttons on his jacket as he descended the stairwell, then stopped to properly tie his shoelaces before he crossed the gardens outside the apartment block. His breath was visible in the cold November air.

He opened a gate and then turned left, heading in the direction of a pay and display car park. In the direction of a white

Mercedes E Class, from which a private hire licence plate had recently been removed. Its engine burst into life.

He didn't pause to speak to the driver, just opened the passenger door and climbed inside.

"Well? You got it?" asked the driver.

Julian patted his jacket pocket with a look of satisfaction.

"Yeah, I got it."

"Good boy. Show me."

He took out a Zip disk and handed it over. The driver looked at it carefully in the low sodium glow of a nearby street lamp, then placed it in a clear plastic bag.

"Do you need a lift?"

Julian shook his head. The driver waited until he'd left the car, and then pulled away into the night.

Nine days later, Emma's husband was dead.

Chapter 2

CALM had replaced the violent explosions in the skies over Sarajevo, but harrowing scenes of a humanitarian crisis still filled the screen. The recently agreed Dayton Peace Accord had yet to be signed, but the ceasefire was holding, and the official end of three and a half years of fighting in the Balkans was in sight.

Danny Churchill cast only a cursory glance at the subtitles as the BBC war correspondent gave a live report from the battle-ravaged Bosnian capital. He didn't need the details. His colleagues on the news and foreign desks would be all over it. For now, he'd make the most of the rare luxury of an early morning session at the gym. Thirty more reps on three more machines, then a quick shower before the dash to the Daily Echo office. He'd be on time, if nothing went wrong in the interim.

The correspondent signed off and the subtitled bulletin continued from the studio. A photograph of a man filled the screen. An arrest had been made in the case of the murdered

7

banker Tom Napier, whose body had been found in the car park of the London office of a Swiss private investment bank, Gersbach and Haller, just over two weeks ago.

And then Danny stopped. Suddenly his enthusiasm for the day was replaced with a growing sense of dread and nausea. A reporter was interviewing a high-ranking police officer, but Danny didn't need to read the subtitles to know the officer's name. The rotund face, thinning grey hair and smug smile of self-satisfaction were unmistakeable.

DCI Graham March was back on the Force, cleared for work despite Danny's overwhelming evidence of his corruption, evidence removal, trafficking, brutality, protection and vice. Evidence he'd compiled to back up the suspicions of his former boss, Clare Woodbrook, before her career as an investigative journalist had come to an untimely end.

March was explaining that a woman had been arrested in connection with the crime but no further details could be given. But then he looked straight at the camera, and it was as though he was looking directly into Danny's soul, daring him to try to prove him wrong.

The laughter stopped as Mike Walker entered the room and took his customary place at the head of the table. Others had embraced the recently introduced "dress-down Friday" culture, but the Daily Echo's editor still wore a suit.

The morning conference was a chance for all heads of department to update their boss and their colleagues on the latest developments in ongoing stories, and shape the direction of the paper for the next few days. Since rising to head of the special investigations department, Danny had been a regular attendee, but his relative youth and inexperience still seemed to irk some of his longer-serving colleagues.

Walker started with one of them: news editor Simon Oakley.

"Tom Napier. An arrest was made?" It was a question rather than a statement.

Simon glanced across the table to Danny before starting his update.

"Indeed, late last night. We're on it."

"The details?"

"Word has it his wife's been nicked. Classic case of domestic reprisal."

"Is it straightforward?"

"Seems so."

"And the police involvement? Our old friend DCI Graham March?"

"Yeah, he seems back on form." Simon glanced at Danny again. "He's doing his best to rebuild his reputation."

"Okay, and you've got reporters digging up backstory? I want to see how they met. Where's the wife from? Pictures of the two of them at parties, maybe on holiday. Happy times, then friends, relatives, colleagues giving the insight on where it all went wrong. There's got to be some dark secret. I need you to find it. Understood?"

"Yeah, all in hand."

"Sorry, I've got to speak up." All eyes turned to Danny.

"Go on," said the editor.

"I just don't see it. I saw the news this morning. It's March. I just don't trust him."

Simon Oakley laughed.

"You've got to get over it, Danny. Forget about him. He's a good cop."

"But he isn't."

"You need to learn to put your personal agendas aside. Don't be sore just because he's back putting away the bad guys. Or girls." The addendum was designed to taunt.

"I'm not sore. It's not personal. It's just I don't trust the man. For God's sake, everyone here has seen what he was up to."

The news editor was a veteran of Fleet Street and didn't welcome younger staff members questioning his work.

"Danny, look, I know you've got issues, but forget him. This is news now, not *features*." The last word was delivered with uncompromising contempt. "The CPS wouldn't prosecute if the evidence wasn't compelling."

"But is it? Really?"

"For Christ's sake. There's a recording of him saying her name - Emma - just before she shoots him. He was gay, she was having an affair. The police found his phone and bullets in her flat. She lied about her alibi. Do you need me to go on?"

Danny shook his head, resigned.

"Let's move on," said Walker. "While you've got the floor, Danny, what's the latest on, what is it? Footballers?"

Danny looked down to his notepad, but he already knew what he was going to say.

"Yes. Premier League players betting on matches. Possible match fixing. It's early days but I'm following leads."

"How's it looking?"

"Promising. I've got a lead with a bookmaker ..." He looked up to the editor, who seemed to be assessing.

"I'm not sold."

That came as a shock.

"It'll be good if it stands up."

"No, it's taking too long. It's not really news. Fletcher, do you have an opinion?"

Fletcher McCarthy was the Echo's long-standing, hard-drinking sports editor.

"Think how much the average Premier League footballer earns, and then realise half of them earn even more than that," he said. "Why on earth would they need to risk everything by betting on matches?"

"That's the point," said Danny.

"I agree with Mike. There's not much there. A couple of paragraphs at best in the unlikely event that there's any substance. Slap on the wrist for the player. It's not really worth more than that."

"Thanks, Fletcher," said Walker. "So, Danny, I need something different. Something bigger. Forget the football story. Move on. Now, everyone, what's our angle on Bosnia? Anything new?"

Danny zoned out of the rest of the conference, until the editor gave a progress update on the newspaper's imminent re-location from its traditional home off Chancery Lane to a new building in London's resurgent Docklands.

Was he losing his touch? Or was the sports editor just protecting his friends in the game by persuading the editor to turn a blind eye? Was March really as reformed as he tried to pretend? He couldn't understand why Simon Oakley was suddenly in March's pocket. What schemes and deals were being concocted? Why was all the evidence of the DCI's appalling history being so lightly disregarded? Why were they not digging deeper and deeper until they could finally put him away for good?

At the end of the conference, as everyone else filed out, Mike Walker told Danny to stay behind.

"Shut the door," he said. Danny did so with a sense of foreboding. It felt like being called in front of a particularly imposing headmaster.

"You need to stop fixating on March. Leave him. It's done."

"Okay, but..."

"Not another word. We ran the stories. He got suspended. He redeemed himself and they let him back in. End of story. End of our interest. You need to pull your finger out. And I need something better than footballers and I need it quick. Understood?"

"I'll try."

"You need to do more than try. Reputations count for nothing

11

here, Danny. You don't need me to remind you. If you're not up to the job, you also don't need me to tell you what the options are."

"I'll come up with something."

"Good. Progress report by the end of Monday. No excuses."

Danny closed the door on his way out, and walked across the open-plan editorial floor, towards his corner office. Simon Oakley was back at his desk in the news department, talking on the phone, but his eyes followed Danny with a cold deliberation that warned of trouble to come.

Danny sat at his desk for a while, thinking, trying to decide which of the other possible story ideas he'd had would be the most compelling. The most likely to save his career. None seemed like the obvious solution.

In the old days, before she disappeared, Clare would have known what to do. She'd been the most feared investigative reporter in the country. Danny had been her researcher. She was a master of spinning plates, of seeing the story when others did their best to bury it, and then fearlessly and relentlessly pursuing the truth until a giant front page splash set the national news agenda for days.

But times had changed. She was no longer in the office beside him. Her name was never mentioned. It was as though her legacy had been forgotten. It was days like this when the true scale of the tragedy hit home.

Feeling disillusioned and devoid of inspiration, he logged off his terminal and decided to leave the office and head home. Staying here wasn't going to help. He just needed time and space to think.

He could continue pursuing March, but without the editor's backing, his career would be over before he managed to deliver a line of copy. And yet the policeman's smug smile and the secrets it hid were taunting him. He didn't like to lose. He liked to fight injustice, and March's escape from censure would forever haunt him.

Danny had no sense of the storm that was about to hit.

Chapter 3

THE problem with a glamorous photoshoot in some sun-soaked paradise island is very much the sun-soaked paradise island part. Don't get me wrong, I'm all for a sunny day if I'm on holiday, and I'm not averse to a paradise island, as long as I get a chance to explore its inner secrets rather than just being stuck turning red on a beach. But for the photographer, a week-long shoot is not a holiday. There's lots of work and responsibility in stifling heat, with precious little time to unwind.

The worst of it all is that when you come back, everyone assumes you've had an amazing time. They don't see the slog of carrying equipment in ridiculous temperatures, the technical issues with lighting, and make-up that won't set. The models who discover cocktails and lethargy just as they, in turn, are being discovered by mosquitoes. And yet I wouldn't swap it for the world. I spent years dreaming of building a reputation as a hot, in-demand fashion photographer. I'd just prefer it if we could occasionally do away with the "hot" part.

The other problem, of course, is that when you get home, to London, at the start of December, you end up shivering and disorientated, not quite getting to grips with either the temperature change or the time difference. I wouldn't swap that for the world either, though, because I love living in London. I love the fact I can fix most of my worries with a nice cup of tea, and I love the fact I need never run out of teabags because there's a shop open twenty-four hours every day, just a few minutes' walk away, in Camden. Even if it's technically a petrol station.

When Danny arrived home, I was lost to the world, half asleep on the sofa, listening to Pulp on headphones. I hadn't even unpacked my suitcase, but I'd managed to have a shower and change into my fluffiest pyjamas. Probably not my sexiest look, in fairness, but there was very little chance of looking alluring after a long haul flight. I'd been trying to make sense of a car magazine, having decided it was time to replace my ageing Honda Prelude, but I hadn't got much further than lusting over a Mercedes SLK before my eyes had succumbed to heaviness.

I jumped when I felt his hand on my shoulder, but the momentary sense of panic was soon replaced by an urge to sit up and give him a great big hug. I should have removed the headphones first. The wire wasn't long enough, and they ended up hitting me on the nose.

"Ooh, that looks sore," he said.

"Don't start. Is it bad?" The skin was peeling but that was my own fault for not being liberal with the factor fifty.

He smiled, and we embraced, and I remembered another of my favourite things about being home.

"How was Mauritius? Did you have a fantastic time?"

"It was hard work but I think it'll be worth it. I've got some Polaroids somewhere I can show you. More importantly, how are you? Did you miss me?"

"I always miss you. It's lovely to have you home."

"Or did you just miss me beating you at chess?"

He smiled and joined me on the sofa, resting his hand on my leg. Danny and I have an understanding. We're the best of friends. We share a house. In fact, we've lived together since our student days. It's six years now and counting. We're not lovers, although we do love each other in our own particular ways. I spent most of that time loving him in all sorts of ways that I didn't dare mention in case it ruined a friendship, but I've successfully managed to move on now. That's my official version of events, anyway, so I'm sticking to it, and trying to persuade myself that it's true. In recent weeks we've had an ongoing chess tournament, in which I'd won the last five matches.

"How's the gym going?" I asked. "Have you had the audition for Gladiators?"

"Haha. I'm *not* trying to go on Gladiators."

"You clearly are. Got a little thing for Jet, have we? Lightning?"

He laughed.

"I really have missed you. But could you go away again?"

"Let me feel your arms first."

"No."

"Just a little squeeze."

"No."

"Spoilsport. What is the point of going to the gym if you don't want to show off your lovely arms?"

He moved away slightly, out of my reach.

"You just reach a certain age when you need to look after yourself."

"Oh, I forget you're nearly thirty. Thirty, Danny. Halfway to sixty."

"I'm twenty-six."

"That's close enough. It's like you're turning into a proper grown-up. And how's work?"

"God. Don't even ask."

He closed his eyes and leaned back.

"That doesn't sound good. Still looking into the footballers?"

"That's been knocked on the head. I've got to come up with something new by Monday."

"Not good. What happened?"

"Mike decided against it. It's like the whole thing's a conspiracy. It's getting worse."

He sighed, and I really did feel for him.

"What are you going to do?" I asked.

"First and foremost, almost certainly end up making a cup of tea for you."

"Excellent plan."

"And then spend the weekend trying to come up with something. I've got a few other things on the go, but nothing that's particularly earth-shattering."

"Can you go back and have another crack at Graham March?"

By his expression I gathered that was the wrong suggestion.

"I've even been warned off that. You know the absolute injustice? He was on TV this morning. Remember the bank bloke who got found dead in the car park? March has arrested his wife, and suddenly he's basking in the glory on breakfast TV."

"That doesn't mean he's not up to something."

"No, he's obviously up to something, but I've been told to lay off him."

"Why, for heaven's sake?"

"You tell me. Friends in high places."

We lapsed into a thoughtful silence until Danny broke it by asking me questions about the trip, and, eventually, getting the hint that a cup of tea would be very nice indeed.

"So, what should we do tonight?" I asked when he returned. "I'm thinking we should phone out for a takeaway and then I was going to have an early night, but if you want to rent a video I'll try to stay awake."

"No, you're okay. Takeaway's good, but I should probably start trying to brainstorm. See if I can surprise myself."

"That reminds me, you had a parcel."

"A parcel?"

"It's on the desk, in a Jiffy bag. Have you been ordering some of your special interest films while my back's been turned?"

"I get those sent to work."

I hoped he was joking.

He moved across to the desk on the far side of the room, and then returned with the package.

"Is it an early Christmas present?" I asked.

"I've got no idea."

Inside the parcel was a box. There was no covering letter. Danny looked at me.

"Do you think it's a bomb?"

I laughed. "Is it ticking?"

He raised it to his ear, then shook his head.

"Go on, then," I said.

Danny peeled back the edge of the Sellotape and then removed the lid. The contents were covered in bubble wrap. He started to remove that too, until he was left with two mobile phones and their respective chargers.

"That's weird. Have you ordered a new phone?" I asked.

"No. Have you?" I shook my head.

He passed one to me for closer inspection. And no sooner had I started to play with the flip-down front than it started to ring.

Chapter 4

I STARED at it as though I'd never come across a phone before.

"What should I do?" I asked.

"Answer it?"

I hesitated, then pressed the green button.

"Hello," I said, with considerable caution.

"Anna?"

"Speaking." But immediately I recognised the hint of a long-faded Wearside accent, and felt an involuntary glow. "Clare?"

"Hi, yes it's me."

"Wow, where are you?"

"You know I can't answer that."

"Okay, how are you?"

"I'm fine, doing okay. Is Danny there?"

I looked at him. He was asking questions with his eyes.

"He is. He's right beside me."

"Are you on your own?"

"Yes, it's just the two of us."

"Perfect. Can you press the button again and put me on speaker?"

"Which one?"

"The green one."

"One moment."

I pressed the button.

"Are you there?"

"I am. Hi Anna, hi Danny. How are things?"

"Clare," said Danny. "Long time no speak. How are you?"

"I'm okay, Danny. You got the phones then?"

"We did, we just opened them."

"Excellent."

Danny looked at me. I shrugged. I didn't have a clue either. Clare had been his boss at the Echo before she'd turned into an international criminal and exceptionally accomplished fugitive. But despite her faults, and my natural misgivings (not least about Danny's obvious devotion, never mind the time she'd pointed a gun at us) she'd earned my respect in unforeseen ways. We hadn't so much as heard her voice in over a year, but she had a habit of turning up when she was least expected.

"There's one each," she continued. "There are two numbers programmed in. One for the other phone, and one for me. If you need to call me, use these phones. Do not - and I cannot overstress this - use them to call anyone else. Okay?"

I looked at Danny again.

"Okay," he said. "Does that mean we can call you whenever we want to?"

"Of course." She said it as though it was entirely normal, as though her regular disappearing-off-the-face-of-the-earth act was not a thing.

"Are you back? What are you up to?" he continued.

"Danny, I'm never back, and I've never really gone away. But technology moves on, and there are a couple of things I wanted to talk to you about. How's work?"

"Ticking along. All going well. I won't ask you the same."

"Excellent news, and no, probably safest."

She wasn't joking about the safety. Clare moved in some dark circles. After a couple of minutes of small talk, in which we caught up while simultaneously learning nothing, she finally came to the point.

"I saw Graham on TV this morning." She'd never been a fan.

"He's the flavour of the month at the moment apparently," said Danny. "I've been told to lay off him."

"Who by?"

"Mike."

"That's weird. Although it's one of the things I wanted to talk to you about. Did it seem feasible to you, that it was the banker's wife?"

"I've not really been following the story. But no, I very much suspect not, not if he's involved."

"Exactly. I don't want to say too much on the phone, but I'm absolutely certain that Emma is innocent."

"How come?"

"Let's just say, I've come across that particular bank and I've heard of a few of the people involved. I think you should investigate it."

Danny's expression was tainted by frustration.

"The news department's already on it. You know what Simon's like. That's the last thing he'd want me to get involved in."

I tried to sneak a quick feel of his arm while he was otherwise distracted, but he was too quick for me.

"Danny, listen," Clare continued. "You've got to come up with a new story by Monday."

"Whoa, how did you know that?"

"The same way I knew you weren't telling the complete truth when you said it was all going well. What are you doing tomorrow? Could you give me an hour of your time to go through everything that I've learned? The pair of you?"

I was secretly quite excited about the thought of meeting

Clare again, and was hoping Danny would say yes. I found her fascinating, even though I hadn't always been her biggest admirer.

"I'm free all day so yeah, of course," said Danny. "Pick a time and tell me where and I'll meet you there. Anna's nodding as well."

"Fantastic. It'll be great to see you both again."

My heart did a little excited leap.

"So when and where, then?"

"Well, there's the thing. It will be really good if you could pop down to see me at my country residence."

"You've got a country residence?" I said, suspecting there was definitely more to that than she would ever let on.

"Let's just say it's temporary," she said. "Did you get any other post this morning as well as the package?"

Danny looked at me.

"I think you had a couple of bills or junk mail," I said.

"That sounds promising," said Clare. "Can you go and open them?"

"Very mysterious," I said, while Danny went over to the table.

"Hopefully you'll find a couple of train tickets."

"Train tickets? Where on earth are you?"

"I'll tell you that tomorrow," she said.

Danny returned with the envelope, opened it and found the tickets.

"Got them," he said.

"Perfect. Sorry about the early start, Anna. You must be exhausted after your trip, but bring an overnight bag and I'll make it up to you. Any problems, you've got my number. I look forward to it." She paused. "Take care, and enjoy the takeaway. Oh and Danny, The World's Strongest Man is coming on TV in a moment. You might be able to get some tips. I've got to dash but I look forward to seeing you tomorrow."

There was laughter in her voice as she disconnected the call.
I turned to Danny.

"How did she know about my trip?"

Danny sighed.

"You know, if it was anybody else I'd be freaked out."

"Or the takeaway? Do you think she's still bugging us?"

"I don't even want to begin to think about it."

Danny looked at the tickets, and then looked at me. He handed them over.

"Where on earth is Totnes?" I asked.

"I think it's Devon."

"What? Surely she's not being serious?"

Apparently she was.

DCI Graham March knocked on the door of the office, but didn't wait for a response before walking in.

The man on the other side of the desk put down his pen, then stood up and reached over to give him a warm handshake.

"Quite a success," he said. "You've done very well."

"I try my best," said March with a smile. He didn't wait to be offered a seat before taking his place on a low sofa in front of a bookcase.

The man walked across to a cabinet and took a bottle of whisky and two crystal glasses from a shelf. He put the glasses on the coffee table in front of March and poured a measure into each.

"A toast to new beginnings," he said.

March nodded and took a sip.

"I assume it's cast-iron?"

"Beyond reasonable doubt," said March.

"Can you give me a one-minute summary?"

March settled back into the well-worn leather of the sofa, and coughed to clear his throat.

"I had my suspicions from the outset," he said. "I mean, it's usually the wife when it's a domestic. The secretary found the body. Nice girl, bit ditzy - would, though, if she asked me to."

Both men laughed at the innuendo.

"Then she discovered a voice message on her office answerphone," March continued. "It was Tom saying 'Emma, no!' just before she pulled the trigger. His phone wasn't found at the scene, but we discovered it in their flat, down the side of the sofa. Stands to reason the killer took it, and stands to reason therefore it had to be Emma."

"And the bullet that killed him?"

"From the same batch as the murder weapon found in the flat."

The man looked pleased, and raised his glass in tribute.

"When did you go to see her?" he asked, after taking a drink.

"I went with the lovely DC Lisa Miller to break the news. The evidence was found later. Miller asked Emma where she'd been the previous evening and she said she'd been at a charity fundraiser in Birmingham and only arrived home about half an hour before we got there. Said she had been stuck in traffic on the M1. I looked at her car as we left, and there was frost on the bonnet, so I knew she was making that up."

The man nodded.

"Then the next time we went to see her, she admitted to an affair, and told us Tom had been going to a gay club. So, there's your motive as well. After that we found the evidence. I mean, obviously I'll get the credit, but I'll make sure that the team are congratulated for their efforts. Tragic really, and a bit of a waste, because she had a nice face on her, but professionalism shines through."

The desk phone started ringing. The man got up to answer it then put his hand over the mouthpiece.

"I've got to take this," he said in a low voice. "I'll see you at the club later, and we'll have a proper celebration."

March nodded, finished his whisky, and then turned to leave the room, closing the door gently behind him. It was good to have friends with influence.

Chapter 5

PADDINGTON Station was full of noise and diesel fumes, even at half past nine on a Saturday morning. Danny and I took our seats in a first-class carriage of the InterCity 125, courtesy of Clare's generosity. I wasn't convinced we'd still be admiring the altruism in a day or two. Danny tried to show off his new muscles by lifting our overnight bags onto a luggage rack that was beyond my reach, but the bags weren't even particularly heavy, and I think he made a bit of a meal of it.

"Do you think this is slightly weird?" I asked when he'd settled down beside me.

"It is, completely, but if nothing else it'll be good to see her again," he said.

"Assuming she even turns up. It feels a bit like we're characters in an Agatha Christie book, heading to a remote location, where we'll meet up with a group of strangers and all get murdered, one by one. She's even got us travelling from Paddington, for heaven's sake."

Danny laughed.

"We shall stick together then," he said. "At the first sign of anybody being poisoned, we're on the first train back."

"What if we're stuck on an island and the ferry captain's the first to be poisoned?"

"Look for the Belgian bloke with the moustache and stick close by him."

The journey passed more quickly than I'd imagined, partly because I was enjoying the relative novelty of the first-class carriage, and partly because I was still worn out after my trip. I woke up in time to enjoy a genuinely scenic stretch of track that rang along the Devon coastline. I'd never been to Devon before, but imagined it would be full of rolling fields and grazing cows, with thatched cottages and tiny, winding country lanes. It looked like I wasn't too wide of the mark as we approached our final destination.

"What now?" I said, when we'd disembarked at Totnes. It was a tiny station and felt a very long way from home. A gate from the platform led directly to the car park with a taxi rank on the right, but there was no point getting a taxi as we hadn't the first idea where we were going.

"Presumably she'll pick us up," said Danny.

"Can she do that? Can she be seen in public? She's supposed to be on the run."

He didn't get a chance to answer before we were approached by a small man with a moustache, carrying a card with our names on it.

"What if he's Belgian?" I hissed, as he approached, and I got a warning nudge for my troubles.

"Danny Churchill? Anna Burgin?" he asked, in a West Country accent, much to my relief. We nodded. "I thought as much. Come on then, my lovelies."

He led the way to the taxi rank, where a yellow Peugeot 405 was waiting.

"Where are we going?" I asked, as he left the station car park

27

and pulled into traffic. I say traffic, but it was nothing like the relentless pace of life in Camden.

"Not far, my dear," he replied, and then started asking us about our journey, and what we did, and started pointing out some of the local landmarks. We passed a spectacular water wheel at the side of a building, crossed an incredibly narrow single-track stone bridge over a beautiful river, and then drove past an even smaller train station.

"Did you see that?" I asked, nudging Danny. "An actual steam train. That's amazing." It was like stepping back in time, to a more innocent era. Even the road signs looked like something from a forgotten age.

Eventually we pulled up outside a pub called the Sea Trout Inn. I tried to give the driver money but he said it had all been paid for. He opened the doors for us, and retrieved our bags, before giving us a cheerful wave and leaving us stranded, seemingly in the middle of nowhere. Even the air was different. It was so much cleaner than London, albeit with the faintest hint of a farmyard tang.

Danny took his new mobile phone from his pocket.

"I'll ring Clare," he said. Then he looked at me with a bemused frown. "No signal."

"We are so getting murdered."

"Not if I can help it," said a voice from behind us. "Welcome to Staverton." We both turned and there she was, grinning mischievously, as though a carefree tourist rather than international fugitive and part-time assassin. She had yet another new hairstyle, even darker, but it suited her.

"How do you do that?" I said.

"Come on, follow me," she said, ignoring my question. "What have you done to your nose?"

"Don't start."

We picked up our bags and followed her through a cosy-looking pub, and up a small flight of stairs. She opened a door and led us through into a double bedroom.

"Your home for the night," she said.

"Have you gone into the hospitality trade?" asked Danny.

"No, but I'm not far away."

"And did you book a double deliberately?" I asked.

"Are you two not together yet?" The look of innocence was almost convincing. But Clare didn't do anything by chance. As ever, I was slightly in awe of her.

"Sort yourselves out and I'll meet you downstairs," she said. "Twenty minutes?"

We were down in five.

Clare rose as she saw us, and headed our way. I was rather hoping for something to drink, but instead she told us to follow, and led the way outside. It was cold in the early December afternoon, especially compared to Mauritius, and I was grateful for my scarf.

"I'll make sure we're back in time before they close after lunch," she said, "but let's just go for a little wander."

It looked like a tiny village in the middle of nowhere, but Clare was big on intrigue. We made small talk as we walked down a single-track lane. Just before it disappeared into the woods, she turned and led us through a gate, into a beautiful churchyard.

"So," she said at last, "I suppose you're wondering why I've brought you all this way. Thanks for coming, by the way."

"Something to do with the shooting of Tom Napier," said Danny. "You said you had your doubts."

I decided to hang back a little while they talked shop. I wasn't quite sure why I was there, but I was enjoying myself anyway. I tried to spot the oldest gravestone, but they were so weathered it was impossible to read most of the inscriptions. So many lives had ended, but in a bizarre way it was strangely uplifting to know they were at rest in such a peaceful setting. Talk of murder seemed out of place, even in a graveyard.

"Exactly. March has arrested his wife, but I don't think she did it. None of it makes much sense," Clare continued.

"Agreed, although I don't have any particular reason aside from not trusting the man. I said I wasn't convinced at the conference yesterday, but nobody wanted to listen. Apparently the evidence is compelling."

"I do miss the morning conference." I looked up at Clare when she said that, and caught a wistful expression. "But you know what compelling evidence means? It means she may have done it, which is always a possibility, or - much more likely - it was a professional job with a successful cover-up."

"But why? And why are you interested in it?"

We came to a gate. Danny opened it and we all filed through, into an even narrower lane. Clare took a deep breath, then paused to light a cigarette. She offered us both the packet, but we refused as she knew we would. One of these days I'll accept, just to shock her.

"Danny, you're familiar with the Bosnian war, with Serbia, Croatia and all of that?"

"Of course."

"And you know it's officially ending?"

"Yeah, the agreement's done, aside from being officially signed."

"Exactly. Well, imagine the guns haven't stopped, so much as faded in volume. Bear that in mind, because it underpins everything."

"Okay. Curious."

She took a deep drag of the cigarette. Looking pensive, she continued.

"I've spent a bit of time in Bulgaria recently, and I've heard Tom Napier's name mentioned on more than one occasion."

"Wow, okay. In relation to what?"

"I'm coming on to that."

"What were you doing in Bulgaria?"

"This and that. Making a living. Didn't we set a load of ground rules about these kind of questions?"

"We did, but if you want me to get involved in something, you may have to tell me."

"Oh, Danny."

When it was clear that he wasn't going to let her off the hook, she resumed.

"Look, when the Wall came down, the Bulgarians voted the Communists back in. They don't like to make a fuss. And lots of people in the party were given suitcases full of cash to buy factories. The trouble is, they don't know how to run them. I know people in other countries, like Germany, who do, so there's an opportunity to match buyers and sellers, okay?"

"And it's all, you know, legal?"

"Obviously. Who do you think I am?"

"Can I get away with not answering that?"

I couldn't help but smile. Luckily, Clare did too. There was always a strong possibility she could shoot us if we made her angry, but so far she'd always been on our side.

"Anyway," she continued, "Bulgaria has a border with Serbia. It's about two hundred miles long, so it's significant. And the Bulgarians make it their business to know what's going on next door. We're not talking idle gossip. We're talking security services, government officials, that kind of thing."

"Spies?"

"Exactly."

I was already starting to feel a sense of foreboding.

"Despite the close links to Serbia, Bulgaria was one of the countries supplying arms to Croatia and Bosnia, all routed through Vienna," she continued. "The UK was even involved, unofficially. There was supposed to be an embargo, but there was money to be made. And now the war's ending, there's chaos everywhere, plus a rush to move assets out of the region to avoid the potential of hyperinflation."

I could see Danny was intrigued, but was as clueless as I was.

"Okay, but how does this relate to Tom Napier?" he asked.

"Well, to cut a long story short, one of the people wanting to move money out of Serbia was a nasty local bastard called Miroslav Nikolić. Miroslav wanted to invest through Gersbach and Haller in London, and Tom was handling it for him."

"Illegally?"

"No, all above board, at least on the surface. But recently Tom had a bad run and lost a lot of money, which didn't seem to go down very well."

"Kind of like a Nick Leeson?"

"They were talking about Leeson on the radio this morning," I said. "He's just been sentenced."

"Indeed, but not on that scale. Though it was painful enough for Miroslav."

Clare stopped as we reached a railway line. In the distance we heard the sound of a train whistle, and then the sound of a steam engine puffing, getting closer.

"You'll like this," she said.

She wasn't wrong. A few seconds later, the train appeared around the corner, chuffing its way towards us. The driver tooted his whistle, and I felt the compulsion to wave. It was like stepping fifty years back in time.

"It's mainly for tourists, but I love it here," she said, once the train had passed. We crossed the line, then made our way over a weir onto a pebbled island surrounded by trees, with the river flowing past. It was utterly tranquil, and I imagined about as big a contrast to the Bosnian battlefields as it was possible to be. Maybe that was the point.

"I still don't understand your connection," said Danny, leaning on a tree.

"I've got a contact in Sofia called Georgi," Clare continued. "He's one of those in the know, if you know what I mean. He's been keeping an eye on Miroslav and his money movements, and when he heard about the shooting he mentioned it to me. I suppose he thinks it's on my patch."

"So, the thinking is what? It's some sort of punishment hit, and this Serbian killed him?"

"It could be punishment, or perhaps revenge, especially if the money was needed for something urgent." Clare picked up a stone and skimmed it across the river. It bounced five times before settling and sinking. "Not necessarily, though."

"How come?" asked Danny

"This is where it gets a bit complicated."

Pebble skimming looked like good fun. My first attempt bounced six times. I was ecstatic.

"Beginner's luck," said Clare, albeit with a smile. I knew she'd now need to do seven.

"Complicated, how?" asked Danny.

"It could have been Miroslav," she replied, "but equally maybe someone targeting him for working with the Serbians in the first place. Maybe someone from Croatia, wanting to continue the battle in a boardroom, or maybe even a rival Serbian gang. Possibly Russians, Germans, or pretty much anyone."

"Or maybe just a random mugging?"

"It's not that. Don't forget the cover-up. His phone and matching bullets were found at their flat. Either way, Tom was at the heart of it. He's been involved with some bad people. That made him a target before he even lost the money, but then when it all went wrong it got ten times worse."

She tried again and matched my six.

"The entire region's awash with guns after the war," she continued. "Anybody could have shot Tom, but whichever way you look at it, it's unlikely to be his wife. Any of the above would have the expertise to frame her."

"You've got no idea who it could have been, though?" asked Danny. "This Georgi hasn't heard anything?"

"No, Georgi just alerted me to Tom a few weeks ago. I've got another colleague who's been taking a bit more of an active interest."

"Is this going to get even more complicated?"

I couldn't resist joining in.

"I like the way you say colleague, as though you share an office."

"Okay, associate then."

"Who is he? Or she?" asked Danny.

"He's a German I've done some work with. Otto."

"And what does Otto do?"

"That's not important."

"It might be."

Clare paused. It looked like she was assessing the risk of revealing too much.

"Otto helps me find buyers in Germany. Let's leave it at that."

"Okay," said Danny. "Does he have any ideas?"

"That's what I'm trying to find out, but I've struggled to get hold of him. He's not always the most accessible."

Danny paused and attempted to skim a stone. It went straight in without bouncing at all. Happy days.

"Did Tom have any specific enemies that we know of?" he asked.

"It's a shady world, Danny, that's what we've got to find out. We need to find out what happened and..." She stopped.

"And?"

"Well, if it was a cover-up and Emma has been framed, we need to discover why our old friend Graham was so keen to arrest her. Was he simply naive? Or, more intriguingly, was he on the payroll?"

And that was it. No matter how dangerous this all sounded, that was the moment that Danny was hooked. And the moment that changed our lives forever.

Chapter 6

MIROSLAV Nikolić sat in the back of a black Mercedes, parked on the top level of a multistorey car park near Harrods in Knightsbridge. His chauffeur was standing outside, leaning on the bonnet of the car, waiting out of earshot.

The London Evening Standard lay folded on the seat. Tom Napier's face stared out from the front page, along with that of his wife. The photograph was from a high society charity fundraising event from the previous year.

Miroslav turned to the man next to him.

"You did well to keep me out of it," he said.

"My pleasure. I didn't see the need to bring your involvement to anyone's attention."

Miroslav flinched at the word "involvement".

"Very wise, Graham. Let's make sure it stays that way. And I trust we can keep this between us."

"It goes without saying."

DCI Graham March took a business card from his wallet.

"If there's anything else you need, or anything happens, this is where you'll find me."

"I already have your card."

"This is the one for what I like to call my freelance endeavours, if you know what I'm saying."

"I think I do."

Miroslav looked out of the window, across the rooftops of west London.

"But I am merely a businessman," he added. "I would hope that it is unlikely."

"Of course. But you never know. I am keen to foster good international relations."

"I'm sure you are."

March reached out and shook hands with the Serbian, then opened the door, and headed for his own car on the far side of the car park.

Miroslav watched him go and then tapped a number into his mobile phone.

"Update?"

"Everything is progressing well. Nearly at Timișoara. Do you need me to speak to anyone?"

Miroslav thought for a moment.

"Maybe. I'll let you know. Extreme times may call for urgent measures."

"But you're happy with the progress?"

"I'll be happy when I don't need to think about this any more."

He cut the call, then signalled to the chauffeur, who got back behind the wheel.

"Where to now, sir?" he asked.

"Straight home," said the Serbian. He had some planning to do.

We left the riverbank, and started walking back towards the pub.

"Come on, I'll buy you lunch," said Clare.

As we settled back into a steady pace, I made a confession.

"You know, I'm ashamed to say it, but I've got completely lost with the war and who's on which side," I said. "It's been on the news every night for about the last three years, but it just seems like endless fighting, and nobody ever really explains it."

"It's been horrendous," said Clare, opening a gate for us, and then following us through. "The Serbs have done some horrific things, but Croatia did much the same to Serbia when they joined with the Nazis in the Second World War. This time, Serbia started fighting with Bosnia. Croatia joined in to help the defence, but then started attacking Bosnia as well. The whole thing has been tragic, really. And some of the atrocities..."

"I know. It doesn't even bear thinking about. I do feel privileged to come from a country that's fundamentally peaceful."

"I know what you mean." She put her arm through mine, which was oddly reassuring. "But believe me, you appreciate it even more once you move abroad."

It was there again. Every so often I got a glimpse of the real person behind the mask, the real emotion behind the calm, controlling façade. She could be ruthless, and kill a man in a heartbeat, but occasionally there was a tinge of something that seemed like sadness. No matter how much money she'd made since crossing to the dark side, she had deep regrets. I longed for the day that she'd trust me enough to let me in. She must be needing a friend. I wasn't sure she'd ever had one.

"How do I speak to this Otto?" asked Danny, bringing the subject back to the present.

"I expect he's lying low," said Clare. She suddenly looked a bit shifty. "And that is a bit complicated as well. You haven't asked me how he came to be investigating Tom."

"That sounds ominous," said Danny.

"Not really, just delicate. You heard Tom was gay and Emma was having an affair?"

"Apparently."

"Well, the man she was having an affair with was working for Otto."

"He was *what?*"

"He was only supposed to get close to her, to find out more about Tom, but he was a typical man. Took things too far once he got an ounce of encouragement."

"Jesus."

"Emma worked for a charity dealing with Romanian orphanages, and all of that, trying to do good in the world, using her social position to give something back. All very noble."

"Not really the mindset of a murderer."

We started back across the churchyard.

"Exactly, but she obviously had a weakness. She met him at a fundraiser and seems to have fallen for him. You can't blame her. Tom was clearly occupied elsewhere."

"At his gay club?"

"At the very least. The trouble is, if the police had looked too closely at Julian, they could have started asking some very awkward questions."

"Did they not try to find him?"

"I've read the reports. Apparently March thought she was making him up. He put minimal effort into finding him and gave up. The charity she said he was working for had never heard of him, so March decided she'd invented him to fake an alibi. That's fundamentally shit policing from Graham, but quite handy for us."

"And Julian can't have been involved in the shooting?"

"No, Otto is one of the good guys. If I can track him down I'll see if he can put us in touch with Julian to see what he knows. In the meantime Georgi may be able to give us more information on Miroslav." There was a pause as we navigated a pile of leaves that somebody had carefully swept together, then Clare turned to Danny. "So, what do you think? Do you think it'd make a story?"

"It's definitely a story if there's something in it, but I think it sounds very dangerous."

"There's always danger, Danny. But you've got a quite-possibly-innocent woman on remand. You can fix that, write a brilliant exposé, and wipe the smug smile off March's face. Quite the hat trick."

Danny nodded, but I didn't like the sound of it. Gun-toting Balkan gangsters sounded terrifying. I rolled my eyes but nobody noticed.

"And I can help you, within the boundaries of officially not existing."

It seemed like the deal was done. There was little point in me raising an objection on the basis of my experience in seeing how things could get out of hand.

"So where should we start?" asked Danny.

Clare started to smile. It looked like she was up to something.

"I've got a plan for that, but I'll tell you this evening. The most important thing at the moment is lunch."

Clare asked the waitress at the Sea Trout Inn for a table for three, although the entire place was empty. I decided the other guests, if there were any, must be out, making the most of the countryside.

The waitress gave us lunch menus, and returned to the bar. Clare said it was her treat. I wondered if it was still a bit early for a Sauvignon Blanc before remembering it never is, so asked for a large one. Danny opted for a pint of Dorset Gold, which was some form of beer, and we both decided on the club sandwich. Clare went to the bar to place the order and returned with the drinks, including a glass of wine for herself.

"So, is this your local?" I asked.

She smiled at me, and lit another cigarette.

"You want to know if I've moved here?"

"I did kind of wonder. You seem very much at home."

"I pass through occasionally. I used to spend the summers here when I was little. My mum grew up in Staverton, so we came back during the holidays."

"That's a hell of a way from Sunderland."

She laughed.

"Many happy hours playing I-Spy on the motorways. Anyway, what's new with you two? Are you an item yet? And if not, why not?"

"We're very much the best of friends," said Danny.

"And you know my less than stellar record with men," I added, then immediately regretted it.

Danny perked up and I sensed imminent disaster.

"Oh go on, this sounds interesting," he said, every inch the investigator.

He looked at me, then Clare, waiting for one of us to speak. I blushed. I don't keep secrets as a rule, but the night Clare helped me out of a tricky situation with a former boyfriend called Mitch was very much one of them.

I felt Clare's leg nudge mine under the table as she came to my rescue again.

"Nothing too sinister, Danny," she said. She stopped speaking. A moment later, a man appeared at the far end of the bar. It was as though she had a sixth sense. Maybe that's what helped her hang onto her liberty. The man looked our way, but then turned and left again.

"It's okay, he's a local," she said, probably more to herself than us. She flicked her cigarette into the ashtray and turned back to Danny.

"This was last year while you were in the hospital. Anna and I had a long chat. She was telling me about her student years. Todd wasn't it?"

"It was." How on earth did she know about Todd? That was a chapter of my life that I never discussed with anyone.

"I'd almost forgotten about him," said Danny.

"Yeah, well let's change the subject." I took a sip of the wine. "I heard a brilliant joke about herbs and fish, but I can't tell you it now. It's neither the thyme nor the plaice."

They both looked at me as though I was a bit odd. I continued, unperturbed.

"What about you then, Clare? Are you still single or have you finally met someone?"

"It's interesting that you assume I've been single," she said.

"Wow. Weren't you? You never mentioned anyone, so I always assumed."

"And Danny can tell you the golden rule on that."

"Never assume anything," he said.

"God, not this again." I looked to Clare. She had the expression of a benevolent aunt, albeit an incredibly glamorous one. "So?"

"So what?"

"So have you got a boyfriend?"

"Why would I want a boyfriend? I'm thirty-three."

"Well, you know, for all those things that are better shared with someone."

"You mean sex?"

"Well, I..." I blushed again. She laughed and turned to Danny and started quizzing him about the imminent office move. Clearly she missed her former life as a journalist.

Conversation paused as the waitress approached with the sandwiches. I was ever so pleased. Not because I didn't find it fascinating, but because I was absolutely famished.

"Are you not eating?" I asked when I realised there were only two plates.

"No, I'm okay," she said. "You two tuck in."

I didn't need asking twice.

When we'd finished, the waitress hovered at the bar, looking in our direction. It was long past closing time.

"Let's continue this later," said Clare. "I've got some things to do this afternoon, but I'll come and pick you up around seven and take you to dinner and tell you about how we can get started. Plan?"

We both said yes. Clare stood up, and gave us both a hug.

"It's good to see you both again," she said. I could see her looking at me, sensing my nervousness.

"It'll be okay, Anna," she said. "It may sound dangerous but I'm sure it'll be fine."

I had my doubts. And, as it transpired, with very good cause.

Chapter 7

DCI Graham March pocketed the change and picked up the drinks. Detective Constable Lisa Miller was waiting for him in a booth towards the back of a quiet bar, close to their station near Holborn.

He put the drinks on the table, then squeezed in next to her. Lisa moved slightly to her right, to give him more room. March closed the gap again.

"A toast to a successful outcome," he said, chinking his pint glass against Lisa's white wine.

"To teamwork," she said.

"I have to say, I've been very impressed with your contribution," he continued, once they'd both taken a sip.

"Thank you. It was a good fun case, if you take the gore out of it. You're confident it'll stand up in court?"

"Oh, no question. You saw the evidence. You helped to uncover it." He smiled. At twenty-seven she was only around half his age, but he could recognise potential, albeit not just in policing.

"You could go far, with the right guidance," he continued. "Are you ambitious?"

"I like to think so."

"That's good. What I like to call very encouraging. I'll put a word in for you. Stick close to me, and you'll go far."

"I'll bear that in mind," she said.

March took another drink, then put his glass back on the table, making sure his knuckles brushed the back of his DC's hand. Lisa moved her hand away.

"Is it true what they say about redheads?" he asked, after a moment.

"That depends who 'they' are. And what you've heard."

"Oh, you know. Just the usual. Fiery, independent, passionate lovers."

"We tend to take no nonsense, if that's what you mean."

She tried to edge away again, but there was nowhere to go.

"Ah, that's a good thing. I like a girl who gets straight to the point. Knows what she wants and isn't shy about getting it."

"I bet you do. And do you meet many of them?"

"My fair share. I've got considerable influence, as you might have heard."

"I've heard all sorts, boss."

"Hey, keep the 'boss' for when we're on duty. Call me Graham when we're in private."

He winked. Lisa drew a breath.

"Okay. Graham."

"And I've heard the scurrilous rumours to which you refer. I'm not naive. But the truth is, I've ruffled a few feathers over the years. What's the expression? You can't make an omelette without cracking a few heads." He laughed at his own joke. "All I'd say is, judge me as you find me. I can be your best friend. Your closest ally. I've been around the block, know the ropes, got the scars to prove it, but I've nailed plenty of nasty bastards along the way. I get things done."

Lisa took a sip of her wine.

"I've heard that too. You must work long hours."

"You don't join the police if you want the nine to five."

"But do you ever get to see your wife? She must be very understanding."

March's expression cooled, almost imperceptibly.

"She knows which side her bread is buttered, if you pardon the colloquialism."

"I shall bear that all in mind, boss. Graham," Lisa continued. "Hopefully we'll get to work together again soon."

"I'm sure we will. In fact I'll very much make sure of it. I'm developing what I like to call a soft spot for my favourite DC." He winked. "I've got big plans for you."

"That's intriguing. Sadly, though" - she paused while she finished her drink - "I've got to get home to relieve my babysitter, so I'll have to let you tell me another time." She put the glass down, but she couldn't stand up unless March moved to give her room. He didn't.

"That's a shame. I was hoping we could celebrate long into the night."

"I'd love to, but maybe after the next one?" She smiled. "I'm sure we'll have plenty of opportunities. But if you don't mind, I just need to squeeze out?"

"Of course."

March moved slightly, but not enough that she could exit the booth without rubbing against him.

"Can I give you a lift home?" he asked.

"Thanks, but no. I've got the car."

"Okay." He stood up. "Take care DC Miller. Remember, I've got my eye on you."

She turned to leave, walking slightly more quickly than when she'd arrived.

———

Twenty minutes later March walked down the steps towards the basement of a run-down building near King's Cross. He put his key in the lock, and once inside, followed the corridor until it opened into a dimly lit room. Two men were there: one gagged and strapped to a chair, the other holding a baseball bat.

"And what have we here?" asked March. The man in the chair was in no state to speak, so the one with the bat answered.

"I'm just stressing the importance of making payments promptly," he said.

"Very good. Has there been a problem?"

"A small one, but we're discussing it."

March nodded.

"It seems like you're doing a very good job. It's important to always be professional in front of a client. Especially such a pretty boy."

"Would you like to join in?"

March thought for a moment.

"It looks like you've got it very much in hand, Jimmy," he said eventually. "I just popped in to pick up some petty cash."

He moved to a safe that was bolted to the floor in the corner of the room, and turned the dial. When the door swung open, he withdrew a handful of twenty-pound notes, then closed the safe and reset the lock.

"I've got an appointment with a lady," he said. "I will leave you two to continue your chat."

And with that he left the basement, grateful that the sounds from within couldn't make their way to the street.

I suspect early December isn't Devon's peak tourist season. Clare picked us up in a taxi and then led us to an Indian restaurant in the centre of Totnes. It was less than a quarter full, even at prime time on a Saturday evening.

In fairness, she looked striking in her black leather skirt, matching tights, matching jacket and equally matching new haircut. Every inch the femme fatale, which was appropriate in many respects, although also slightly disquieting. I felt hopelessly underdressed in a sweatshirt, jeans and my favourite Dr Martens boots. And even smaller than usual given her four-inch heels. For somebody who was supposedly in hiding, Clare was doing incredibly well at being the centre of attention.

We had a plate of poppadoms while we waited for the main courses: chicken dhansak for me, and a jalfrezi for Danny. Clare, typically, ordered one of the chef's specials that I'd never previously heard of and would never be able to remember.

"So, you said you had an idea on how to get started?" said Danny.

"Yes," she said. "I've arranged a trip for us."

"A trip? Where to? When?"

"Bulgaria."

"What?"

"Tomorrow, just for the night. To meet Georgi."

That seemed a bit dramatic.

"What time are you flying out?" I asked. "And where from? We appear to be in Devon."

"Not till the afternoon, so you've got plenty of time to get back in the morning. Heathrow."

Danny was looking agitated.

"I'm really sorry, but I can't do that," he said.

"Why not?" asked Clare.

"This is going to sound pathetic, but my passport expired last month and I haven't renewed it. So sorry. It's been hectic."

She reached into her bag and passed across a brown envelope.

"There you go," she said.

"What's that?"

"A new one. Just till you get the proper thing."

"Clare, I cannot fly out of the country on a fake passport," he said in little more than an agitated whisper.

"Why not? You did when you came to see me in Geneva. You need to learn to live a bit."

He didn't have an answer to that.

"Early start, then," I said. Danny still didn't look happy. "Don't worry, I'll make sure he gets there."

"You're invited as well," said Clare.

"Me? Really?"

"Of course. We're a team."

"Can I stop you there. I'm just a photographer. I'm not like you two. You don't need me. I love a trip, but I'd just get in the way."

"Of course we need you."

"Why?"

"Because you're good. And Georgi will be delighted to meet you."

That was an immediate red flag.

"I'll stop you there again," I said. "I appreciate this is important but I'm knackered as it is, and I'm definitely not going if I'm just supposed to be some sort of arm candy, having you pimping me out for the sake of a story."

"That's not what I meant."

"Sounded like it."

"Well, it wasn't. We're better than that. It's because he loves a bit of photography. Do you know Zenit cameras?"

That took me by surprise.

"Of course, Russian SLRs."

"Perfect. Well, I've never seen him as excited as the day he said he was giving away his Zenit because he'd just bought himself a Nikon."

"Good taste."

"There you go then. I wouldn't ever ask you to do something I wasn't willing to do myself."

"I'm not sure that's particularly reassuring."

I broke off a piece of poppadom and loaded it with lime pickle and the green yoghurt stuff that I can never remember the name of.

"Who actually is this bloke?" asked Danny.

"Georgi? Officially ex-military. Party member. Unofficially ex-secret service."

"And you've known him how long?"

"About a year, year and a half."

"Is it going to be safe?"

"To visit? It's probably safer than here. He's not the sort of person you mess with, so if he's on your side you're in a good place, and you'll want to stay there. I should just say, though, Georgi and Otto don't know each other."

"That's handy. How come?"

"I keep them apart. It keeps me in employment."

"Okay, and whereabouts in Bulgaria?"

"Sofia."

The main courses arrived, and the conversation continued although there was little more about the case, or the imminent trip to Bulgaria. Clare was adept at dodging any personal questions, no matter how much I tried. By the time the bill arrived we'd spent a couple of hours discussing everything but learning nothing. She was still an enigma.

"Let me get this," said Danny in a show of welcome chivalry. But when he offered his Switch card to the waiter, he was told that the bill had already been paid. Clare just sat back, shrugged, and lit a Silk Cut. I felt a conspiratorial nudge on my leg under the table again.

"I've arranged a taxi," she said. "I'll come with you back to Staverton and then go on from there. Then I look forward to seeing you tomorrow. You'll need to get an early train back."

"Will we be able to get a taxi in the morning okay?" asked Danny.

"It's already done. It's booked for seven."

"Seven?" That seemed a touch enthusiastic.

"It's going to be a busy day." She took an envelope from her bag and passed it to us. "These are your flight tickets, hotel details and some spending money."

"Can I not just stay in Devon for a bit? I like it here. I could have a lovely lie in while you two go off and save the world."

But I didn't mean it. I was secretly looking forward to the trip. I had no idea what purpose I was going to serve, but most of all I was hoping to spend more time with Clare. Despite her troubled past and habit of shooting people, I couldn't help but find her company intoxicating.

We went outside to where the taxi was waiting. Clare put her arm around me.

"We just need to find out who shot Tom Napier," she said. "Trust me. Everything will be okay."

I wanted to believe her. I really did. But things had a habit of not quite going to plan.

Chapter 8

W E were up by six, to leave enough time for a quick shower and early breakfast before the taxi was due to arrive. There was a note under our door from Clare, wishing us a safe trip home and saying she'd see us in Sofia.

"How did she even do that?" I asked. "She must have come back."

Danny was still half asleep.

"And how come she's not actually flying with us?" I continued.

"What do you think?" he said, propping himself up in bed.

"I think she passes through closed doors like some sort of ghost."

"You're probably not wrong."

"I suppose it comes from officially being dead. Has anyone cottoned on to the fact that she actually isn't yet?"

"March for definite but he's an idiot."

"Interpol?"

"No idea but you'd have to hope not."

I put the note into my bag, then took the first shower to make sure I got a dry towel. These things are important, and I was forever marvelling at Danny's tactical naivety.

The rest of the morning passed in a blur of sleep deprivation. Danny tried to do some work on his notebook computer on the train, but the battery was dead. He considered plugging it into a socket marked "cleaner only" but decided against it, for risk of frying the thing. He consoled himself that at least he had a mobile phone signal again.

"That's a point," he said. "How did Clare phone us on a mobile phone on Friday, when she was in Devon and there was no signal?"

"Presumably she wasn't in Devon," I said.

We were back home by lunchtime, but only had time for a swift repack before making the dash to Heathrow. Danny insisted on taking the Piccadilly Line for the sake of speed and convenience. I tried to object on the basis that the Underground was unnatural, but there wasn't time to seek an alternative. I just had to take a deep breath and confront my fears.

The flight left on time, and despite my best endeavours to stay awake, I was jolted out of a lovely dream when the wheels hit the tarmac. After successfully clearing passport control - you have to hand it to Clare, she knows a thing or two about forgery - we collected our bags, and went in search of the taxi rank. We quite possibly got fleeced, but twenty minutes later we were being dropped off outside our hotel. It was a small place, opposite what appeared to be a disused former nightclub.

My first impressions of Sofia were mixed. I felt a bit like Dorothy from the Wizard of Oz as we travelled over the yellow brick roads, but overall it seemed to be in need of basic repairs. Understandably, it looked like a city, and quite possibly a country, in transition.

Clare had cheekily booked us a double room again, but I

didn't mind really. Despite being completely over Danny, at least as far as I was telling everyone, I didn't mind sharing a bed for old times' sake. We were adults. We could sleep next to each other without any shenanigans. We'd done it countless times before. And while Danny tried to connect his notebook to CompuServe via the hotel's phone system, I was very happy to test the comfort of its mattress.

———

I was having another lovely dream when I felt a hand on my shoulder, gently trying to rouse me. I opened one eye, then, not quite trusting it, opened the other. Clare was looking down at me.

"Where on earth have you come from? Where's Danny?" I asked, in a state of confusion.

"I'm over here," he said. He was at the desk, with the notebook screen open. He seemed to have changed his clothes, and Clare looked majestic in a fitted dark grey overcoat. I was still in the jeans and sweatshirt I'd been wearing in Devon, and not for the first time felt I was doing the fashion world a professional disservice.

"Have I got time for a quick shower?" I asked. Clare nodded.

"Take your time," she said.

I shook myself awake, grabbed a change of clothes and my make-up bag, and disappeared into the en suite bathroom.

Forty-five minutes later I emerged, looking like shit. There were bags under my eyes, my nose was still peeling, and my black dress looked considerably lower-budget than Clare's off-catwalk couture.

"I'm assume we're not going to be walking far?" I said, thinking of my choice of footwear, but then noticed a room service pizza and suddenly lost interest in the answer, even if it meant redoing my lipstick.

Danny unplugged his notebook and put it away in the hotel room safe.

"So," I said, while I attacked a second slice, "is there anything we should know?"

Clare was standing by the window, looking out at the city through a film of rain.

"No, I think we just play it by ear," she said, turning back towards us. "I'll lead the questions. We'll see what he can tell us and see where it leads."

"Where are we actually going?" I asked.

"It's the best hotel in Sofia," she said. "The Vitosha New Otani. Vitosha's the volcano you can see when it's daylight."

"You mean this isn't the best hotel in Sofia?" I looked around at the tiny room and furniture that seemed to have withstood years of service. "And you didn't book us a room there because?"

She laughed.

"Because it was short notice. And it may pay to keep some distance."

"That sounds ominous."

Clare moved to an armchair beside the bed, and crossed her legs. She was toying with a packet of unfamiliar-looking Victory-branded cigarettes but didn't attempt to light one.

"This is Sofia," she said. "It's a great city. There are lots of really good people and incredibly low crime. But it's also a country that's finding its way post-Communism."

"How come Bulgaria managed it peacefully and Yugoslavia ended up having a civil war?"

"How long have you got? Yugoslavia was made up of separate regions that hated each other for all sorts of reasons. Bulgaria's different. Did you notice the lack of bright colours?"

"Yeah, it seems to need a lick of paint."

"That's deliberate. It's part of the culture. They don't want to draw attention to themselves. They just want stability. When the Wall came down and they had free elections, they voted the Communists back in."

"Wow."

"The trouble is, there was a lot of corruption. Still is. They're concerned about rising inflation. We can trust Georgi but we just have to bear that in mind. It's not the same as being at home."

"Do you mean he's dodgy?"

"No, but we need to be careful. Remember, no mention of Otto, and definitely not Julian, okay?"

"Understood."

I finished the pizza, swigged a little bottle of white wine from the minibar and retouched my make-up. By the time I re-emerged from the bathroom, Danny and Clare were waiting for me, ready to head into the unknown.

Chapter 9

THE taxi splashed through rain-soaked streets. I snuggled up close to Danny in the back seat while Clare, up front, engaged the driver in what I presumed was small talk. I don't know which language they spoke, but it definitely wasn't English.

Before long, we pulled up behind a huge black Rolls-Royce outside a hotel that looked completely out of sync with my expectations of eastern Europe. The driver got out and held our door open. A doorman held an umbrella to protect us from the weather for the walk to the hotel entrance. All four strides of it. Clare gave him a tip. I just smiled and pretended I knew what I was doing, and linked arms with Danny. He looked exceptionally smart in his dark navy suit and white shirt.

Clare led us through an opulent marbled foyer and into a small, wood-panelled bar. She didn't need to ask directions, and I didn't need to be Sherlock Holmes to deduce this was probably every bit as much her local as the Sea Trout Inn in Staverton. Aside from that, though, the two places couldn't have been any more different. I'd felt far more at home in the other one.

As we walked into the bar, a well-muscled man in perhaps his early forties rose from his chair and moved towards us. He greeted Clare with seemingly genuine enthusiasm, a great big hug, and a kiss on both cheeks. He tried the same with me as Clare introduced us, and then shook Danny firmly by the hand. Despite Danny's gym work, I could see him wince at the strength of Georgi's grip.

But there was a second man at his table, and from the look that flashed momentarily across Clare's otherwise calm, perfectly made-up face, she hadn't been expecting him.

"Let me introduce you to my friend," said Georgi. "Clare, Danny, Anna, please meet Aleksander Kovač."

"Wonderful to meet you," he said, rising from his chair. He was considerably older, and looked well fed.

"Aleksander is here from Croatia," Georgi continued. "Your reputation spreads far and wide."

Clare's mask of calm professionalism returned.

"I'm not always sure that's a good thing," she said, shaking his leather-gloved hand.

"Far from it - I have only heard good things. Georgi tells me you have been very diligent."

"I try."

We ordered drinks at the bar and then joined our two hosts at their table. Clare took a chair on the far side, against the wall, with a clear view of the rest of the bar and the open doorway to the hotel lobby. Always watchful, always on guard. I'd hate to live like that, with such a constant paranoia, but I had to admire her success in self-preservation.

Danny sat next to Clare. I sat on his other side.

Clare lit a cigarette while the two men opted for cigars. There were a few minutes of small talk. The drinks arrived and then Georgi asked me about my work and my favourite camera and lenses. I mentioned the Nikon F4 that I'd lost on a stakeout with Danny last year and he sounded genuinely upset for me.

"And in the studio?"

"I've got a Hasselblad for that, but don't even start me on the trauma I've had with those over the years."

"Really? I thought they were the best that money can buy?"

"They are, they're beautiful. It wasn't so much the camera as something that happened when I was a student. But honestly, you don't want to know."

Clare's ears seemed to prick up like those of an excitable puppy hearing its lead being touched.

"That sounds intriguing," she said.

"Another story for another day," I said, wishing I'd never mentioned it.

I'd longed to meet someone interested in me and my work, rather than just seeing me as some sort of gatekeeper to a glamorous lifestyle of model girlfriends. Today wasn't that day, though, and talk soon progressed to the famous names I'd worked with, and mythical parties at which it was assumed I'd spend every evening. I tried to explain that beauty was only skin deep, and that while many of the models were lovely people, a fair few were high-maintenance divas, but nobody is ever interested in the reality. The fantasy is far more compelling.

As the conversation developed I started to get more and more marginalised, until eventually business took over completely. Luckily, a second round of drinks arrived.

"So, what's your role?" Clare asked the Croatian.

"I'm much like everyone. Just looking at the end of the war and making plans."

"Do you work here in Bulgaria or are you still in Croatia? What do you do?"

"I have some business interests."

"That's very vague."

"I don't mean to be. But you have to understand, we've all been through hell in the past years. The war is ending but the country is a mess. It's the same in Bosnia, even Serbia. We are all living in countries and economies that need rebuilding."

"So, you're in construction?"

"In a manner of speaking."

"And you wanted to meet me because?"

"Because maybe we can help each other. Although I see now is not a good time to discuss it."

Clare looked over to me and Danny. I was beginning to understand the game, even if I didn't know the rules.

"You can discuss things in front of my friends. But if you prefer, please give me your card and I will contact you."

Georgi stepped in.

"Everyone is planning for life after conflict," he said. "Our neighbours are all trying to redefine themselves for a new international future."

Aleksander nodded.

"We just want peace. Prosperity. Maybe one day you'll even let us join your European Union," he said.

"And do you think Dayton will give you this peace and prosperity?" asked Danny, in his first meaningful contribution.

"I don't know. I hope so. But I think it's designed to end the war rather than hold the peace. It's better than most of the other plans, but we shall see. I hope so. But Serbia... Whether they will stick to it? Who knows?"

"Do you think they won't?"

"They were losing the war, so they may do, but there's no long-term plan. Bosnia is still very... what's the word... made up of small parts."

"Fragmented?" offered Danny.

"Yes, fragmented. And I think there will be problems with Kosovo and Albania. We shall see. We can pray but there's nothing so dangerous as a wounded animal."

I perked up at this.

"Is that actually true?" I said. "Surely if it's wounded it would be less dangerous? It wouldn't be able to run so fast."

Aleksander smiled.

"I like you," he said. "You have a nice view of the world."

I didn't quite know how to take that. Danny gave me a look.

"Georgi tells me you're interested in the legendary Miroslav Nikolić?" he continued.

Clare took over.

"He's crossed the radar," she said.

"Interesting. And may I ask in what way?"

"There was a shooting. A bank employee back in London. The police have made an arrest but we think there's maybe more to it. We believe the man who was shot was investing money for Miroslav."

"Who was arrested?"

"The victim's wife."

"So it's, how you say, a crime of passion?"

"Possibly. But possibly not. We don't know so we're just exploring. The bank apparently lost a lot of money. So we're looking into motives and opportunities."

"And your role in this?"

"I'm just an interested observer."

He laughed.

"Your reputation would say otherwise."

"I'm a journalist," said Danny, joining in. "Clare's helping me. If there's another truth I want to find it. If there's an injustice I want to expose it. And if there's a bigger picture I want to see it."

"It's early days," Clare continued. "We will continue to look."

Kovač nodded.

"Miroslav makes it hard for us."

It seemed like an odd thing to say.

"What do you know about him?" asked Clare, letting it pass.

"He is an ambitious man. Ruthless. He has a certain... reputation."

"I can imagine. Georgi was telling me about his links to a transport company."

"Really?" Aleksander looked at our host and shrugged. "I don't know anything about that."

I'd finished my second drink and was looking at the others to see who would crack first and order a third when suddenly Clare looked at her watch, her expression hardening. The change was subtle, almost imperceptible, but I was beginning to recognise the signs.

"Well, it's been a pleasure meeting you, Aleksander," she said, standing up. I followed her glance to the entrance, but if something had spooked her I had no idea what it was. "And Georgi, wonderful as always. But sadly we must leave you now."

"So soon?" said the Croatian. "But we were just starting to get to know each other."

"Unfortunately our schedule is tight."

Danny finished his drink, and we both stood, following Clare's lead. Handshakes were exchanged. Both men kissed my cheek. I tried not to recoil at the aroma of cigar smoke.

"Let me give you my card," said Aleksander. Clare took it from him, and slipped it into her jacket pocket without looking at the front. "It would be a pleasure to continue this conversation when you have more time."

"Indeed it would. Goodnight to both of you. I'm sure I'll be in touch."

I looked at Danny, but he seemed to share my confusion. We followed Clare through the lobby to the entrance, where a line of taxis were waiting. None of us spoke. Clare nodded to the driver of the first, who got out and opened the door. As we climbed inside she said something to him, possibly in Bulgarian. I had no idea. It certainly wasn't English again, and didn't sound like German. Either way, he seemed to understand, and once we were all inside, he pulled out and joined the traffic on the main road heading back towards the city centre.

I started to speak, but Clare raised her hand to stop me. It all seemed rather strange. It seemed stranger still a few minutes later when we reached our destination. It was a hotel, but it wasn't ours, and I began to realise I had no idea where we were.

Chapter 10

CLARE led us inside, again without a word. She walked past the reception desk without acknowledging the staff, and pressed the button by a bank of lifts. Almost immediately the doors opened, and all three of us got inside. She pressed the button for the top floor, and only once the doors closed did she speak.

"Sorry about that," she said.

"What happened?" asked Danny.

"Something wasn't right."

"I got that impression," I said. "Where are we? Is this your hotel?"

"I've never been here in my life. We'll go back down in a moment but I just need to make sure we're not being followed."

"You're scaring me."

"Anna, don't worry."

"That's easy to say. What actually happened?"

"It was Aleksander. He shouldn't have been there. I gave him the benefit of the doubt because I thought I could trust Georgi, but then when he started to lie to me, I knew it was a bad idea."

"How did he lie to you?" asked Danny.

"It wasn't so much the lie as that he knew I'd see through it."

"About the transport company?"

Clare nodded.

"I'm not here to play games. It's too dangerous." The doors opened at the top floor and we left the lift. Clare indicated to the staircase and we started to head back down, the arduous way. After a couple of flights, there was a noise from below. We stopped, immediately. It sounded like a door closing. I couldn't hear much over the sound of my own heartbeat but strained to listen for movement nonetheless.

After maybe thirty seconds, Clare indicated for us to continue. Her right hand was poised near the inside pocket of her jacket. I didn't even want to think about the reasons why.

"I don't think they'll be following, but I'm just playing safe," she said at last.

Eventually we reached the ground floor. She looked through the glass door, scanning the lobby for threats, before leading us back outside. Again there was a line of taxis, but this time we ignored it. Instead she turned right, walking up the street away from the hotel. We followed. We crossed the road a couple of times, took several turnings, then paused, doubled back, and finally crossed a couple more roads before finally she seemed satisfied. The yellow bricks in the roads were treacherously slippery as a result of the earlier rain.

A couple of corners later I recognised the welcoming glow of our own hotel entrance. How she'd done that I had no idea. I was so grateful to be back I didn't have the heart to complain about the promise she'd made when I was choosing shoes, and was thankful the alcohol had done something to dull the pain.

Once in our room, Clare turned on the TV and then started speaking, barely audible over the noise of a strange-looking Bulgarian game show.

"I'm sorry," she said, "but at least that's proved something."

It's proved you're paranoid, I thought, but I didn't say it aloud.

Danny nodded, seemingly more attuned to her thought process. She reached into her pocket and withdrew the business card, studied it for a moment and then smiled.

"You noticed he was wearing gloves?" she said.

"I did. I assumed he must have eczema or something," I said, realising how naive I sounded.

"No, he was just very keen to give me this without also giving me a fingerprint. Look at it. A PO box and a mobile phone number. Again, it's what it doesn't say that's important."

"In what way?"

"Because he knows that I know that this is worthless. It'd be no more use in contacting him than standing on the roof of a tall building, shouting his name. Even assuming we knew his name, which is almost certainly anything other than Aleksander."

"But why?" I asked. "Why go to the trouble of meeting you if all he's going to do is talk nonsense, tell lies and then give you a fake business card?"

"Because it's a warning. They want us to know they're watching, but they don't want to tell us why. The subtext is that we should back off."

It seemed to make sense, sort of.

"Are you saying he was connected to Miroslav?" asked Danny. I took off my shoes, feeling the urge to lie on the bed.

"It's possible."

"But he was supposed to be Croatian. I'm not an expert but I don't think they get on."

"He could have been Croatian. Or Serbian, Bosnian, Slovenian, Macedonian, even Bulgarian. Pretty much anywhere. We didn't see his passport, not that that would have proved anything."

She removed her jacket and hung it over the back of the desk chair, being careful, I imagined, that nothing would fall out of the pockets and land with a metallic thump on the threadbare carpet.

For the first time since I'd known Clare, she seemed unsure about something.

"Are you okay?" I asked.

She nodded.

"Not worried?"

She did one of those "kind of unsure" expressions. I didn't know whether to be relieved at the show of human emotion or just be really, really scared.

"You remember I said Tom Napier was investing money for Miroslav, but it was a long story?" she said at last.

"You did," said Danny.

"Well, it's not quite that straightforward. I think I'd better bring you up to speed, but we may all need a drink for this. It's time to go back to the beginning."

She opened the little fridge that served as a minibar. Thankfully it had been refilled in our absence. I accepted a small bottle of the Bulgarian equivalent of Prosecco. Danny went for the local beer. Clare chose mineral water, which seemed weird when she was the one who had suggested we might need alcohol. It caused a momentary sense of panic. If she needed to be on high alert, maybe we should abstain too, but that thought didn't last long when I considered there was fizzy wine on offer. I'd already had several, and coupled with the last knockings of jet lag, I was already some considerable distance from my sharpest. She passed me a glass and I unscrewed the fake cork.

"There's something I need to tell you both now that I didn't want to say before the meeting," she continued, moving back to the armchair. Danny had joined me on the bed. "You may have wondered how I ever got involved in all of this. Why I first started taking an interest in Tom and what he was up to at the bank, and what made me aware of Miroslav."

"I thought it was something to do with your business over here," said Danny. "But you wouldn't tell us even if we asked."

"Kind of. But you have to believe me in this. Despite everything that's happened since I left the Echo, I'm still the same person really. I still look out for the bad guys and have an overwhelming urge to stop them."

"Cheers to that," I said, raising my drink, then thought it really would be appropriate to take things more seriously.

"So, Tom or Miroslav are definitely the bad guys?" asked Danny.

"And again it's a bit more complicated than that. It's possible, but that's based on rumours and it's hard to know what to believe when it comes out of a place like this. Everyone has an agenda."

"But there was enough to make you interested?"

She nodded, then took a drink of water and leaned forward, lowering her voice even further.

"You know I mentioned the Balkans were awash with guns? Well, one of the things I most like about England, one of many things, is that there's very little gun crime."

"Are you being ironic here?" That was Danny. It made me smile.

"Self-defence isn't a crime, Danny."

"It's not always been self-defence, though, has it?" That was brave, I thought.

"I'd argue it was, in the broadest sense," she said. "You can sit here, pondering semantics all you like, but the fact remains, the reason there's not much gun crime is because it's extremely hard to get hold of a gun. As I well know. It's a massively undersupplied market. Agreed?"

We both said yes.

"Well, just a few miles from here, across the border, is the most heavily armed region in the world. Literally millions of guns, on all sides, in the hands of civilians as well as the armies. And do you know what that means now the fighting's over? If there's confidence that the peace will hold, then you're suddenly looking at a massive export opportunity."

"You're suggesting to Britain?" asked Danny, several steps ahead of me.

"Possibly. It's seen as a rich country. There's already a black market but it's tightly controlled. Demand far outstrips supply. Imagine how appealing that looks if you've got hundreds of guns to sell, and you want to maximise the price you get for them."

"Do you know this for definite?"

"I don't know much for definite, but it's a logical conclusion. And imagine the carnage on British streets if every mugger, criminal, political extremist or even disaffected schoolchild suddenly had easy access to war-grade handguns and assault rifles. It doesn't bear thinking about. The irony is that the UK has been complicit in the smuggling of arms into the region, and now it's looking like payback."

She paused to let that sink in.

"But surely we've got border controls to stop that?" said Danny. "Customs?"

"We have, of course. But, Danny, does that stop drugs? People trafficking? You've seen that for yourself. If you've got the nous and a few contacts, then anything less than a couple of tons is pretty easy to shift round Europe."

"I'm not even going to ask how you know that," I said.

"It's common knowledge."

"In your world."

She ignored me.

"So, that's been bothering me, a lot," she continued. "I didn't want to think about it, but I couldn't help it. And then as the war started coming to an end, it became something I started to focus ever more on. I wanted the theory to be proved groundless."

"But I get the impression it wasn't?"

"Maybe. But I don't know yet. Everything really came into focus over the last few weeks, once I heard about Tom Napier. I knew he was working with Miroslav, and Miroslav has a reputation as a proper ruthless nasty bastard. Otto started to look into it for me, and then... Well, we know what happened next."

"But wouldn't the British police and MI5 and whoever else be aware of the risks?"

"You'd hope so."

"But you don't think so?"

"Let's just say I don't have absolute faith in either of them, Danny. Not when you've got idiots like Graham March in charge, and when he's seemingly got friends in high places willing to overlook some of the stuff we know he's been up to."

"I'll give you that."

She suddenly looked wistful again, as though there was a warmth hidden deeply beneath the veneer of cold professionalism. It didn't show often, but occasionally there was a reassuring glimpse, if only I could coax her out of her shell one day.

"I want to move home at some point," she said, "but to a country where every Saturday night, people are falling out of bars and nightclubs, and having good old-fashioned punch-ups, not where they're shooting each other. This all worries me a lot. But, like I say, it may be groundless."

"And is that what you wanted to tell us?"

She pursed her lips together, and her eyes sharpened again.

"No. That's just the background. I'm just coming up to the really bad part."

Chapter 11

DC Lisa Miller kissed her daughter goodnight and removed all of the soft toys from the cot, apart from the favourite rabbit, Flopsy. She gently closed the door, leaving the night light on low, and then returned to the front room and the welcoming embrace of an ageing armchair. Any minute now there would be a gentle knock at the door, but until then she would close her eyes and breathe deeply, and try to find an inner calm. It wasn't going to be easy.

The job was the one thing, apart from her daughter, that she truly loved. The months spent training at Hendon, together with the subsequent years of pounding the streets, had finally led to the day when she'd swapped her uniform for the prefix "Detective". It felt like she'd arrived. It was daunting, but the nerves caused by the added responsibility were countered by the feeling that she was finally able to make a difference. That she'd be able to pit her wits against the worst of humanity and make the world a safer place. And then one morning she woke up with a suspicion that all her plans might have to change. Radically change.

There was never a doubt that she'd keep the baby, despite the huge challenges of rearing a child on her own. Her partner had abdicated responsibility and departed her life, long before the arrival of Jessica. But any concerns about her ability to provide a safe home, and how she would manage to raise a child on her basic salary, with her unpredictable working hours, were swept away in a flood of emotion the day she looked into her newborn daughter's eyes.

The first day back at work was torturous, and not just because it meant being parted from Jessica. So much had changed in such a short time. DCI Graham March had been known to make life a misery for colleagues, but when she'd left for maternity leave he'd been serving a suspension, following newspaper allegations of corruption and worse. She thought she'd seen the last of him, but somehow, he'd managed to worm his way back, despite a supposedly thorough inquiry. She'd heard the rumours, of course, and knew of his reputation. At first she managed to keep her distance, but then her luck ran out, and they were partnered together on the Tom Napier case. Pitting your wits against the worst of humanity was supposed to mean thieves, drug dealers and murderers, not one of your own.

Seeing the man and his methods close up had done nothing to quell her concerns. And now, even worse, he'd made it clear that she was the latest in a long line of his "chosen ones". She knew the risks of making an enemy of him, and the potential damage to her career and her ability to provide for her daughter. Who knew how far his tentacles reached? And then there was his tendency for violence when he didn't get his own way...

She rose to answer the door, and welcomed her mother with a hug and a promise that she'd be back as soon as she could. She wasn't looking forward to this, but it had to be done. It had to be done for Jessica.

Pulling her coat tight against the winter chill, she got in her car and navigated the streets towards an unfamiliar address. She found a parking place and locked her car, suddenly aware of her own vulnerability. She was brave. She'd proved that on countless occasions, but the sodium glow of the street lamps created the ambience of a crime scene that was waiting to happen.

At the block of flats, she followed the signs in the dimly-lit corridor until she found the correct door on the third floor. If she knocked, there would be no going back. She paused, suddenly doubting herself. The whole idea was madness. How much worse could it be to just go home, and lose herself in a bottle of wine? But it had to be done. For Jessica. She raised her hand, took a deep breath, and knocked at the door.

———

The really bad part? That sounded ominous. I was beginning to feel the fake Prosecco had been a bad idea after all. Or maybe I should just have several more.

"I started making a few more enquires out here," said Clare.

"Through Georgi?" asked Danny.

"Yes, among others. Call it my survival instinct, if you like."

"You say that as though you're worried."

"I work to minimise personal risk."

"But there is some?"

"Always." She didn't elaborate, which was unsettling. "I've put a few feelers out, looking for anything suspicious. Anything out of the ordinary."

Danny was sitting up straight, giving her his full attention. I closed my eyes and took a deep breath.

"So here's the thing about Miroslav," she continued. "There's a small haulage company based in Macedonia. They spent the war taking relief supplies into Serbia completely illegally, but the authorities turned a blind eye because it was helping to avoid a humanitarian crisis. Food, oil, other essentials. Officially there's an embargo, and officially the borders were closed, but they'd go up through Bulgaria and in over the border there. With me so far?"

We both nodded. I finished my drink. I definitely fancied another.

"Now the war's ending, you'd think that slowly business would get back to normal, but that's going to take years, if it ever even happens," she continued. "But once the embargoes are lifted, there's going to be a huge influx of supplies into Serbia, Bosnia and the rest from all over, and our friendly family haulage company is no longer going to be controlling the back routes for the black market."

"Is this the transport company you mentioned to Aleksander?" asked Danny.

"I'm coming on to that, but for now, just picture the scene. Lots of lorries, suddenly empty. The drivers are experienced in crossing borders that shouldn't be crossed, which means they're experts in smuggling. So if you were based in Serbia and you wanted to ship a batch of handguns and assault rifles out of the country for the highest bidder, who are you going to turn to for the logistics?"

Danny breathed out deeply.

Maybe it was the alcohol, but I suddenly had a terrible thought.

"Christ, you're not suddenly turning into an illegal arms dealer, are you?" I asked.

"No, of course not."

"Clare, don't take this the wrong way, but guns scare me. If that's your world you can keep it, but I'm going home."

"I'm not involved in guns."

I did my slightly disbelieving face.

"That's not strictly true," I said. "You've got one. I've seen it."

"I know one end from the other if that's what you mean."

"It's arguably a bit more than that."

"And just as well, for your sake." She had a point. I had a

sudden flashback to the night she'd come to my rescue the previous year. "But what I mean is, I'm not involved in selling them. I don't like the things. I've only used one when it's been strictly necessary."

"Again, I'm not one hundred percent sure that's the case."

"Shhh," said Danny, giving me a look. Clare gave me a look too. Then I remembered she quite possibly had a gun in the inside pocket of the jacket hanging on the back of the chair, and I decided to shut up.

"Is this all hypothesis or do you know this for definite?" asked Danny, apparently keen to get back on the subject.

"It's a bit of both. It started as a hypothesis. But then something significant happened. Georgi told me about a new haulage company he'd spotted being formed in Bulgaria. Nothing unusual there in itself, but this one was called Serdica International Logistica, or SIL for short, where Serdica is the old Roman name for Sofia. I've seen photographs of their trucks. They've only got two, carrying containers. And guess where they bought them from?"

"The company in Macedonia?" said Danny.

"Exactly. Georgi made some enquiries to see who owned the new company and that's where it gets very interesting. None of the listed directors actually exist. It's a complete ghost operation. But obviously someone is behind it, and to cut a long story short, if you follow the trail of shareholders back from Sofia, you end up in Serbia. And a company called Sokobanja Industries."

"SI again."

"Quite. Sokobanja is a Serbian spa town. It doesn't have industries, but it does have a very interesting former resident."

"Miroslav?"

"Exactly."

"And by a quirk of fate, Sokobanja Industries has an account at the London office of a certain Swiss investment bank, with an office in London."

"Gersbach and Haller?" said Danny.

Clare nodded.

"Was that the bank Tom Napier worked at?" I asked.

Clare nodded.

"Shit."

It took a moment for us to let all that sink in.

"Are there any crisps in the minibar?" I said. "Or chocolate?"

Clare went back to the wardrobe and returned a moment later with a KitKat. She passed it to me. She passed me a second bottle of drink as well, without needing to be asked. Telepathy again.

"So the logistics company is owned by Miroslav. It's possible they're going to be smuggling guns, and if Tom's lost the money he's going to be in a lot of trouble," said Danny. "And if he knows too much he's going to be in even more."

"Precisely. And that's all the more reason why Emma's not even in the top ten of the most likely suspects."

"Maybe Aleksander didn't know about the transport company," said Danny. "I mean, if it's top secret, isn't it possible that he just hadn't heard of it?"

"You heard what he said. Miroslav made things hard for them. That was probably the only true thing he said all night. He wanted us to know he was on the other side. But everything else he did and said, or rather didn't say, only served to obscure his real identity. Oh, and there's one more thing."

I didn't think this was going to be good news. It wasn't.

"SI Logistica doesn't seem to have any clients. But the two trucks are currently heading north, through Romania. They were last tracked near Timişoara yesterday, but two days ago they were seen in Serbia, about 30 miles north-east of Belgrade."

"Picking up guns?" asked Danny.

"It's possible. So we need to stick close to Miroslav, find out what happened to Tom, and then find out everything we can about the shipment - because if it is guns, and they're heading to Britain, we need to do everything we can to stop it. If we can't..."

She fell silent, letting the thought sink in. Much as I loathed the idea, I was beginning to realise we were in this for the duration.

———

From within the third-floor flat came the sound of bolts being drawn and a chain clinking. The door opened slightly, and Lisa noted the immediate look of confusion. Detective Sergeant Amy Cranston was her superior and clearly hadn't been expecting a visitor. But her expression almost immediately gave way to concern.

"DC Miller?" she asked.

Lisa nodded, then pulled a strand of red hair back from her eyes.

'I'm sorry to come unannounced. I didn't know where else to turn. It's about Tom Napier."

"Has something gone wrong with the case?"

Lisa paused. In a world in which she was increasingly unsure about who she could trust, it was time to put her fate in the hands of instinct.

"Actually, if I'm honest, it's not about Tom Napier. It's about someone else."

"Let me guess. Graham March?"

She nodded.

DS Cranston opened the door, and took a step backwards.

"Come in," she said. "I think it's about time we had a conversation."

Chapter 12

W E caught an early flight home, despite a headache-related reluctance to get out of bed on my behalf. There are times when I really wished I smoked. Then I could give up and feel brilliant and full of energy and suddenly have loads of money, rather than spending most of the mornings feeling a bit shit.

It was lovely to be home. Camden hadn't always proved to be the safest of locations in recent years, but it seemed comfortingly less nerve-inducing than Sofia.

I popped to the supermarket to get fresh bread, milk and dishwasher tablets (there's always something that bumps the price up). By the time I got home, Danny was attaching Post-It notes to the wall like he'd watched too many TV crime dramas and was trying to audition for a role. I wasn't sure how much help it was. Most seemed to contain only question marks.

"Talk me through it," I said, once I'd made us both a cup of tea.

Stepping back, Danny took a deep breath.

"I'm just trying to put a bit of structure on it," he said, then sighed. "We're not massively further forward. We start from Tom, but all we really know is that somebody shot him."

"We know that March thinks it was Emma."

"And there's the evidence of the phone call, and the phone and bullets, but I think we can agree we're not convinced. But still, she gets a Post-It. Then there's Miroslav Nikolić. Who is he? What is he up to? Does he have a motive? Yes, possibly more than one: either revenge because he's sore about losing the money, or a need to silence Tom because he knew what he was up to, whatever that might be. And clearly easy access to guns."

"But how would he have got the phone and bullets into Emma's house?"

"We don't know but that's going to be the same for everyone."

"Okay."

"Then the rest is a bit vague. Aleksander. Who is he? What's he got to be so secretive about? Georgi. He's Clare's friend, but what was he playing at yesterday? Can we trust him? I'm not seeing any evidence."

"She won't like that."

"That's tough. But we don't know him and we're unlikely to ever get a straight answer on anything from her."

"Ooh, fighting talk."

Danny laughed.

"She just lives secrets. But she said herself, there's a lot of corruption in Bulgaria, and he's already brought someone along to a meeting who shouldn't really have been there, and seemed to have some other agenda. Until we get to know him better, I'd treat him with absolute caution."

"And the last column?"

"All the others. Otto. Who is he? Clare's friend, but what does that actually mean? Julian. He was working for Otto and got close to Emma. Clare says he wouldn't have pulled the trigger, but that's definitely something to look into. And then there's always the possibility that the attack could have been completely unrelated to any of this. Tom was gay. Was it blackmail, or something connected to the club he went to? Was it somebody at the bank? Or a rival firm? Was it a mugging that went wrong? Or something completely unrelated? Mistaken identity, or just a random hit by a madman?"

"And if it's any of those, how did the evidence end up in the house and what was the voicemail all about?"

"Exactly. And so the last of them all is Emma. Maybe she did do it, and March was right and I should give up and have a change of career."

"Excellent. Do that. Could you get an ice cream van? I like a Mr Whippy."

"I don't even want to think about what sort of latent fetish is going on inside your head."

Danny leaned on the back of the sofa, looking at the wall, searching for inspiration.

"I've got some work I must finish at the studio this week, but I can help you when I can," I said. "Anything to take my mind off Christmas."

"I can't keep getting you to do my work for me," he said.

"You can. Clare said it. We're a team. And I've got my assistant now. She's good."

"I thought you were getting annoyed by her?"

"No, not as a person. It's just her name."

"Diana?"

"Exactly."

"What's wrong with Diana?"

"It's just a bit scary, whenever anybody calls out for her. It sounds like 'Die Anna'. I don't want to sound morbid, but it freaks me out."

Danny laughed. One day he should try being me.

"Well, any help you can give me is much appreciated, if you're sure."

"My absolute pleasure. As long as it doesn't involve getting shot at. What's first?"

"We need to get into the bank, speak to the secretary who found the body. Go back to the beginning and start from there."

"Was that the beginning? Or was that the end?"

"Good question."

"I've got another one. Do you know her name? And how are we going to get into the bank? I imagine it's not like a branch of the Midland."

"I'm going to have to think about that. In the meantime, I need to go into see Mike and pitch it as a story."

"God. Good luck with that. I've got to place a film order. Are you coming back here after?"

He said he was and we agreed to have a brainstorm on his return. After he left, I fired up the PC and loaded CompuServe. I started reading as much as I could about the collapse of Yugoslavia, because to my shame, I suddenly realised just how little I knew about the biggest war in Europe for fifty years.

Danny knocked on the open door of his editor's office, took a breath and walked in.

"What have you got for me?" There was no time wasted on pleasantries.

Danny explained that he wanted to look into the Tom Napier case. He explained about the link to Miroslav Nikolić. Maybe there was a bigger story than just a domestic dispute. Maybe there was an element of police corruption, gun running, corporate espionage, and an elaborately planned cover-up.

Mike Walker frowned.

"Are you sure it's not just a vendetta against Graham March?"

"Not in the slightest," said Danny. "I think it's bigger than that."

"And your source for all of this hypothesis?"

That was difficult. Clare Woodbrook was once the newspaper's most celebrated employee, but now her name was poison.

"I've spent the weekend in Bulgaria."

"You've done fucking what?"

"I've been speaking to people who know Miroslav. Ex-Bulgarian secret service."

"How much the fuck did that cost? Do I need to remind you about the need for prior approval of expenses?"

"I'm not claiming for it. There's no cost to the paper. It was something I believed in."

That stopped him, although if Danny expected praise for taking initiative, it was not so easily earned.

"I'm not comfortable with this," said the editor after a moment of contemplation. "Simon isn't going to be happy. You heard him on Friday. He's got two reporters digging up backstory."

"And what have they brought you?"

"So far? Nothing."

"Precisely."

"You should work with Simon, tell him what you know."

"I think Simon's got an issue with me."

"Yeah well, I'm not here to be your nanny."

"All right, I'll put it another way. I'm not sure he's entirely impartial."

"What the fuck does that mean?"

"I mean he's pals with March."

"That's a fairly serious allegation."

"It's not really an allegation. Judge for yourself."

Mike stood up, and walked past Danny to the door of his office and closed it.

"Okay," he said, through an inscrutable expression. "I'll give you three days to see what you can come up with. I want something on my desk by the end of Thursday or you give up on it and hand everything over to Simon. Agreed?"

"Three days? It's going to take longer than that to do this properly."

"Danny, when I said 'agreed?' it was rhetorical. Thursday. End of. No excuses, and no extensions. I haven't got resources to have two separate departments on the same story. Christ."

"I'll have something by Thursday."

"Good lad."

The editor returned to his desk.

"Anything else?" he asked.

"No."

"Get a fucking move on then."

DCI Graham March fastened his coat and picked up his keys, just as his wife, Rafaela, opened the front door carrying four Safeway carrier bags.

"Are you going to give me a hand with these?" she asked.

"I'm just going out."

"Is that a 'no' then?"

"That's an 'I'm just going out'."

"Fine. Sod you."

She brushed past him to the kitchen, and lifted the bags onto the counter.

"Where you going?" she asked.

"Business to attend to."

"Eating out?"

"Probably."

"Good. Don't rush back."

He left her to it. One day she'd appreciate just how lucky she was, but today he was in a good mood, and domestic issues were far down the agenda.

He had to be at the club in a couple of hours, but the journey would take less than a quarter of that. There was plenty of time for half an hour of relaxation. There was a new girl, and that was always a highlight, especially when services rendered were on the house, in exchange for merely ensuring that the relevant authorities focused their attention elsewhere.

He'd lie back and enjoy her touch. She'd be grateful for his guidance. Everyone would benefit. And in the meantime there was almost certainly a medal of commendation to look forward to, and a rather profitable sideline that was just starting to flourish. Everything was going very well indeed. It was good to be back.

Chapter 13

B Y the time Danny arrived home from the office, I'd
succumbed to the temptation to cook for us. It never
ends well, but sometimes when I've been travelling I just
end up craving a potato. And even I can put a few of those in
the oven.

The problem was forgetting to take them out again before the
whole affair turned into a charcoal-encrusted shambles.
Surveying the wreckage, I phoned for a takeaway, as I sensibly
should have done in the first place.

On the upside, the driver said my nose was looking better,
although it comes to something when the only man who pays you
a compliment rides a moped with a box on the back. And in any
case, I think he was just being polite after I gave him a tip.

Once we'd cleared the plates away, we continued our
brainstorm. Danny checked his email. There was one message,
from Clare, saying that she still hadn't tracked down Otto.

"So, the bank?" I said.

"I've been thinking about that," said Danny. "We need to go
and see them, but I want to speak to their IT department as well,

to see if there's been any unusual activity. Do you remember Wedge?"

"What? *The* Wedge? How could I ever forget Wedge? Are you still in touch?"

Wedge shared a house with Danny when they were both students, although I never got to the bottom of what he was supposed to be studying. He took a shine to me, but his preference for spending money on drugs rather than rent meant that both Danny and he got evicted. In fairness I'd forgotten all about him.

"Occasionally. I've got his number. Last I heard he was working as a sysadmin."

"He's actually got a job? I didn't see that coming. What's a sysadmin?"

"Kind of a techie geek. He looks after computers and network servers and all that kind of stuff for a magazine company. I was thinking I could give him a call and see what he suggests."

Danny went to his bag and retrieved his phone, and then another gadget that looked like a mini-notebook computer, but which he proudly called his Psion. It was like an electronic Filofax.

"Here we go," he said. He tapped in a number on his phone keypad. I moved closer so I could listen to the call, but then Danny put it on speaker anyway.

It started to ring. An answering service kicked in.

"You're through to the answering service of Jeff King," said a remarkably sober-sounding voice. "Please leave your number and I'll call you back."

"Jeff?" I said, after Danny had left a message. The shocks kept on coming. Almost immediately Danny's phone started ringing. He connected the call, and then put it on speaker again.

"The Danster!" said a more familiar-sounding voice. "How are you dude?"

"Hey, Wedge, thanks for calling. All good. How are things?"

"Stop you there, my man. The Wedge has been retired. Sold out to the machine, and reinvented under a new regime of corporate bastardry. But great to hear from you. Still with the goth chick?"

I had to nip that in the bud.

"Technically not a goth," I said, "but yes he is, sort of, as a friend. Hi, er, Jeff. It's Anna. I'm here as well."

"Wow, the dude and dudette. Gorgeous goth girl. How are you? Has he provided you with copious offspring?"

"No, not yet," said Danny, "but there's always time." I gave him a very funny look at that point. "Listen, Jeff, I was ringing for a bit of advice."

"On how to give the ladies a baby? Coolio. You are right to call the expert and I will be happy to dispense my wisdom. Do you want a boy baby or a girl baby? I have a theory on position of conception."

"No, not that, a bit of technical advice."

Danny gave a brief summary of the bank challenge without giving too much away, and then asked if there were any specific questions he should ask that would get him past an IT department's natural reluctance to talk to strangers.

"I just need a way in," said Danny. "Something I can say that'll get them talking, so I can start asking questions."

"I see your problem. Your uncle Jeff can rescue you from the abyss."

"That's good. What do you suggest, then? Anything would be hugely appreciated."

"I can go one further. The world of networks is a network. How long do we have before it's mission lift-off?"

"It's quite urgent. I was hoping to speak to them tomorrow."

"Ten-four for a copy. Leave it with me, sixty minutes max. I'll make some calls and penetrate the cabal. Stand by on standby."

"That's brilliant. You'll call me?"

"I'll ping you the minute there's a breakthrough. Mission accepted. Laters dude."

The phone line went dead.

"For a minute there, I thought he'd turned all sensible," I said. "If anything, he's worse."

Danny laughed.

"We'll see what he comes up with, if anything. Okay. Next?"

His phone rang again. He said yes a couple of times. Then gave his email address and disconnected.

"That was Wedge again. He's going to email instead. Where were we?"

"You're onto the bank tomorrow," I said. "That's progress. What about Miroslav and Aleksander? How you find out whatever they're up to is anyone's guess, but hopefully this Otto bloke can help if he ever surfaces."

"Agreed. We need Clare to come through on that, or maybe give me Georgi's number so I can call him."

"What about Emma herself?"

"Emma?"

"Surely she'd know as much as anyone. It's not going to be easy if she's on remand somewhere, but at least if you could speak to her you'd get a sense of whether she seemed like the murderous type."

Danny thought for a moment.

"You know what I could do? I could talk to Amy."

"Amy, as in police Amy?"

He nodded.

"Didn't we burn our bridges with her over the whole hospital thing?"

"I don't know. I don't think so. I think she understood why we did it. And she seemed to have some sort of deal with Clare."

"Which I never really understood. Amy is the straightest person I've ever met."

"They're united by a common enemy. And if Graham's up to something again she may just be willing to help us. I'll call her."

He tapped away at the Psion again. I'm pretty sure a Filofax would have been quicker, but who am I to question the endless fascination boys have with gadgets? At least it keeps them away from porn. He dialled her number and put it on speaker again. She answered on the fourth ring.

"I need a really, really big favour," he said after they'd had a moment to catch up. "You heard about Graham arresting Emma Napier? The Gersbach and Haller Bank thing?"

"I did," she said.

"Can I speak to you off the record?"

"You can speak to me, but I may not be able to speak to you. It depends on what you want to talk about. I'm not at liberty to discuss live cases. You know that."

"I know. I appreciate that. I'm just working on a theory that there may be more to it than simply a domestic."

"Because?"

"Because Graham March was the DCI who made the arrest, and because I've come across some evidence that may point in another direction."

The line went silent for a moment.

"Interesting," she said eventually.

"You weren't involved, I suppose?" asked Danny.

"Happy to deny any association with it whatsoever."

"You sound like you've got your doubts?"

"Let's just say I'm keen to keep an open mind. What is this new evidence?"

"That's where we need to keep things off the record. It may be nothing. It may be something. I've just heard something on the grapevine."

"And does this grapevine have a name?"

"She does."

Amy either laughed or sighed. I'm not sure which.

89

"Danny, if I can, I'd be happy to help you. But there's a cost associated with that. You have to tell me what you've heard and why you think it's credible."

"Okay." He took a breath. And then explained about Clare, Otto, Miroslav and the rest of them, finishing with his suspicion that DCI Graham March was potentially covering up the truth.

"It may be nothing," he said, "but equally it may be something. But I really need to speak to Emma. I didn't know if you could suggest anything, maybe point me in the right direction? I don't even know where she is."

"Oh, Danny, that's a lot to ask. You want to go and do an interview with her?"

"Ideally."

"You do know she's locked away somewhere?"

"Yes, but I assume she's still allowed visitors, even if it's just her solicitor or someone."

"I hope you're not suggesting you're going to pretend to be a solicitor to break into a prison? They may not let you out."

Danny laughed.

"No, but if there's any way I can see her, it'd either prove there was definitely something in this, or that it's just worth forgetting about."

"It's all very interesting, Danny. The one thing I can tell you is that you're not the first person to talk to me about this. And before you ask I'm not at liberty to say who the other one was. But if there's a legitimate way to help wipe the smug smile off March's face, I may be able to point you in the right direction. Give me a few minutes and I'll be in touch."

She cut the call.

"We're getting there," I said. "I think we should have a celebratory cup of tea."

Danny didn't look quite so enthusiastic.

"It's just the deadline. I've got to have this finished by Thursday or hand everything over to Simon."

"Says who?"

"Says Mike. Honestly, if that happens and the bastard buries it because he's pals with March, I think I'll quit and go freelance."

"He wouldn't, would he?"

"Hopefully we won't have to find out. But honestly, can you see us getting to the bottom of this in less than three days?"

It was a fair point.

"I'll put the kettle on," I said.

By the time I returned with two cups of Yorkshire tea, Danny seemed significantly happier. He was just ending a call and I heard the word "fantastic".

"That was Amy," he said. "She's got me in to meet Emma. She's going to come with me."

"Brilliant news. When?"

"That's the only downside. Not till Wednesday, but that's still a world better than nothing."

I put the teas down.

"That is progress," I said. "Now we just need Wedge to come up with something magical and first thing tomorrow it's full steam ahead. You know what you need to take your mind off things?"

"Dare I ask?"

"You need a game of chess."

"God."

Graham March poured himself a generous measure of brandy, and powered down his PC. That was enough for today.

His home office was his sanctuary. Once it had been home to an array of folders, full of information about people of interest, whether friend or foe. The labels were frequently interchangeable. Technology, though, afforded new opportunities. It was the future. And the information was compiled with the future in mind, either to influence and cajole, or simply for the sake of reprisal. And where reprisals were concerned, the more thorough and comprehensive the better.

It was more secure on the computer. He could password-protect reports in Ami Pro, and then keep a backup disk in a hidden place in case, as had happened once before, the sanctuary of his office was breached. There would be no such problem this time. Life was all about learning. All about information. And all about making sure the information was secure.

He was thinking of going back downstairs, but Rafaela was there, watching TV. He could hear the canned laughter. It was a new comedy, set in a police station, called The Thin Blue Line. He couldn't stand the programme. At least dramas like Cracker and The Bill attempted to represent a police station properly, although they only ever gave half of the story. Of course, he could turn it over, but there would be a row, and really, what was the point?

He was saved from further rumination as his mobile sprang into life. Not his work phone, but the personal one he kept for out-of-hours interests.

As the caller spoke, March's expression darkened. Was he aware that a journalist was sniffing around Emma Napier? Just a word to the wise, straight from a source at Holloway. Maybe it was something he should be aware of? And yes, the journalist's name. Danny something? Yes, Churchill.

March ended the call. It wasn't going to happen again. Not this time. It was time to sort this once and for all.

He picked up the phone and dialled a familiar number.

Chapter 14

Tuesday, December 5th, 1995

D ANNY rose early, giving into the restlessness caused by the pressure of the looming deadline. He logged in to CompuServe and reread the email that had arrived last night.

Wedge had come through, with not just some questions to ask, but a contact within the IT department at Gersbach and Haller. A friend of a friend who would be willing to speak off the record, as long as he could talk away from the office. Danny dialled the number, hoping it would be early enough to catch him before he left for work, but not so early that he'd wake him.

"Is that Jonathan? Jonathan Killin?"

"Speaking." The voice sounded sleepy, which was hardly surprising. It was still dark outside.

"Hi, this is Danny Churchill. A friend suggested I should give you a call."

"Hi, Danny. I've been expecting you."

"It's not too early, is it?"

"It's never too early." The way he said it implied a willingness

93

to speak that took Danny by surprise.

"I don't know if you know, but I'm just making tentative enquiries into the Tom Napier case," said Danny. "It may be nothing, but I'm trying to find out a little bit more about Tom, what he was working on, and if there was anything else that could have led to somebody wanting to shoot him."

"You don't think it was Emma then?"

Something about the way he said it hinted that he shared the doubts.

"It's been suggested," said Danny.

"I'm not sure how much help I can be," said Jonathan. "I didn't know Tom very well."

"Did he have a reputation in the bank? Was he a risk-taker? Was he popular?"

"Like I say, I hardly knew him, but all those guys have a certain, how can I put this, 'arrogance'. I don't think he was any worse, but I'll tell you what has been happening. There's been a lot of activity within the compliance department over the last few weeks."

"Compliance?"

"It's a very tightly regulated business, Danny. We've got our own internal compliance department. The last thing we need is a visit from the regulator."

Especially if you've just lost a small fortune for a Serbian gangster, thought Danny.

"Were they looking into anything in particular?"

"I'm not sure. They certainly came to us asking for access to server logs and email archives. That's company confidential stuff though, so there's no way I could give you access to that. It's not just my job that would be at stake, it'd be illegal."

"Understood. No, don't worry, I wouldn't ask you to do that. I'm trying to find out if maybe Tom had any enemies or anybody else who stood out as being a potential suspect, that maybe the police haven't looked into."

"Have you had many dealings with private banks?"

"Not on a journalist's salary." Danny laughed.

"They're secretive places by definition," Jonathan continued. "Clients come to us because they want services that they maybe can't get from more mainstream places, and one of those is definitely discretion. I mean you know the whole thing about Swiss banks, right? I look after the infrastructure and make sure it's as secure as it needs to be to ensure that it could never be hacked. But we're just a satellite office. The main HQ is out in Switzerland. Listen, I'm going to have to go, but I'll keep an ear open and let you know if I come across anything, okay?"

"Brilliant. Just one last question before you go. Why?"

"Why what?"

"Why are you willing to help me? You don't even know me."

"I heard you were a good guy, and let's just say I don't exactly have much loyalty if there are things going on there that shouldn't be."

Even though I'd already been in the shower, I still felt I had the look of a zombie as I wrapped myself in my bathrobe and stumbled to the kitchen for an essential cup of tea. Danny was in the front room, and as I passed, he called out. I said I'd make tea for us both and then he brought me up to speed on the overnight developments, once I'd delivered it.

We had a plan of action for the day. We were going to attempt to talk our way into the bank so we could speak to Lucy, Tom's former secretary, and find out her take on the events. It was hard to gauge Danny's mood. He looked tense.

I started quizzing him on the logistics of the plan, but was stopped, mid-flow, by somebody knocking so hard on the door I thought it might splinter. Danny went to answer it while I looked out of the window. Worryingly, there was a police car directly outside, with its blue lights flashing although thankfully they hadn't turned on the siren.

"Danny Churchill?" asked a figure, looking rather resplendent in a uniform.

"That's me."

"And is that your car outside, the white Toyota RAV4?"

Danny took a step forward and looked to the left where his car was parked just ahead of mine.

"It is. Why?"

"Can you tell me where you were between the hours of midnight and 2AM this morning?"

"I was here, fast asleep. Why? What's up?"

"We have a report that a car matching the description of yours was involved in an accident near Kilburn in the early hours of this morning, but the driver failed to stop."

"Well, it wasn't me, and it wasn't my car."

The dishy-looking policeman didn't seem to be convinced.

"A witness made a note of the registration number, and it matches the registration of your car," he said. "Would you like to step outside with me?"

I moved to the front door as Danny followed the lovely policeman and his slightly less-striking colleague down the steps to his car. Even from there I could see the damage. The policeman pointed out the front of the car where the driver's side headlamp was smashed and there was a big dent on the front bumper and wheel arch.

A couple of minutes later they returned to our flat and Danny led them through to the front room.

"That's absolutely ridiculous," he said. "I was here all night. I haven't gone anywhere."

"And can anybody corroborate that?" asked the policeman.

"I can," I said.

"And who are you?"

I told him my name.

"And you're what? His girlfriend?"

"Flatmate." And available, I felt like adding.

"Well, I'm afraid that the evidence is rather stronger than the mere say-so of a flatmate," he said.

"What evidence? What exactly am I supposed to have hit?" asked Danny.

"The evidence is the damage to your car and the eyewitness statement confirming your registration number. Thankfully nobody was killed or seriously injured, but failing to stop and report an accident is still a serious offence. Obviously we need to take paint samples to make sure, but if they match then I'm afraid an alibi provided by a flatmate is at best worthless, and at worst an attempt to pervert the course of justice. Has anybody else had access to your car?"

"No, of course not," said Danny.

"Can you explain the damage? It looks fresh to me."

"No, the car was absolutely fine when I parked it there yesterday. I've got no idea how it got smashed. All I know is that it wasn't me." Danny looked at me as though he suddenly thought I might have borrowed his car, but that would have been madness. I've got one of my own and he knew I didn't like his.

"Can you give me the keys to the car, please?"

"What for?"

"We need to take it away for examination. It's up to you - I can arrange a tow truck, but you really don't want the expense of that on top of everything else when this comes to court."

Danny just shook his head.

"This is absolute madness," he said. "I was here all night. Both of us were. And I haven't hit anything."

But the policeman didn't seem interested in his denials. He made Danny hand over his keys and then sign some sort of form before warning us we would hear more soon.

"Before you go, I'm going to take some pictures of the

damage," I said. I quickly put on my shoes and a coat, and headed down with my camera.

It was bitterly cold outside, with a biting wind, and a few flakes of snow in the air. My shutter finger soon stiffened as I took pictures. Close up, the damage certainly looked bad. I could see some red paint mixed with the white of the wheel arch.

By the time I'd finished, the two policemen were ready to leave.

"What on earth just happened there?" said Danny, once we were back on our own.

I didn't know what to say. The whole thing seemed surreal. It wasn't going to be a cheap repair, but I had a worrying sense that it might turn out to be the least of our problems.

DCI Graham March connected the call.

"Well?" he asked.

"All done," came the reply.

"And he believed you were genuine?"

"Worked like a dream."

March chuckled.

"Nice work. Where's the car now?"

"It's in the compound. We'll release it back again in a few days, but in the meantime hopefully he'll have something to worry about other than Tom Napier."

"Perfect."

March ended the call, pocketed his phone and smiled. That was one favour called in, but there were many more people who owed him, both inside the Force and elsewhere. It had truly been an ingenious plan, but in the grand scheme of things, it was no more than an an encouraging start. By the time he finished, Danny Churchill would have ceased to be a problem. It was time to press on with phase two.

Chapter 15

THE Gersbach and Haller building was in the heart of the City of London, close to Liverpool Street station. It's not an area I often frequent, unless venturing out to one of the lovely Indian restaurants on nearby Brick Lane, although I did once have a date in the vicinity, in an overpriced wine bar. The less said about that the better. I'd had to fly to Milan the following morning, and I'd been very, very poorly.

As Danny pointed out, the only logical option was to take the Tube, and I had to agree. It *was* the only logical option. However, logic was not taking into account my entirely reasonable distrust of Underground trains, nor the walk to the station in freezing cold conditions, wearing my smartest navy skirt suit and heels. Danny couldn't drive, for obvious reasons, so I got behind the wheel of my soon-to-be-replaced Honda Prelude, and said I'd worry about parking it when we got there.

That backfired badly when I saw the eye-watering expense of a couple of hours in the closest multistorey car park, but I kept quiet and hoped he didn't notice.

We had a plan. Not much of one, in fairness, but it was the best we could concoct at short notice. Danny waited outside, in the shelter of a bus stop, while I went on a sortie. I didn't look like your typical bank raider, but that was kind of the point.

Gersbach and Haller shared an upmarket office block with several other companies. It all looked rather formal and imposingly affluent. A revolving door led to a marbled lobby that could have equally graced a five-star hotel. I walked straight past a huge reception desk to the lifts, hoping my outfit made it look like I belonged there, so I wouldn't attract the attention of an overly inquisitive security guard.

Thankfully, the lift buttons were labelled as well as numbered. Within a few seconds I was being whisked upstairs at speed. I'm not a huge fan of lifts either.

The doors opened to another impressive reception area, with a giant G&H logo etched into a vast mirror behind a curved light oak desk. Two women sat behind it, wearing headsets and looking like a formidable yet impossibly glamorous pair of gatekeepers. To my left, a corridor was lined by matching light oak doors. To my right, there was a larger open-plan office, full of activity, with people moving furniture. At the side of that I could see some glass-partitioned rooms. A man in a white shirt and paisley tie walked past me, carrying a fax machine, as I approached the desk.

"Can I help?" asked one of the women, in a voice that implied helping was the very thing she was least willing to do. Her name tag identified her as Peggy Holland.

"It looks very busy through there," I said, nodding in the direction of the open-plan space. "I just wondered if Lucy was available?"

"Do you have an appointment?"

"No, but she's a good friend of a friend, so it's kind of a social visit."

"I'm sorry but we don't really do social visits in working hours."

"Of course, I understand that. Just maybe if she was available to have a quick word, I could arrange to come back later?"

Peggy removed her headset and stood up, checking the room behind the glass wall.

"It looks like she's rather busy at the moment," she said. I followed her gaze to a tall, blonde-haired woman in a grey skirt and pale blue shirt, carrying a pile of box files.

"Is that Lucy there?" I asked.

"Yes, but she's very busy with an office move. I can't really disturb her. Leave your name and a message and I will make sure she gets it when she's free."

I doubted that.

"That's okay," I said. "I'll pop back another day. Thank you." I headed back to the lifts, not wanting to prolong the conversation. At least I now knew what she looked like.

I returned to the ground floor and then found Danny out on the street. All we had to do now was wait.

After about half an hour we saw Lucy emerge from the front entrance of the building and turn left. I nudged Danny and we fell into step, a short distance behind. I felt a bit uncomfortable stalking a single woman on the street, but it had to be done.

She crossed the road and after walking for a couple of minutes, avoiding the throng of lunch-hungry office workers, she entered a branch of the sandwich chain Pret. It was perfect. Once she'd selected a baguette, we got into line behind her at the till. Then, all I had to do was choose the right moment to deploy my fledgling acting skills.

As I'd said to Danny that morning, I hadn't done any acting since I was at school, on the night where the rostrum, on which I was standing, collapsed. I was terrified, but the teacher explained it was just a stage I had to go through. He completely missed the gag, which I still think was one of my finest. Either way, we'd decided Lucy would be less likely to think something was weird if she was approached by a woman. But come the moment of truth, I felt way out of my depth.

She paid, then turned away from the counter. It was hard to avoid me. Deep breath time.

"Wow, is that Lucy?" I asked, leaving Danny to order cappuccinos.

She looked at me in the blank way that Londoners have as a defence against speaking to a nutcase. Back home in Manchester we'd have been swapping numbers and arranging a night out by now.

"Lucy from Gersbach and Haller?" I continued.

"Sorry, do I know you?" It was a start.

"No, sorry, it's me that should apologise. I didn't mean to disturb you. I just popped in to see you at the office but you were busy moving things around. I'm Anna."

"From?"

"Not from a company. Just a member of the public."

"Okay." I could tell she was beginning to revert to the nutcase theory. "And you popped in to see me?"

"Yes, sorry. I'm not making a very good job of this. My partner and I" - I indicated to Danny - "we're, er, looking for some investment advice. A friend of a friend suggested G&H. He used to deal with Tom, before, well, you know…" Her eyes darkened and I just had to hope she wouldn't ask which friend. "So he suggested speaking to you. I think you were his secretary? Sorry to bother you, I should leave you to your lunch, but I just thought it was such a coincidence seeing you here."

She looked confused, which I took to be a good thing.

"If you've got the number, you should just phone the office," she said.

"I know. I shall. It's just we're not in town long and - oh, here's Danny. I'll introduce you. Lucy, Danny. Danny, Lucy from Gersbach and Haller."

He gave the boyish smile I always used to find irresistible. It was something about the way it travelled to his eyes, which in turn were perfectly framed by the floppy fringe. She seemed to be impressed too, and noticeably softened. They shook hands.

"Anyway," I continued, "We'll leave you in peace and give you a call."

"No, don't worry," she said. "It's just a bit of a hectic time. I'm moving to a new department now Tom's no longer there. I'm not sure I'd be much help, but I can point you in the direction of someone who would be."

"I can imagine. It must have been a terrible shock," I said.

"It was. It was just, well, horrible."

"Are you around this afternoon?" asked Danny, coming to my rescue. "We can phone you if that's okay, but if you're busy it can wait. Although we're only here a couple of days."

"This afternoon should be okay. I don't know what my new extension will be, but if you ask for me at reception they'll put you through."

"Shall do. How are things there now? I can't imagine what you've been through."

"It's been hard, but..." She shrugged.

"I saw it on the news a couple of days ago," he continued. "They've arrested his wife, apparently."

"Yes, Emma. I don't know anything about that, though. I mean, I knew her, but the whole thing is just, I don't know. It's baffling."

Danny nodded.

"Well, look, lovely to meet you," he said. "Apologies if it's a bad time."

She put her tray on a table and leaned on a stool.

"You're fine. I'm just a bit distracted."

"But your job's still safe?"

"Yes, thankfully. It took a bit of time for them to decide what to do, but it's all change from today on, really."

"That's good. I'm glad you're okay." It was like watching the first tentative stages of flirtation, but she responded with a smile and I increasingly felt like a spare part. I took the drinks and pulled out another stool, so I could at least avoid having to stand in heels while it happened.

"Thank you," she said. "It's been a weird time. It was me who found him." Now she seemed to want to keep the conversation going. It was pitiful.

"Ah, yes, of course," said Danny, with a warm and engaging smile. Jesus. "I remember now. That must have been awful."

"Not the best morning."

"I know. Well, every sympathy for that. But if you're busy we won't take up any more of your time now. We'll call this afternoon and make an appointment. Lovely to meet you."

"And you." She reached out for another handshake. For heaven's sake.

"Come on," said Danny to me. "We'd better head to our next appointment."

I stood up and said goodbye, but she didn't seem to want to shake my hand. I followed Danny out of the door.

"You've pulled," I said, as we started walking. The streets were still busy, and we both had people bump into us.

"She seemed like a nice person." The smile was back, but it was like he was teasing me.

"Where now?" I asked, ignoring it.

"Back home. That should give her time to get back to the office. Well done back there. You did a great job."

I was pleased at the compliment, but tried not to let it show. Mainly, though, I was just glad to do my bit. It felt like we were a million miles away from knowing what had happened to Tom, but at least we'd started the journey.

When we got back to the car park, Danny offered to put it on expenses. But then he started frantically patting his pockets.

"Are you okay?" I said.

"I've lost my wallet," he said, looking deeply concerned.

"Oh, here we go."

"No, seriously. I had it in Pret because I bought the coffees, but it's gone."

"Shit. Did you leave it on the counter?"

"I don't think so. I'm sure I put it back in my jacket."

"Do we need to go back?"

"I'll just run back. Are you okay to wait here? I'll only be a minute."

In fact, it was closer to ten, but the bigger worry was his expression when he returned.

"It wasn't there," he said.

"But we came straight back here. We didn't go anywhere else for you to leave it."

Then I remembered the way those people had bumped into us as we walked back up the street. I hadn't paid them any attention, and couldn't describe them, even if I was asked. But it looked like at least one of them was a pickpocket. I checked my bag, grateful for the fact that it had a clasp. My purse and car keys were still there.

"It's not been your day," I said, as I fed a ten-pound note into the car park payment machine. But the day was far from over.

Chapter 16

DANNY phoned his bank and credit card companies as soon as we got home, reporting the theft. He called the police too, but by the sounds of the call, they weren't particularly interested. I suppose compared to many of the crimes that take place in London on a daily basis, the theft of a wallet is fairly minor, but it was no less annoying and inconvenient for that.

While he was busy making calls, I phoned Lucy at the bank. That was the only upside of the wallet heist. At least it put the brakes on the fledgling romance. I think it was Peggy who answered the call, but once I got to speak to Lucy I managed to make an appointment for us to visit and have a meeting with one of their advisers, Christian Fuller, the following afternoon. Again, she seemed slightly less friendly with me than she had with Danny, and there was a hesitancy in her voice. She said that they were normally quite happy to visit prospective clients at their homes or workplaces, but I reiterated that we were only in town for a couple of days and that we'd be moving around a lot during that time. I think she believed me.

By the time we'd both come off the phone, it was already late afternoon. I just had time to make a cup of tea before I was alerted by the ringtone of my special Clare mobile. I connected the call and put it on speaker.

"How are things going?" she asked.

Danny explained about the progress with the IT department and Lucy at the bank, but Clare's mood changed when he told her about the police visit, car damage, and theft of his wallet.

"That makes me nervous," she said. I didn't associate Clare with nervousness.

"The car thing was weird, but the wallet was just one of those things," said Danny. "That could have happened anywhere."

"Nothing is ever just one of those things," said Clare. "It's too much of a coincidence."

"You don't think it was connected, do you? I don't see how it could be."

"Danny, we're a long way from having visibility of all of the connections. What are you doing this evening?"

"I was going to do a bit of research into the whole Bosnian conflict, and start mapping out what we know, what we think and find where the gaps are."

"You're not going out?"

"No, I wasn't planning to."

"Okay, best not to. That sounds like a good plan. Take care, Danny. And that's not just a platitude. I really mean it. Be careful."

When she ended the call, I announced that I was going for a lie down. Really I should have popped into the studio to check on Diana, to make sure that everything was running smoothly, but I just didn't have the energy, and something about Clare's tone was continuing to unsettle me. I was sure Diana would be okay. She was nothing other than efficient, even if her name caused me problems.

"Before you go, look at this," said Danny. He was reading news reports on CompuServe. "It says there are over 120,000 land mines in Bosnia alone. Just think of that for a moment. How on earth are they ever going to manage to clean that up?"

The more I found out about the war in the former Yugoslavia, the more horrified I became. It had been barbaric. I couldn't believe that something like that could still be happening in Europe in the late twentieth century. There was much about the world that I didn't understand.

———

Danny's work mobile rang. The incoming number was withheld.

"Hello?"

"Danny, a little bird tells me that you've been a naughty boy." DCI Graham March's mocking voice was unmistakeable.

"Graham, to what do I owe the displeasure?" said Danny, letting go of the mouse, and moving over to the sofa.

"That's hardly the way to talk to a Detective Chief Inspector of Her Majesty's constabulary."

"I try not to think about you in those terms. It seems somehow inappropriate, given everything I know about you." He yawned, deliberately.

"Danny, you're surely not still harping on about all that, are you?" March continued. "I was exonerated as well you know, and in fact I'm quite what I like to call flavour of the month at the moment. Luckily for you, my reputation for solving high-profile cases goes before me, so I don't have time to investigate your little motoring infraction. But I will watch the court case with interest."

"You can watch the court case all you like, and investigate it for as long as you want, as far as I care. It wasn't anything to do with me."

March laughed.

"And I hear word from the City boys that you've managed to

misplace your wallet. Now that I could have helped you with, had I not been so busy chasing real criminals."

"News travels fast, then."

"You're the journalist, although I use that term in its loosest possible sense. You never did write that article about my work for the homeless."

"I kind of lost interest after I saved your life."

March gave a derisory laugh.

"You saved my life? Good God, Danny, is there no end to your delusion? I admit I was having a little local difficulty in the midst of an investigation, but it was nothing that I wasn't on top of. Talking of being on top of things, how's little Anna? Has she got herself a boyfriend yet? You must give her my number."

Danny was fast losing patience.

"Is there a point to this?" he asked. "Or are you just calling to gloat because you'd heard I'd had a bad day?"

"I called because I heard you'd been misbehaving."

"I told you, that was nothing to do with me."

"I'm not talking about your inability to drive in a straight line without hitting something. I mean poking your nose into a police investigation that doesn't need your involvement."

"I have no idea what you mean."

"You know exactly what I mean. You want to be careful, Danny boy. If you keep doing bad things they're going to catch up with you. I'll be keeping an eye on you and making sure of it."

Before Danny had a chance to reply, March ended the call. So that was that then. March showing his hand. But what exactly was he up to, and why would he bring attention to himself? Unless it was to hide something altogether darker.

Chapter 17

I CAME to, just after six, and staggered through to the living room to find Danny hard at work on his notebook computer.

"How are things going?" I asked. Danny told me about his call from Graham March. Nothing surprised me any more.

"Are you going to be working all evening, or do you fancy a break?" I asked. "We could go to see GoldenEye if you fancy it."

"I'd love to," said Danny, "but I still need to do lots of research, and write as much as I can to show Mike on Thursday. I could do with a break, but I can't really do the cinema. Sorry."

"No problem. I could do with an early night as well, actually. I'm still all over the place. I'll attempt to cook us something, and then thrash you at chess again if you like?"

Danny looked cautious. In fairness, it could have been at either part of my suggestion. I didn't really fancy cooking, but we'd missed out on lunch and I was starting to feel a bit wobbly.

Not for the first time that day, there was a knock at the door. It wasn't quite as aggressive as the last time, but even so I could see Danny's heart sink.

"What's he up to this time?" he said.

"We're not expecting anybody, are we? Don't worry. Whoever it is, I'll tell them you're not in."

That ceased to be an option when I opened the door. Clare didn't wait to be asked before walking past me. She was carrying a brown paper bag and a bottle of wine.

"I've brought you an Indian," she said. "I thought you might be hungry. Your nose is looking better."

I ignored the nose comment. Clare, as ever, looked flawless.

"How did you know we wouldn't have had dinner?"

She looked at me as though the possibility of not knowing everything hadn't even crossed her mind. I was past the point of thinking it was telepathy, and was fairly sure she was simply bugging the flat. Nevertheless, she wasn't wrong. Hugs were exchanged.

I laid the table and Danny joined us. The wine was a very pleasant-looking bottle of white Rioja, and somehow she'd even managed to chill it.

"The good news," she said as I was serving up, "is that I've tracked down Otto."

"Fantastic," said Danny. "How did you manage that?"

"I knew I'd get there eventually," she said, avoiding a direct answer to the question. "It was just a case of perseverance. He's back in London tomorrow evening so I've arranged for us to go and see him."

"Well done. It's going to be a big day tomorrow, then. We've got Emma in the morning, the bank in the afternoon, and then Otto. If something good comes from all of that, the deadline is on."

"Hmmm," murmured Clare. She took a sip of her wine and then announced that she was going to pop outside into our back garden for a cigarette while we finished the food. I half expected her to climb over the fence and make a run for it, in the traditional manner, but as I took the plates through to the kitchen I could just make her out in the light from the window, talking on her phone.

She saw me in the kitchen, ended the call, and came back inside.

"All done?" she asked.

"Delicious. Thank you so much."

I refilled the wine glasses and took them back through to Danny in the front room. Clare followed me.

"So," he asked her, "what time are we meeting Otto? Did he give you any indication that he knew anything that would be helpful?"

"No, it was only a brief call. He was at the airport. That's a good point, though. Remember when you go to see Emma, not to give any indication that you know who Julian is, or who he was working for. Play dumb and see what she has to say."

"Of course. It'll be fascinating to talk to her, though."

Clare sat on the arm of the sofa. I was impressed by her coolness. The last time she'd been in our flat she'd killed a man. At the time I'd had cause to be extremely grateful. I moved to the armchair and zoned out while they talked shop.

"It is good progress," she said, "but it's just a start really. We still need to speak to Miroslav, and we still need to rule out any connection to the Smoking Gun."

"The what?"

"The gay club Tom used to go to."

"Ah, I thought you meant the actual gun. Do you think the club's still relevant?"

"Maybe. It's definitely part of Tom's past. We should go there."

"Do you think they'd let us in?"

"I don't see why not. It's not like it's anything particularly extreme. As far as I know, it's not a leather and rubber bar, more of a swingers' place for the gay and bisexual market. It's not probably the kind of place to go as a heterosexual couple, but women are allowed. I rang them yesterday. We should definitely check it out."

"Okay." Danny sounded hesitant. "The issue is time. I've got two days before Mike pulls me off the story."

"There's your answer then. We'll go this evening. Unless you've got something better to do."

"You and me?"

"All three of us."

That caught my attention.

"Can I just stop you there?" I said. "This sounds dangerously like a plan, and the last time you came up with a plan I had to dress up in a nurse's uniform and nearly got arrested."

"Yes."

"Well, then. You can understand my reluctance?"

"Not really. Obviously there are theme nights, but on a Tuesday I suspect a nurse's uniform would be overkill."

"Jesus." I started having another flashback. "And the last time I went to a nightclub at your behest, I ended up covered in bruises and had a craving for a Mars bar."

Clare raised an eyebrow.

"I'm not sure I want to know."

"It was your bloody fault. Bentleys in Sunderland, remember?"

"Ah yes. Sorry about that. I've still got the pictures. They were good."

"Thank you. But anyway, my point is, I'm not entirely sure that a gay swingers' club is my natural domain."

"Why not? The longer you have to think about it the more the thought will scare you. It's like jumping off a mountain on a zip wire. Sometimes you've just got to do it."

"Do you regularly jump off mountains on a zip wire?"

"It's a metaphor."

"God." I'd forgotten about Clare's metaphor obsession. "And I'm supposed to be having an early night."

"How old are you?"

"You already know that."

"I know, of course. It was rhetorical. A month off twenty-six."

She knew everything. I didn't think I'd ever had a conversation about birthdays with Clare.

"The point I'm making is: you're still young enough to party," she continued. "And you can't tell me you're uncomfortable with gay people when you work in the world of fashion."

"No, of course not. What I've got a problem with is going along with the plan when I've not had a chance to think about it."

"You're thinking about it now, so that's that one sorted. Danny, are you coming?"

He looked at me. I shrugged. The wine was making me sleepy and really I just wanted to go back to bed.

"Yes, we'll both come with you," he said. I gave him a stern look, but he'd fixed his attention in a different direction.

"You'll be fine," Clare continued. "There'll be loads of hunky men with great arms." That made Danny laugh, irritatingly.

"They're not going to be interested in me, though, are they? Given that I'm neither a man nor gay."

"You can still admire them, though."

I turned to Danny who seemed to be finding the conversation hilarious.

"What's wrong with you?"

"Nothing," he said. "It's just your arm thing."

"What's wrong with liking arms?"

"It's just a bit weird."

"No it isn't. They're nice. Not too muscly, though. I don't want to be crushed, but just a bit of definition. Anyway, you're obsessed with legs, so it's a bit hypocritical to have a go at me."

"Legs are an acknowledged thing."

"Ha! I knew it."

"Yeah, but that's normal. Aren't women supposed to like nice eyes and six-packs and men in touch with their emotions? Not arms."

"If you're going to talk shit, I'm ignoring you." I turned back to Clare. "I don't have an option, do I?"

She shook her head.

"It'll be fun. You'll have a great night. The music will be brilliant."

It was futile to protest.

"Okay. What time are we going?"

"It's nearly seven now. I think aim to leave for nine. Can you be ready in two hours?"

"Twice over."

"Perfect. Danny?"

"Not a problem. I just want to write up a few notes. Can you give me an hour or so?"

"Of course. That gives me a chance to play Anna at chess."

"What?" I said, looking horrified.

"I thought you liked playing chess."

"I like playing Danny at chess, but that's because I win."

Half an hour later, I was in my room, getting ready, feeling elated after a completely unexpected victory. I'd beaten the invincible! I could not have been happier. I slid on ripped jeans over fishnets and then started work on my make-up. The shift in my mood was astonishing, and I was ready to party.

It took a while for it to dawn on me that the chess victory was all part of the plan, and the master manipulator had actually outplayed me completely.

Graham March took his pint and edged through the smoke, past groups of hardened drinkers, to a quiet alcove at the back of the bar. It was the sort of place that he'd frequented earlier in his career, to spend time among the lower reaches of society, and coax them into revealing dark secrets about their criminally inclined acquaintances. Many of the rougher parts of London had been gentrified, but this was an oasis of old-school squalor. A game of backgammon was underway on the next table, but he was confident he would not be overheard, even assuming the two elderly players retained any semblance of their hearing. The floor was sticky, the furniture worn, and the lighting dim. The man was waiting for him.

"What the hell is this place?" he asked in a clipped German accent as March approached.

The detective smiled and squeezed in opposite.

"I thought you'd appreciate the cultural diversity, Stefan," March replied. "How the devil are you?"

Stefan looked at his beer with a degree of distaste.

"I am sure I have been better. What do you need from me?"

"Straight to business. I admire your efficiency. The embodiment of the cultural stereotype."

"I have no desire to spend one more minute in this place than strictly necessary."

"You disappoint me. I thought we would make a night of it." March laughed. "Okay, cards on the table. We have a problem with some mutual friends, but with a little bit of assistance I think we could secure what I like to call an extremely positive outcome."

"Which friends?"

"Otto Schreiber. And, of course, the enigmatic Ms Woodbrook."

Stefan nodded.

"It is always Clare," he said. "I thought we asked you to deal with that problem in Sofia?"

"What can I say? It was all in hand, but I was let down by the hired help. It won't happen again."

"You need to ensure that it doesn't, or you may find you cease to be considered a person of influence."

The warning was stark. He was well aware of what could happen when somebody was no longer considered an asset.

"Duly noted."

"So what is the nature of the problem?" asked the German.

"Otto is making a nuisance of himself investigating Gersbach and Haller. He seems particularly interested in one of their clients, Miroslav Nikolić."

"I am familiar with Miroslav."

"I expect you are. It seems Miroslav is up to mischief, but Otto's interest could potentially cause complications with an ongoing police investigation."

"Since when has the integrity of a police investigation been your top priority?"

"That is cutting, Stefan. I can't pretend I'm not hurt."

"And I can't pretend that I am unfamiliar with your reputation for talking shit."

March took a sip of his pint, and then wiped the froth from his top lip.

"I assume you still have friends in Croatia?" he said.

"Of course."

"And I assume that they would not rejoice in the success of a Serbian gangster like Miroslav?"

"I expect that would upset them greatly."

"And if I could tell you that far from being just a casual observer, Otto has now sensed an opportunity, and is now joining with Miroslav and Clare to bring about the demise of your Croatian friends, would that give them an added sense of urgency to assist with the issue?"

Stefan sat back.

"That sounds rather fanciful."

117

"Exactly my first impression. But it's a verified collaboration. So let me run this by you. I may need to borrow you, and a couple of your boys, but I think you'll agree that my proposal solves many of our problems at once."

He leaned forward, and lowered his voice, and then started to explain the specifics.

Chapter 18

I WAS making great progress with Clare's bottle of wine by the time Danny was ready. He looked particularly fetching in a white T-shirt and faded blue jeans. A Brylcreem quiff would have completed the full fifties heart-throb image, but instead he opted for a bit of gel on the sides and left the floppy fringe to do its stuff.

"Clare, what are we actually trying to achieve here?" I asked.

"We're just having a look around. Seeing what we can find out. Asking if they knew Tom, and generally getting a feel for the place."

"But won't we be conspicuous? I've been to Heaven, but that's my only experience of a gay club. I get the impression this is a bit more... intense."

"We'll be fine. I'm sure we'll blend in."

The confidence with which she said that made something click inside my brain. Why had I never thought of it earlier?

"I hope you don't mind me asking but are you...?"

"Anna, there are some things it's best not to discuss."

"What sort of answer is that?"

"You know me. I'm normally an open book." I looked at her. Either she was deluded or just taking the piss. "But I don't like to discuss personal things. I don't like to classify myself."

"In terms of?"

"In terms of anything. I'm just me. I have issues I'm working through. Technically I don't even exist. That can be quite a burden on occasion. It's like..."

"God. Are you going to do another metaphor?"

"No."

"Thank goodness for that."

I poured the last of the wine as Danny finished off in the bathroom. It was a shame to leave a bottle unfinished.

"I've done some research," she continued, metaphor avoided. Of course she had. "The owner is Ben Lambert so we could try to speak to him. If not, the head barman is Stevie Butler. He'd be best placed to tell us if Tom was a regular, and who he may have been meeting up with."

I sniggered.

"What's so funny about that?"

"Are those their real names?"

"It's what they go by."

"Lambert and Butler? Don't tell me, are the doormen called Bob Benson and Harry Hedges? I had you down more as a Silk Cut girl."

I wasn't quite sure where I was going with that. Thankfully Danny appeared just as she was giving me a look that bordered on pity.

"All set?" he asked. We nodded. It was time to be brave.

I was already in no state to drive and fully intended to be even less so by the time the evening was over. Danny was still car-less, and I had no idea how Clare got around the place, so we hailed a taxi. Twenty minutes later we pulled up outside the club, and a few minutes later we were inside.

At once I was struck by the utterly delicious seediness of the place. Everywhere seemed to be painted black. The lighting in the main bar area was minimal, with coloured neon signs combining with UV tubes to create an instant aura of debauched possibility. Danny's white shirt glowed. Our skin looked tanned and radiant. Music carried through from a nearby dance floor, but the bar area was quiet enough to hold a conversation. There weren't many customers. The action seemed to be elsewhere, but there were a few men dotted around, a handful of women, and some gorgeous-looking transvestites who had clearly spent far longer on their make-up than I had. It may not officially have been leather and rubber night, but both were still in abundance.

Clare led the way to the bar. We both had a martini with lemonade, while Danny opted for a bottle of Beck's. And once those were delivered she suggested going for a walk to explore the place.

I saw things that I could never unsee. As we approached the dance floor, a thumping Hi-NRG version of REM's Losing My Religion blasted through the speakers. I never had one to lose. Sometimes I thank God I'm not religious.

On the far side of the dance floor, darkened corridors led to a series of play rooms. Naked bodies were entangled on vinyl-covered mattresses, watched over by an appreciative audience who might have been awaiting their turn or just enjoying the show. Danny's expression was hilarious, but Clare seemed to be in her element.

She took my hand and led us through an open-plan space which clearly served as the orgy room, and then through to another even darker area full of cages and instruments of torture. A man wearing nothing more than a leather thong was strapped to a cross, while a hooded figure whipped his back. There were men on all fours, wearing collars and leads. I saw a few women. Some were kissing, some were chatting. Others were being impaled with all sorts of gadgetry. The sense of liberation was curiously erotic, but my primary emotion was fear, and relief that I wasn't here alone.

Eventually, Clare led the way back to the dance floor, and dragged me into the middle of it, while Danny stood at the edge, watching. As we gyrated ever-closer to the pounding electronica, I could see him being chatted up. It was genuinely very funny indeed, especially after significant amounts of alcohol. After two songs, however, I began to have a pressing need to answer the call of nature. The toilets were surprisingly clean, but I have no doubt there were industrial quantities of drugs in the vicinity.

We made our way back to the bar.

"Well, that was educational," said Danny. I laughed.

"I liked it," said Clare. She sat on the stool next to me, lit a cigarette, and then started to caress my thigh with her free hand. I looked up in surprise, but she leaned over and whispered "role play" into my ear. I ordered another drink, and quite possibly blushed, but it was so dark nobody would have noticed.

"I don't want to sound prudish," Danny continued, noticing her hand, "but you can kind of understand why someone would be less than keen for their husband to come here."

"But enough to murder them?" asked Clare.

"That's difficult to say. What makes anyone murder anyone? It's normally sex, money or anger, and if he'd been spending a fortune coming here, that could be the hat trick."

"Yes, maybe - but when there's anger, something snaps and there's a violent outburst. But with a gun? That says pre-meditated to me. So unless she'd been planning it for a long time, it still doesn't make sense. Let's chat to the barman."

Clare beckoned him over.

"Hi," she said. "Are you Stevie?"

"Which Stevie are you looking for? You've got a choice of two."

"Stevie Lambert?"

He shook his head.

"I'm the other one. Stevie Dunhill. Do you need to speak to the other one? I can get him for you."

She nodded and said thank you.

"Dunhill?" I said, when he'd gone. "Are they taking the piss?"

"Anna," she said. "What's the name of the place?"

"The Smoking Gun."

"Right."

And then I felt stupid.

"So yes, they've all got made-up names," she continued, "but that's kind of the point. It's the attention to detail that makes all the difference. We don't yet live in a society where everyone can be open about an association with a place like this, so there's anonymity from the top. And yes, they're all cigarette brands because of the name. And I am a Silk Cut girl, but I'm cutting down, before you ask, because apparently it's not good for you."

There was absolutely no evidence of her cutting down, but I didn't like to point that out.

A new man came over, dressed in a leather waistcoat over an incredibly tight white t-shirt. He looked older than the barman, perhaps in his mid-thirties. He introduced himself as Stevie Lambert.

"What can I do for you?" he asked.

Clare smiled at him and took charge.

"Nothing really, I just wanted to say hello. It's our first time here." She put her arm around me and squeezed. "I'm Clare, this is my partner Anna, and her brother Danny. We're not from London but a friend recommended we should come down and check it out. He said you were the main man."

"One of the team. I hope you're having a great time."

"So far so good." She winked. "It's certainly lively. I'm sure we'll be back again."

"It can be." He looked in the direction of the dance floor, where two transvestites were doing a fantastic job of dancing in heels higher than even I'd attempt. "Are you meeting your friend in here?"

"Tom? No, it's kind of awkward. This is sort of our wake for him."

"Oh, I'm sorry. Was he the guy who died?"

"Yes, it was so sad. Such a shock. He used to rave about this place."

She was good. I had to give her that.

"People do," said Stevie. "Customers tend to share their enthusiasm. It's a very open and inclusive environment."

"I noticed. There's a great mix of people."

"Yup."

"Mainly regulars?"

"Yeah, lots of familiar faces but others just passing through."

"Really? On holiday? Or business?"

"Both."

"How can you tell?"

"Accents, the way they dress. You get attuned to it."

"Haha, I can imagine. Did you know Tom?"

Stevie's expression changed. Was it wariness, or was he hiding something?

"Not personally."

"Did he come in often?" That appeared to be one question too many.

"Who are you again?"

Clare took it in her stride.

"Can I level with you?" she said.

"Go on."

"We're not really old friends with Tom."

That seemed to lower the temperature a notch.

"I actually work for Time Out. Tom was a friend but he mainly hung out with one of the team who do the film guide."

The ease and conviction with which she lied was both impressive and unnerving. It came so naturally.

"I've been brought in to spice up the nightlife section, and make it more edgy, if you like. So yeah I heard about this through Tom, and I felt we owed it to him to check it out. But don't worry, I'll only say good things. And it is still a kind of a wake."

"I'd better get you more drinks then," said Stevie, instantly more amenable.

The conversation continued. Yes, he knew Tom. Yes, he was a regular. No, he didn't see him with anyone in particular on the night he died. Yes, we were welcome back any time. When he left us to enjoy the rest of our evening, Clare turned to Danny.

"Not a huge help," she said, "but it's been entertaining." I wondered if it was time for her to let go of me, but at the same time I was quite enjoying the affection. It was rare I ever got any.

"It was definitely worth coming," said Danny. "At least we've got a bit of insight into the kind of bloke he was. It's weird to think that probably all of the people in here have day jobs. It's hard to picture some of them in an office."

"Especially the ones in the collars," I said. "It's good, though, that they can come here and let off steam. And if they enjoy it, all well and good."

Clare finally let go of my leg.

"I expect you two need to be getting back. Early start tomorrow?"

"It is," said Danny. "I'm meeting Amy first thing then heading off to see Emma."

"You say that as though you're trying to get rid of us," I said.

"Well, you know, the night is young." She winked, then I think she saw my shocked expression. "No, my party days are over. I'll see you into a taxi and then I'll be heading back."

"Where are you staying?" asked Danny.

"Tonight?"

"Yes, while you're in London."

"I move around, Danny."

"There's no point in me asking you, is there?"

"Didn't we have ground rules about that kind of thing?"

"And I think we also agreed to abandon them."

We made our way out onto the street. When we'd successfully hailed a cab, hugs were exchanged. Danny and I settled into the back and she waved us off. A thought occurred.

"We can't just leave her," I said.

"I was thinking exactly the same," said Danny. "Should we follow?"

I nodded, a smile creeping over my face. If nothing else, it would be exciting to see where she ended up. Danny spoke to our taxi driver and asked him to stop around the first corner. The driver protested, accusing us of wasting his time, but a big tip solved that one. We got out of the cab and doubled back. Clare was walking down the street, in the opposite direction.

I found it hard to suppress a giggle, but Danny put his arm through mine and told me to be quiet. We fell into step, a good distance behind. She seemed to be heading in the vague direction of Holborn.

She turned into a side street, disappearing from view for a moment, so we quickened our pace to minimise the chance of losing her. We got to the turning just in time to see her turn right at the end of the street, back onto another main road. We followed again. But when we got to the end of the street and looked right, there was no sign of her. She could have taken a taxi, or another turning.

"Well, that wasn't very successful," I said. "What now?"

"Go to bed the pair of you," said a voice from behind us.

We turned, and there she was, standing defiantly, arms crossed, right where we'd just walked. I couldn't see how it was possible.

"How did you even do that?" I asked.

"I'll see you soon," she said.

This time, when we hailed a cab, she took the first one and then disappeared into the night. We didn't bother to follow again. We should have known it was pointless. And Danny had a very big day ahead.

Chapter 19

Wednesday, December 6th, 1995

I HAD work to do back at the studio, as Diana had asked me to pop in to go over some contracts, but I offered Danny a lift to his meeting with DS Amy Cranston.

Holloway prison was only about a mile away from our home in Rochester Square, so it should have been a two-minute journey. But as is the nature of things, we left later than planned and then got stuck in traffic on Camden Road, so by the time we pulled up next to her, we were considerably late. Amy didn't seem best pleased.

"You do know I'm going out on a limb here," she said as she got out of her car.

"I'm sorry," I said. "My fault." We shook hands. I liked Amy. We'd spent a lot of time with her over the past couple of years, and she deserved absolute respect. She was dedicated to her job, incorruptible, but fair and reasonably tolerant when Danny and I pushed the boundaries. She obviously had a job to do, but she shared Danny's loathing of DCI Graham March and everything he stood for.

"What exactly are you hoping to get from Emma?" she asked after we'd done the pleasantries. "You'd better not let me down."

"Can you trust me?" asked Danny.

"Can I trust a journalist? Do you want me to answer that truthfully?"

He laughed.

"Well, I hope you can. I'm working on the basis that if Graham arrested her, there's probably a reasonable chance she's innocent. And if she is, she may be able to point me in the right direction to find out who actually killed her husband."

"And how is Clare. Is she back in the country?" She didn't miss a trick.

Danny looked hesitant.

"Truthfully? I don't actually know. She was in London last night, but Clare being Clare, she could be anywhere by now. Is she still on your wanted list?"

"Officially, of course, but she's not a priority. Not for me, anyway. I can't speak for March, though. I think he'd love to get her."

I didn't fancy his chances there. I knew whose side I'd rather be on.

"I can imagine," said Danny. "Do you still see much of him?"

"Not as much as I used to, but more than I'd like."

"I don't understand how he still manages to keep his job."

"Danny, that's the million-dollar question, where the million dollars are presumably being passed around among his associates. Let's just say, I think he has connections."

"What I don't get is that presumably for the Napier case he was the SIO?"

"The what?" I asked, interrupting.

"Senior Investigating Officer," said Amy. "Yes, he was."

"But he was still heading up a team," Danny continued. "Didn't anyone else in the team think there was something odd about it?"

Amy paused, as though thinking how best to phrase things.

"He can be quite influential, and quite domineering," she said at last. "I've spoken to the DC on the case. She's yet to fall under his charm, but she's young and not long been back from maternity leave. It's difficult to speak out when you're not the most experienced. I can vouch for that."

"Can you tell me who it was? Would I be able to talk to her?"

Danny was relentless, but Amy looked hesitant.

"I'm not sure that would be wise."

"It could help. If she's got any suspicions she could maybe point me in the right direction. I'm very much up against it on the deadline."

He did his puppy eye thing.

"Let's just see how things go, Danny. She's called DC Lisa Miller but do not attempt to speak to her without me giving you the nod. Okay?"

"Lisa Miller?"

"Yes. Why? That sounds like you know her."

Danny and I looked at each other with something approaching alarm. We didn't particularly know the person herself, but we knew the name.

"No, not really," said Danny. "It's a long story. I shall tell you later."

He checked his watch.

"Should we get going?" he asked.

Amy looked at me.

"Don't worry," I said. "I'm just the driver. I'm leaving you to it. Danny, best of luck. And thank you, Amy, for helping."

We shook hands again and I returned to my car. There was work to be done for both of us, but a women's prison held much more appeal to Danny than me.

Danny and DC Amy Cranston were buzzed through from security, and then escorted to a meeting room that resembled a school canteen, albeit one from a very old school, and with the chairs and tables bolted to the floor. They were told to wait while somebody went to fetch Emma.

"How do you know Lisa?" asked Amy while they waited.

"I don't," said Danny. "But remember when Clare went missing?"

Realisation hit.

"Yes, of course. I'd forgotten about that part of it. Small world."

"We should introduce them. See if we can spot the difference."

Amy laughed.

"You are being careful with Clare, aren't you? You do know what she's capable of?"

"I do, and I am. I'm not saying she's a reformed character, but it seems like her heart's in the right place most of the time."

"She's good at making you think that."

"Don't you agree?"

"I think you just need to be careful, that's all."

"But last year, you could have arrested her and didn't..."

Conversation stopped as Emma was brought into the room by a prison guard. Danny had only seen her in pictures. She looked older in person, without make-up, her features drawn. Her movements were wary, as though she was scared, living in a world of which she had no comprehension.

"Emma," said Amy, "please sit down, and thank you for agreeing to see us. I'm Amy Cranston, a detective sergeant in the Metropolitan Police. This is Danny Churchill. He works for the press, but I can assure you this is not directly for a story, so you have no need to worry."

Emma took a chair. The prison guard moved to the side of the room, but kept a careful watch.

"Why are you here?" she asked, in a tired voice, eyes darting from one to the other. "Do I need a solicitor?"

"No, please let me assure you, this is entirely off the record. Nothing you say will be used in court in any way. This is not an official police interview."

"I'm sorry, I don't understand."

Amy looked at Danny, who took over.

"Hi Emma, I'm Danny. Like Amy, I'd like to thank you for agreeing to see us."

"I'm pleased at the break to be honest. But I don't get why you're here."

Danny offered a reassuring smile.

"I'll explain. But again, really there's nothing to worry about. I work for the Daily Echo, which I expect you know." She nodded. "The paper has been running stories about the case. But, I don't work on the news desk and I'm not really here in an official capacity. I'm here because, well, not to put too fine a point on it, I've got serious doubts that you did it."

"I didn't."

"Exactly. And I believe you. I'm on your side. And yes, ultimately I'd like to write a story, but one in which you're released and the person, or people, responsible are brought to justice."

Emma frowned.

"But why? Why you?"

Danny looked at Amy, who raised her eyebrows.

"Because, let's just say, I've already come across the DCI who arrested you, and I don't always trust his judgement. I'd like to ask you some questions, if that's okay, to hear your side of things and work out if we can find some lines of enquiry that I can pursue."

"Are you being serious?"

"I am. I can't promise anything. And some of the questions may be a little bit awkward, but let me assure you, I'm not here to write an exposé or take advantage of you in any way. If at any point you want to stop, you can say so. I just want to find out the truth. Amy can vouch for me."

Emma looked at the DS, who nodded.

"I don't know what to say, but, well, thank you."

"And you're happy for me to ask anything?"

She shrugged.

"Of course," she said at last. "I've been through the mill in the last few weeks, and any sense of dignity has long gone. Ask anything."

"Okay, perfect. Just be as open as you can. So first: I assume you didn't do it?"

She laughed, with a bitter sense of irony.

"Correct."

Danny smiled and opened his notebook.

"That's handy, or this would have been quite a short chat."

Emma returned the smile. Danny thought she looked tense but he was keen to help her relax.

"Okay. To begin: the police report said you were having an affair."

"Yes." She looked away then down at the floor. "To my eternal shame. I don't know what I was thinking."

"Hey, it happens. Were things not good at home?"

"Sorry, did you say your name was Danny?"

He nodded.

"That's the thing - things were fine at home. We got on brilliantly, like best friends, but the trouble was, that was all it was. I try to be a good person, you know? I work for a charity. I know I'm lucky, or at least I was. Tom had a good job. A great job. We were very well off, and that was my way of giving something back, and doing some good in the world. I've never hurt anyone. I wouldn't know how to."

"But why the affair?"

"It was just weakness. Just the human need to feel loved. To feel safe in someone's arms."

"You didn't think it would hurt Tom?"

"Tom? No. Not in the slightest."

"But how? Because you didn't think you'd be caught?"

Emma sighed.

"No, I didn't think I'd get caught, but it wasn't that. It's what I just said. We were like best friends, but there was no passion. Listen, Tom was gay. I didn't know until all this came out, but it makes sense looking back. We hadn't... been intimate in a long time. I'm sorry, but I really do think I'm a good person. Yes, okay, that was bad, but don't I have the right to be happy? Is that really a crime? And it certainly doesn't make me a murderer."

"So why not leave him?"

"Because we still got on. We were like brother and sister really. Childhood sweethearts. We loved each other, we just didn't have that kind of relationship."

Danny nodded, then paused and changed position. He consulted the list of questions he'd prepared at home.

"What happened that night?" he asked eventually. "The one where Tom caught you with - er..."

"Julian. We went out to a restaurant. It was lovely. It was fireworks night and we made a joke about how romantic it was. We came back, had a drink and then went to bed. Tom was supposed to be out of the country. I don't know where. He didn't tell me. But then he came back unexpectedly in the middle of the night. He was furious - although ironically not with the infidelity but with the security risk. He'd been very stressed."

"The security risk?"

"Yes, he was paranoid about security. Occasionally he'd bring work home with him, and it was always highly confidential. Even I didn't get to look at it."

"Okay, and he kicked Julian out?"

"Yes."

"But you carried on seeing him?"

"Oh God." She nodded, but looked close to tears.

Danny waited.

"Take your time. Are you okay?"

"Yes. I'm sorry."

"No need to apologise. Did Tom know it was continuing?"

"No, we kept it secret. I didn't expect it to last. It was just a bit of fun. I'm getting older. That was it in a nutshell. Just fun."

"When did you last see him?"

"Julian? That was the night Tom died."

"I read the reports. You said you were at a fundraiser in Birmingham."

"I was."

"And that you stayed at a hotel up there that night. But when DCI March spoke to the hotel they said you'd had a booking, but you'd already checked out that morning. "

"I know."

"So why did you say you'd stayed there?"

"I don't know. I panicked. I was in shock about the whole thing. I didn't want to say what I'd really been doing. I know I should have done."

Danny looked at Amy.

"You should," she said, joining in, "but that doesn't make you a killer. March discovered the lie. I've read the reports. He checked your car and found a layer of frost, and when he called the hotel they confirmed you hadn't been there."

"I know."

"So that meant you didn't have an alibi."

"I know. But I did. I was with Julian. I know I shouldn't have said what I did, but it was embarrassing. It was the way that policeman was looking at me, like I was some tart having a midlife crisis. I felt under pressure, and I said I'd still been in Birmingham when I knew I hadn't."

Amy leaned back in her chair, and Danny resumed his questions.

"You met Julian through a fundraising company?"

"I did."

"But when March spoke to them, they'd never heard of him. You see, this is where you've got a problem. March investigated the affair but he didn't find any evidence. So even when you changed your story, your alibi didn't stack up."

"I know, but he didn't look very hard. I gave him Julian's number. Don't you believe me?"

"I do, of course I do. And I'm sorry if this comes across as confrontational. I don't mean it to. I'm just trying to see it from his point of view so I can see what he was thinking, and find out where the gaps are."

Amy joined in.

"According to the case notes, March called the number you gave him, and the person who answered denied any knowledge of you."

"I know. I don't understand that. Unless he was just scared of being involved. But I didn't kill Tom, and I know Julian didn't either. He was with me that night."

"At your house?"

"No, we met at a hotel. In London. Tom knew I was away so wasn't expecting me home. As far as he knew, I was staying in Birmingham."

"Which hotel?"

"In London? It was one Julian used when he was in town. The Shelford. It's not very big."

Danny looked to Amy again.

"Did anyone other than Julian see you there?" she continued.

Emma shook her head.

"I was in Birmingham till late. I left the fundraiser early, but I still had to drive back. The M1 was horrific. I didn't get to London till past eleven. There was nobody on reception when I arrived. I was relieved as I thought that was embarrassing too. I knew Julian's room number so just went straight there."

"You can see why this all looks suspicious, though?"

"Of course. I'm not stupid. Occasionally I do stupid things, but never to hurt anyone."

"And you've got no idea why the person answering Julian's phone denied any knowledge of you?"

"I told you. I just assumed he was scared. Maybe he's married. Please, let me give you his number. Could you talk to him for me?" She looked at each of them, imploringly.

"Of course. I'll try," said Danny.

Emma gave a mobile number, and he wrote it in his notebook.

"That still doesn't explain why the fundraising company had no record of him," he continued.

"I know. Maybe the whole thing was a lie. Maybe he just made up stories to get to know me. It's horrible. You think you know someone, but ..." Her voice drifted off.

"Okay. I'll call him and see what I can find out. I can't make promises, though."

"I understand that."

"That brings us on to physical evidence," Danny continued. "Tom's final words were a phone call to his secretary, recorded on her voicemail, so there's no doubt he had his phone with him when he was attacked. And yet the phone wasn't recovered from the scene. It was found in your house."

"I know. I can't explain that."

"Along with bullets matching the one that killed your husband."

"I can't explain that either."

"But you can see why March decided you must be guilty?"

"Yes, if you believe the evidence, but somebody else must have put it there."

"I believe you, but you understand why I have to ask these questions?

"Of course. I'm just grateful you're taking an interest. I just wish I was more help."

"You're doing very well."

"Thank you." She smiled.

"Did anyone else have access to your house between the shooting and the phone and bullets being found?" Danny continued.

"No. I mean, I had a few well-wishers round in the immediate aftermath, but nobody I didn't know."

"Can you give me their names?"

"It was mainly family and friends. My sister, a couple of people from work. My boss. Tom's secretary came round with flowers from the bank, and then one of his colleagues, Christian. Give me your notepad and I'll write them all down for you."

A couple of minutes later she passed the notebook back. Danny looked at the list. There were no obvious suspects.

The prison guard coughed.

"Time's up," he said.

Danny looked up.

"Okay. But one last question. The obvious one really. Do you have any idea at all who did this? Who shot Tom and why they're so intent on framing you?"

"I've thought about little else for the last three weeks. But no, sorry. It doesn't make any sense."

"He didn't have any enemies you can think of?"

"No, not that I know of."

"Did he ever mention anyone called Aleksander? Or Georgi?"

"Not to me."

The guard took an impatient step forward.

"Time, please," he said.

Danny nodded, and he and Amy stood up.

"I'll do what I can," he said. "Stay strong. And for what it's worth, I still believe you."

"Thank you. You know it's the little things that hurt the most.

It's horrible here but I can cope with that. But I wasn't even allowed to go to the funeral. My own husband."

The tears in her eyes looked genuine. Danny and Amy were escorted back to reception, and Emma was left to an uncertain future in her cell.

Chapter 20

DANNY phoned me when he left the prison. Amy had offered him a lift, so I arranged to meet him by the wall fountain in Festival Gardens, next to St Paul's Cathedral. It was walking distance from our appointment at the bank.

Leaving Diana to sort out some paperwork and equipment repairs at the studio, I drove home to get changed. If I was to impersonate a wealthy investor again, I'd have to struggle into the suit and smart shoes, with a few bits of sparkly jewellery. I don't have any real diamonds, but Danny had an impressive Ceylon sapphire ring that used to belong to Clare, so I found that and borrowed it. He wouldn't mind. I tried to tame my hair by pulling it back and fastening it into a kind of avant-garde chignon type affair, but that's never particularly successful.

This time I didn't take the car, but instead hailed a taxi. Lesson learned on that one. Danny was there before me, and he looked me up and down as I approached.

"Very smart," he said.

I frowned.

"Are you just saying that?"

"No really, you look great."

"Thank you. I tried." It always amazes me how easily men are swayed by smart shoes and a glimpse of hosiery, but I suppose it shouldn't. I've photographed enough in my time.

"How was Emma?" I asked.

"It was good. I really felt for her."

"Oh God. Losing your heart to the wealthy widow?"

"You're terrible."

"I just speak my mind. Did you get the sense that she'd done it? You'll have to be careful if you did, because you'll get her released and then start going out with her, and next thing we know they'll be scraping up bits of you in the car park at the Echo."

"What's got into you?"

"Nothing, I'm just teasing. Seriously, how was she?"

"You're weird. She was fine. She seemed really scared but no, I definitely don't think she did it."

He gave me a summary of the conversation. It amounted to more questions than answers, but I agreed there was something very strange and possibly incredibly dangerous about the whole situation.

"I should call Clare and give her a quick update too," he said.

I leaned against the wall, wishing I'd stopped for lunch, while Danny called Clare on the private mobile. When the call connected and he started to give her a summary I stood up and walked a few paces down the path, trying to get a better view of the cathedral. It was one of London's most famous landmarks, but I'd never been inside. I turned back to Danny. He was still on the phone. Just then a hand suddenly gripped my shoulder, and I nearly screamed.

"Where the hell have you just come from?" I said when I turned and saw Clare standing directly behind me. "I was literally just looking in that direction and you weren't there." She smiled, and carried on talking to Danny.

He ended the call when he saw the pair of us, and then started to walk towards us.

"Should you even be out in public?" I asked. "In daylight?"

"Anna, you worry too much."

"I'm not the one on the Wanted posters."

"Exactly. Don't worry. I wouldn't do anything without assessing the risk. Nice ring by the way."

I immediately tried to hide my hand behind my back. I don't know why. She'd already seen it. In any case, she'd acquired an even more impressive replacement since losing the first one, and I knew she didn't want it back.

Danny arrived and she gave him a hug. In previous times I'd have been jealous, but I was pretending to myself that I wasn't.

"So that sounds all very interesting," she said to him. "Well done for going. I must thank Amy."

"Are you speaking to Amy?" I asked.

"In a way." She left it at that. "In the meantime, I've been on the phone to Otto."

"That's good," said Danny. "Any news? Is he still up for meeting tonight?"

"Yes to both. Julian's in London and I'm waiting to hear back about meeting him, but hopefully you'll be able to see him early this evening too, and then come to meet Otto after. I'm just waiting to see which hotel he's in."

"He stays at the Shelford apparently. I've got his number."

"Have you ever been to the Shelford?"

"No. I don't even know where it is."

"Okay, well let me tell you, he won't be staying there. He may have met Emma there for a romantic liaison, but he'll be staying somewhere more central. The Shelford is more High Barnet. Otto's calling with the details later."

"Excellent - that's all good progress then," said Danny. "I think we're actually getting there, although I'm not really sure where 'there' is."

"And we've got the meeting at the bank in a moment," I added.

"Perfect," said Clare. "What are you doing after the bank?"

"I'm going back to the office," said Danny. "I'm going to try to speak to Mike if I can, to give him an update. It depends how it goes here, though."

"I'm going home to get changed," I added. "And I know this sounds really dull but I've still got a suitcase to unpack and piles of washing to sort out."

"Good. Well, I'll be in touch later. I'd offer to walk you to the bank, but I suspect there's fairly heavy CCTV so I'm heading in the other direction. You don't need to follow." She laughed. "Very best of luck. I hope it goes well."

And with that, she was gone.

"It's like she just materialises out of thin air," I said when she was safely out of earshot.

Danny gave me a squeeze.

"Don't worry about her. I'm sure she knows what she's doing."

"That's what she said as well." But my natural inclination was to worry. Especially when I got a sense that things were about to become very concerning indeed.

Chapter 21

THIS time I didn't feel quite so much like an imposter. Peggy gave me a look of recognition when we got out of the lift, but then focused her attention on Danny, which was slightly irritating on several levels.

"Can I help you?" she asked as we arrived at the desk.

"We've got an appointment with Christian Fuller," I said, making sure she could see the ring.

"I'll just see if he's available."

He'd better be, I thought. She asked us to sign the guestbook while she made a phone call.

"Please take a seat. Somebody will be along shortly," she said, as she replaced the handset.

After a couple of minutes, Lucy appeared.

"Hi," she said with a smile. "We meet again. Follow me."

She held open the door and then led us through the open-plan area to one of the partitioned meeting rooms.

"Are you working for Christian now?" asked Danny, as we entered the room.

"Not as such, but we're still in the middle of changing things over. Take a seat and he'll be with you very soon. Can I get you a drink? Tea? Coffee?"

We asked for tea, which was a risk. I'm fussy about tea at the best of times. She left us on our own to take in the surroundings. I looked at Danny.

"Do you have a plan?" We hadn't really discussed the specifics of what we were trying to achieve.

"Sort of. I want to find out about Tom, but we may have to be patient. See how it goes. We may not get much today but hopefully we'll get a sense of the place."

"So the long game?"

"Exactly. I'm hoping he may talk a bit, though. He'll be keen to establish some sort of commonality."

Lucy reappeared, carrying two mugs with G&H branding. It was a suspiciously quick return, so I didn't hold out much hope for the quality of the contents, but the accompanying biscuits were a nice touch.

"I've just seen Christian," she said. "He's on his way. I'm just across the office if you need me." She said that last bit specifically to Danny, and may as well have winked as she did so, or started to unbutton her blouse. Honestly, it was getting annoying.

I didn't have time to comment, however, as Christian arrived just as she was leaving. He looked in good shape, probably in his mid- to late thirties. His expensive-looking suit was accessorised with equally expensive-looking glasses and a very big watch. We stood up and shook hands.

"So, Mr and Mrs Churchill?" he said. I didn't like to correct him. I'd long thought that if I'd married Danny I'd have been AC to his DC, and the entire thing would have been electrifying.

"Danny and Anna," said Danny as we all sat down.

"Welcome to Gersbach and Haller. Lucy gave me a brief summary, but maybe you could tell me how you think we may be able to help."

I sat back while Danny launched into a surprisingly

impressive speech about our current investment portfolio, our preferred risk profile, the offshore funds we were already exposed to, and a summary of our mid-term and long-term investment goals. It was all utter nonsense, of course, but as with Clare in the gay club, I couldn't help but be impressed by the brazenness of the fiction. Clearly I'd never be able to trust a word he said again. Occasionally Christian looked in my direction, as though seeking verification of a point, but I was happy to nod and act subservient to my husband, the financial whizz.

When Danny finished, Christian took over, explaining about the services the bank could offer. It all sounded suitably impressive. Danny asked a couple of technical questions, but the answers were delivered with the professional smoothness of an accomplished salesman. After about half an hour, in which I discovered the tea was not as bad as I feared, although a long way short of Yorkshire, and in which I also managed to resist the natural temptation to dunk the biscuits, Danny thanked Christian for the overview and said it was definitely something to think about.

"Out of interest, how did you hear about Gersbach and Haller?" Christian asked, as the meeting drew to a close. This was the opening we'd been hoping for.

"A friend recommended you. He knew Tom, and suggested we speak to him," said Danny. "I was shocked to hear about what happened."

"Yes, we all were. It was truly tragic."

"I hear they've arrested his wife. Did you know her?"

"We'd met socially, but I didn't know her all that well."

"But did she seem the type?"

"Danny, darling," I interrupted, working on a hunch, "I don't think you should be asking things like that." Good cop, bad cop. I nudged his leg.

He looked to me then up at Christian.

"You're right. I'm sorry." He paused. "It's probably not

something you want to talk about."

Christian shrugged.

"There's not much I can say. I mean, obviously it was a terrible time for everyone, but no, to answer your question, I had no idea that she could have been responsible."

"Has it affected things much at the bank?" I asked. "You mentioned you like to give a personal service. I can imagine it must have been a shock to Tom's clients too."

Christian sounded hesitant.

"Yes, I suppose, but obviously it was a unique situation. At least I hope it was. If you come on board with me, I'll attempt to last a little bit longer." He laughed, but as jokes go, I thought it was weak, and not particularly appropriate.

"That's a point, though, actually," said Danny. "Obviously if we do move to you we'd be looking for things to be carefully managed. There is a slight concern that if you're now taking on all of Tom's clients, you may already be too busy to give things proper attention."

"No, you don't need to worry about that. We're part of a team. I took on some of the work, but the accounts were spread out among all of us. I can assure you the level of service you'll be given will be just as thorough as before."

"That's good to know." Danny stood up and I followed. It was time to put into practice the next bit of the plan.

"Can you just point me in the direction of the bathroom?" said Danny.

Christian looked wary.

"I can show you," he said, "but..."

"Don't worry about me," I interrupted. "I can wait with Lucy and she can take us back to reception, if that's okay."

"Yes, that's a good idea."

As Danny went off, I went over to Lucy's desk.

"Everything go well?" she asked, clearly wishing that it was me who had gone to the bathroom, and Danny who was now waiting with her.

"Yes, all good. I still can't get over the Tom thing, though. I still can't believe it was you who found him. That must have been awful."

"Yes it was, but I'd rather not talk about it any more, if that's okay. I still find it very upsetting."

"I can imagine. I'm sorry." There was definitely something in her eyes. Was it annoyance? Grief? Fear? I couldn't be sure. It was time to change the subject, but I was short of inspiration. I latched on to the first thing I noticed. "I do like your necklace, by the way."

She looked down at her pendant.

"Thank you."

I was getting desperate.

"Is everything settling down now?"

"Seems to be."

"That's good." I saw Danny approaching but tried to hide my relief. "Well, hopefully if things work out we'll see you again, but if not then the best of luck."

"Thank you."

I waited for Danny to join us, then Lucy said she would see us out. When we reached reception, she shook his hand again, so I offered mine, just to spite her. Her grip was surprisingly firm, which made me regret it immediately.

We took the lift back to the ground floor. As the doors closed and we were on our own, Danny started to speak.

"Well, that was interesting," he said.

"Was it? I'm sorry if I wasn't much help."

"No, you did well. I was just thinking about something Emma said, when I asked if anyone had been to her house since the shooting. She mentioned his secretary brought flowers, but also Christian."

"So he went to see her?"

"Yes, but it sounded like a separate visit, not with Lucy. Just now he told us he hardly knew her and that they'd only met socially. So why did he go round to see her? To plant the evidence?"

"You don't think...?"

"That he did it? I don't know. I didn't get a sense of any motive, but he could have definitely left things behind. Did he look like a killer to you?"

"What does a killer look like? I suppose if we knew that, we'd know what we were looking for. He seemed very slick but had a hint of the arrogant salesman."

"That's what I thought."

The lift doors opened and we walked in silence across the lobby, back to the street.

"He's definitely on the list," said Danny, once we were outside. I fastened my jacket against the cold. "Maybe he was jealous of Tom's clients. Maybe he wanted some of the commission."

"But you've still got the voicemail message. Tom saying 'Emma, no!'."

"What if that wasn't the context? What if the exact conversation was something like, 'Do what I tell you or I'm going to tell Emma' and he makes the call at just that moment, presumably for help, and says 'Emma? No!' not to her but to try to stop whoever it is from speaking to her."

"Could be." I stopped to think about it. "But if that's the case, and you can explain how someone else left the stuff in the house, then that would explain how they framed her. It doesn't explain why."

"No, that's what I was thinking. Unless she was just an easy target."

Danny said he had to go to the office, but wanted to borrow money for travel as he didn't have his wallet. I gave him a twenty-pound note.

"I'm going to speak to Mike and see if I can plead for an

149

extension on the deadline. I'll tell him what we've discovered. He's got to see that the whole arrest and charge is fundamentally unsound."

But when Danny got to the office, it transpired that his editor's patience was the very least of his worries.

———

Danny felt the watchful gaze of Simon Oakley on him as he stood by the door to his editor's office. It was unusual to find it closed. Mike was always around at this time of the afternoon.

Danny looked out across the open-plan editorial department to see if he could spot him, but there was just the usual sight of journalists tapping away at computers or talking on phones. Everyone seemed as busy as usual. Everyone, that is, except Simon, who was leaning back in his chair with uncharacteristic calm, a faint smile taunting Danny, as though he knew things he wasn't letting on.

There was no sign of Mike, so Danny headed to his own office to wait for him there. But as he approached, he was surprised to see the door standing open, and four people talking inside. And as he got closer still, he was even more surprised to recognise Mike and one of the company's lawyers, speaking to two men he didn't recognise. He knocked apprehensively on his own office door.

"Sorry, am I interrupting anything?" he asked. Mike turned, but his expression was straight from the Arctic.

"Is this him?" asked one of the men.

Mike nodded.

"Sorry, what's going on?" asked Danny. For the first time, he noticed the equipment stacked on his desk.

"We need your phone, and notebook computer if you have it," said one of the men.

It took a moment to process.

"What's happening? Can somebody please let me know what is going on?"

The other man spoke.

"We have a warrant to search your office and remove equipment in relation to investigation into potential offences. I am not at liberty to discuss the details, but your cooperation would be duly noted."

"What offences? This is ridiculous."

"Phone tapping," said Mike, with evident disapproval. "Among other things, apparently."

"But that's madness. I wouldn't even know how to tap a phone. Christ, is Graham March behind this?"

But before Danny could say anything else, he was escorted away by the company's young lawyer, who was doing his best to control the situation.

"I have to advise you to say nothing more until we've had a chance to conduct our own internal enquiry," he said.

"You can make whatever enquiries you like. I haven't done anything."

"That's what we will determine. In the meantime, you can imagine how seriously we have to take this."

"But it's utter shit. It's fucking corruption. I'm being victimised by Graham March. He tried to accuse me of a hit and run, for God's sake, and now..."

"Danny, let's not make this any more difficult than it is already, okay? We have no option other than to suspend you while the investigations are ongoing. On full pay, obviously."

"I'm sorry, but this is an absolute outrage."

"Please, if you'd like to just come down to reception with me. I need to make sure you leave the building."

"I'm not going anywhere. I'm going in there and telling them to fuck off."

"I'm afraid that's not an option."

Danny looked at the lawyer. He didn't know the man's name,

but he'd had dealings with the legal department while verifying that previous stories were safe to run. He knew it was pointless to argue, but that didn't make it any less unjust.

"What happens now?" he asked, struggling to sound calmer than he felt.

"You leave it up to us. We will be in touch."

"But that's ludicrous."

"I'm sorry but there's nothing more to say on the subject."

Within a few minutes, Danny was being shown through to reception and relieved of his security pass. A minute after that, he was standing on the street, looking back at the Echo building, feeling as alien as the day he'd first arrived on work experience, nearly six years before. His entire career had been based in that building. Nothing made sense. Nothing seemed fair.

Chapter 22

DANNY stood for a while, trying to make sense of his future, unsure whether to go home, or go to the pub. Whether to fight for his career or search for oblivion at the bottom of a glass.

"You're looking dazed," she said. "What's up?"

He turned, and looked into the familiar, all-knowing eyes of his former boss.

"Clare, I..." But he didn't know quite what to say.

She took him by the arm and led him away from the front of the office, and down a small pedestrianised street to a coffee shop.

"Something's happened," she said, as she led him inside, and then ordered two cappuccinos, both without sprinkles. "Talk to me."

"I've been suspended."

"Shit. Have they been looking at your browser history?"

"I'm being serious. Bloody phone tapping. Escorted out of the fucking building."

"You're not kidding?"

"Of course not."

Clare let out a deep breath, as though struggling to process the information.

"Wow," she said at last. "It's a fabrication, obviously?"

"What do you take me for? Jesus."

"I'm sorry. I don't know why I said that. I was just... what happened?"

"Oh, you don't want to know. It's March, obviously. I just expected a bit more support, that's all."

"Danny, you're not making much sense."

They took their drinks to an outside table, despite the December chill, and he explained about finding the men in his office, and how he hadn't been given a chance to defend himself. How he'd been suspended, and the feeling of utter hopelessness while some power play he had no control over put at risk everything he'd ever worked for.

"And you know the worst of it? It wasn't the accusation, it was the smug look on the face of Simon Oakley as I was led away, the bastard. He fucking knew what was going on. He's so in March's pocket. If they find any evidence, I bloody well know who put it there."

Clare had regained her composure. "There are two ways of looking at this. One, it's just March playing games, trying to mess with your head, and lashing out at you in some form of vendetta. Or two, he's running scared because he knows that of all the people in the world, you're the one with the guts and determination to actually keep pursuing him until his past finally catches up. Not even his past, but everything he's still up to now."

"That's lovely of you to say, but he just seems ever more untouchable. I don't know what the bastard has got on everyone, but it's like he's controlling everything. Nothing sticks. Everything he says and everything he does is like an anathema to justice, and yet he gets away with it. How? Why can nobody else see it?"

"I can see it. You can see it. Amy can see it. But he's a tough one to beat. He's firmly entrenched with his own little power base. It's never going to be easy, but we will get there."

"Will we?"

"Of course we will."

"But how can you say that? Who even are you any more?"

"Whoa, Danny. Where did that come from? I'm on your side here."

He leaned back in his chair and rubbed both hands over his face. Clare took the opportunity to light a cigarette.

"Can I have one of those?" he asked, eventually.

Clare laughed.

"No. You bloody well can't. I've got you into enough trouble already."

"Isn't that what you always said, though? It's a career that leads to alcohol and nicotine?"

"I may have done. But seriously, stick with the alcohol. In any case, Anna would never forgive me. I'm scared of her."

Danny smiled at the thought of his flatmate.

"You're not scared of anyone."

"I am. You haven't seen the way she looks at me."

"She's five foot nothing and seems to worship you."

"I thought she was five two? And I don't know why that would be."

"Believe me, it wasn't always the case. But since last year, since Aurelia, since everything that happened. She used to go off in a strop if I even mentioned your name, but now it's like you're royalty."

"Oh, Danny." Clare laughed and flicked ash. "She's brilliant. Treasure her."

They settled into a thoughtful silence. Aurelia's terrified face still haunted both of them. As did the knowledge of Graham March's role in the ring that trafficked her from Poland.

"But seriously," Danny said at last. "What do you reckon? Is there actually any point any more?"

"Well." Clare frowned as though thinking hard. "The way I look at it, this could actually be a good thing."

"What are you talking about?"

"On the upside, if you're suspended it means you don't need to worry about the deadline."

"It also means I'm officially not allowed to work on the story."

"That's not going to stop you, though, is it?"

"God, you're priceless."

"But you're not - are you? All it means is that if the Echo fire you, you can take it to the highest bidder. Go freelance. I recommend it."

"Your kind of freelance?"

"No, not that, obviously."

Danny paused to drink his cappuccino than looked directly into Clare's hazel eyes.

"Do you ever wish you hadn't done what you did?"

She stubbed out her cigarette.

"Ground rules, Danny."

"Oh, fuck the ground rules. Can you stop hiding behind a veil of frigging self-made mystery and stop treating me like a child? I want to get to know you."

"And again, where did that come from?"

"Can you actually answer a question for once?"

She sighed, looked like she was about to speak, then sighed again.

"I'm sorry," she said at last.

"Sorry? For what?"

"For everything."

"Not good enough."

"What do you want me to say?"

"I want to understand you. I want you to say anything that helps me do that. You're a good person. You fight for the underdog, and expose the corrupt. Your whole career was about seeking justice and trying to put things right in the world. And then..."

"Then what?"

"And then you went mental, if you excuse the expression. We're in a public place so I'm not going to spell it out, but you bloody well know what you did. Did something happen? What happened to the person you were?"

"She's still here."

"But is she?"

"Of course."

"Oh, don't give me that bollocks."

Clare sat back, idly toying with the ring on her finger. She picked up her packet of cigarettes, took another one out, and tapped the filter on the table, but then looked at it, rather than lighting it.

"What do you want from me?" she said at last.

"What do I want? I don't want anything. I just care about you. There, I said it. Always bloody did and always bloody will, and it breaks my heart to think that you are... I don't know how to say it. Damaged? You know what? I don't care what you did. I mean, obviously I do, and I'll never understand it." He leaned forward, voice dropping to a whisper. "You killed people. Actually killed them. For greed." Settling back in his seat, he let his voice return to normal. "But the thing that cuts me up is the effect it's had on you as a person. I worry about you so much, more than you'll ever understand. I hate to think of you living in some twilight world, hiding, and paranoid. I just want to wrap you in cotton wool and make everything okay, and I know I can't do that, and I can't have that, and the most heartbreaking part of all of it is that it's entirely self-inflicted. So there, cards on the table. I don't want anything because the one thing I want is the one thing I can't have, because you made it impossible. But despite that I still want it. Does that make sense? I don't know if you'll ever understand what that all did to me. But worse than that is trying to understand what it must have done to you. And despite everything, I still think you're brilliant and yet so deeply bloody flawed. God you piss me off, and yet I'd still walk to the ends of the earth to do anything for you, because you are you, and irreplaceable. There you go. Rant over."

"Wow." Clare sat silently for a moment, and lit the cigarette.

"And I wish you'd stop smoking as well."

"Oh, Danny. Some things I have no control over."

"That's bollocks as well. I've never known anyone more in control."

"I don't mean things. Real things. Tangible things. I mean inside my head."

"That's what I'd love to understand. What goes on inside your head."

"Good luck with that. If you work it out, please tell me. In the meantime, can we go back to the matter in hand?"

"So you're not going to help me to see the real you?"

She reached out and put her hand on his. He put his other on top, relishing the touch of warm skin, rubbing the back of her hand with his thumb.

"Danny, this is the real me. I'm here. I'm not going to let you down. I can't dwell on the past. Accept me for who I am, and yes, understand that I have flaws and big, unsurmountable issues, but we are where we are, and where are just at this moment is trying to free someone wrongly charged with murder, and finally nailing our bastard policeman." She squeezed. "Okay?"

"Okay. But don't think I won't try again."

"I'm flattered that you care. Really. And I honestly don't deserve it, but let's park that for now. In the meantime, I've got some good news."

"Go on."

"I've spoken to Otto and tracked down Julian. He's agreed to meet you this evening, at 6.30."

"Well done. That's encouraging."

"I don't know if it'll help but it'll definitely be worth a try. Take Anna if she'll go with you, and then come to meet me after, okay? I'll be with Otto, so you can talk to him as well. We will get to the bottom of this, I promise you."

"Shall do."

She passed him a piece of paper.

"That's all the details. It's the Belgravia International Hotel, and that's the room number. And Danny?"

"What?"

"Please don't worry about me. I will talk to you one day and answer any question you have, but let's get this sorted first. Deal?"

He nodded.

"Deal."

They stood to leave. Danny watched Clare go, not knowing where she was heading, and as ever, wondering if he'd ever see her again.

Chapter 23

I'D spent all week since returning from Mauritius in a state of sleep deprivation, but finally gave in to the inevitable. When I woke up, it was with a sense of complete disorientation, not knowing if it was morning or evening or even which day of the week it was. On the floor was the still-daunting pile of washing, mocking me for my inability to simply put it in the machine and press two buttons.

Somebody tapped on my bedroom door.

"Hold on," I called. It had to be Danny, assuming it wasn't merely a very polite burglar, but I couldn't have him seeing the state of my room. I staggered to my door, opened it a fraction and peered through the gap.

"Are you all right?" he asked.

"Fine, yes."

"Have you got somebody in there?"

"What? I'm not some sort of floozy."

"It's just the way you're holding the door."

"Yeah, well." I stepped out onto the landing and closed the door behind me. "How may I assist?"

"Have you just woken up?"

"May have done."

"Sorry to wake you, but we've had a few developments."

"That sounds good."

He did one of those "maybe" faces.

"I'll make you a cup of tea," he said, "then bring you up to speed."

A few minutes later I was in the front room, admiring my Ikea Kandinsky print, and listening to Danny telling me about his suspension, and how Clare had managed to arrange a meeting with Julian. It was a lot to take in.

"So, are you up to a trip?" he said, at the end of it.

"If you think it'll help. Have I got time for a shower?"

"If you're reasonably quick."

Twenty minutes later, I was back in the front room, after a fairly rushed attempt at making myself look presentable. I was pretty sure that the fashion industry would one day decide to excommunicate me, on the back of my apparent inability to do make-up in a rush to anything like a professional standard, but nonetheless I had my jacket on and car keys ready by the time Danny announced we should leave.

We drove in relative silence, carving through the early evening traffic, and arriving close to the Belgravia International Hotel with ten minutes to spare. It was raining heavily, so we sheltered under an umbrella as we made the short walk to the hotel.

As we got closer, I nudged Danny.

"Is that Christian?" I asked. A man in an expensive-looking suit was striding down the hotel steps in front of us. He didn't see us, but raised his collar, and set off in the opposite direction, walking quickly against the rain.

"It looks like him," said Danny. I thought about calling out, but he was already too far away, appearing to be in a rush to escape the weather. In a moment a taxi had whisked him away into the evening.

A uniformed doorman gave us a look as we arrived at the

entrance of the hotel, but we both just said good evening and walked past. We already knew Julian's room number, so we made our way past reception and straight to the bank of lifts. The concierge tried to stop us and asked if we needed assistance, but Danny just waved as though he was a resident.

It felt hauntingly similar to both my attempt to access the bank, and Clare's detour in Sofia. But this time at least we knew what we were doing, and that we were expected.

"It's exciting," I said to Danny as the lift bell chimed our arrival on the fifth floor. But my excitement diminished when we finally reached Julian's door. It was slightly ajar. We knocked, but there was no answer. Danny knocked again and then called out, but still nobody replied. He looked at me. I shrugged, and then he pushed the door open.

The room was in darkness, but the light from the hallway was enough to illuminate a bank of switches on the wall. Danny flicked all three, and the room was filled with a yellow tungsten glow, perfectly illuminating the horror within. I recoiled in shock, struggling to fight a rising nausea.

Julian, if that was who it was, was lying on the bed, but most of his brains were spread across the headboard. There was blood everywhere and a terrible smell. I fell against the wall, my legs suddenly failing to support me. Danny was speechless. We both stood in a shocked silence, unable to quite comprehend the scene. I'd seen dead bodies before, but nothing had prepared me for the sight of one that had come to quite such a brutal end.

Danny grabbed me and dragged me out into the corridor, pulling the door behind us. He took his handkerchief and wiped fingerprints from the door knob, and then reached in and did the same on the light switches, before finally closing the door completely. Neither of us could speak. Danny stood still, apparently in shock. I grabbed his arm and tried to pull him in the direction of the lifts, but he seemed lost in thought.

"Christian?" I said. "It's got to be."

Danny nodded and seemed to emerge from his trance. We sprinted down the corridor, past the lift, then ran down five flights of stairs to the ground floor, slowing our pace only as we crossed the reception. But once outside we picked up speed until we reached the car. The moment Danny's door clicked shut, I floored the accelerator, trying to put as much distance between us and the hotel as I could.

"Shit, shit, shit," said Danny, as I turned a corner. I braked sharply, pulling in to the side of the road. In truth, I didn't feel up to driving.

"What the hell just happened?" I asked.

"I don't know," he said. "All I know is that we've just run from a murder scene, and the concierge could identify us. For fuck's sake."

"Let's ring Clare," I said. I didn't wait for a response before reaching for her secret mobile. But when I called the number it went straight to voicemail. Suddenly it seemed like we were very much alone.

Chapter 24

I T took a few minutes before my breathing returned to any semblance of normal.

Danny continued trying Clare's number. Eventually it was answered. He put it on speaker.

"Danny, how are things?" she asked.

"Seriously not good," he replied. He explained about finding Julian's body, and how we'd seen - or thought we'd seen - Christian Fuller leaving the hotel just before we arrived.

"It's got to be him, surely," said Danny. "He must have found out about whatever Julian was up to and gone to silence him before he had a chance to speak to us."

"It definitely sounds like it," said Clare. Her voice was laced with something I'd never heard before. Fear? Or maybe just uncertainty. Whichever, it wasn't good. "It's going to come as a shock to Otto. But listen, I don't like this at all. I don't think it's safe for you to stay at home. It's getting far too dangerous."

She didn't need to persuade me on that.

She gave us the address of a place she said was a safe house, in Camden, not far from our home.

"The concierge will give you a key," she said. "Use the name

Charlotte Sadler. Dash home now as quickly as you can. Pack a few things for an overnight stay. I don't know how long, but a few days, okay? I'll meet you there as soon as I can."

"Fantastic, shall do."

"You know what, Danny? Hit and run, phone tapping, now murder. I'm impressed at your villainy. My influence is clearly rubbing off."

"You're not even funny," said Danny.

"I try."

"It's seriously not the time. Should we call Amy?"

There was a momentary pause, as she presumably tried to weigh up the consequences.

"Yes, do that," she said. "But after that, switch off your mobile and leave it disconnected, okay? If we need to talk to each other, we've got these. Anna, can you drive home while Danny makes a call?"

I didn't need to be asked twice. The car was back in gear and I screeched away, then hit the brakes hard, and executed a U-turn. I floored the throttle again, producing a characteristic VTEC howl, pinning us back into the leather seats until I inevitably had to slow for traffic. Danny called Amy on the speaker as I powered away from a set of traffic lights and then had to slam on the brakes again to avoid colliding with a cyclist.

"Christ, Danny, what on earth have you got into?" she asked after he'd given her the summary.

"It's not me - I'm just trying to find out the truth."

"For God's sake be careful."

"Surely that's got to make it even less likely that Emma is guilty?"

"I'm not in a position to give my opinion on that. Where are you now?"

"Heading home to get some stuff."

"Have you got somewhere you can go?"

"Yes, Clare's given us an address."

"Good. Go there, and keep a low profile. March is going to be all over this, and the minute he recognises you from the description he's going to come to get you. Don't make it easy for him, okay? He'll be on the rampage."

"Understood."

"Let me make some enquiries. I'll call you."

"I'm turning my phone off. Can I call you?"

"Yes, that's not a bad plan. Okay. I'd better go. Speak soon."

By the time we reached Rochester Square I was terrifyingly aware that time was working against us. At any moment we could be linked with the murder, and as soon as that happened, the police would be on our case.

We ran inside and grabbed a few clothes and other essentials, and were both back in the car less than five minutes later.

Danny looked up the address in my A-Z. Clare was right, it wasn't far away. But as we turned out onto Camden Road I could hear a wail of sirens, getting closer. I pulled out and floored the accelerator again, then watched blue flashing lights speed up in my rear-view mirror. The police cars turned right down the junction we'd just exited. I didn't hang around to see where they were aiming for. There wasn't much doubt.

"Jesus, that was quick," said Danny. I could only just hear him above my heartbeat.

"Do you think they'll come after us?"

"I bloody hope not."

"It was almost too quick."

"Exactly what I was thinking. It was like they were tipped off. Unless they knew about it already."

"Do you think March was watching? Do you think he's involved?"

"You know what, I wouldn't put it past him."

Within a few minutes we pulled up outside an impressive apartment block, probably only a mile from home. Rarely, for

London, it had its own car park. I left the Honda in one of the visitors' bays and we hurried inside.

"Can I help you?" asked the security guard at reception.

"We've come to collect a key. Charlotte Sadler," I said.

"Ah yes, I've been expecting you."

He reached behind and took a key from a cabinet.

"Flat thirty-two, third floor," he said. "The lift is behind you."

The contrast to the last room we'd entered couldn't have been starker. Clare had described it as merely a safe house, but the flat was beautifully appointed. A cream leather sofa dominated the front room, facing a giant TV, with a coffee table standing on a sheepskin rug in between.

"Wow," I said, then followed Danny through to a kitchen that looked almost unused. The Poggenpohl units and granite worktop were pristine. The bathroom was similarly luxurious, with wall-to-ceiling travertine tiles, and a gorgeously inviting walk-in shower. There was only one bedroom, but it looked like something from a five-star hotel. A giant double bed was covered in crisp white cotton sheets. Clearly no expense had been spared.

"What is this place?" I asked.

"I don't know," said Danny. "Do you think she lives here?"

"It doesn't look like anybody does, but it's lovely. Can we stay forever?"

Danny smiled, then returned to the kitchen.

"I am sorry about all of this," he said, as I lay down full-length on the sofa. "I had no idea what was going to happen today."

"It's fine, it's not your fault."

"I'm just looking to see if there's any milk."

"Is there?"

"Brand new, semi-skimmed. Cup of tea?"

"That sounds delightful."

"Or actually there's wine?"

"Even better."

A few minutes later, Danny brought two glasses of wine

through. He joined me on the sofa, which meant I had to turn and sit up properly. But before he had a chance to settle, there was a knock at the door.

"That'll be Clare," he said. He got up and walked across to the door. But when he opened it, the person standing there wasn't Clare. It was DCI Graham March, looking exceptionally pleased with himself.

"On the run, Danny old son?" he said.

Chapter 25

"ARE you going to invite me in?"

"No," said Danny, standing his ground.

"That's a shame, I'm coming anyway." He pushed past and then approached me on the sofa.

"Ah, lovely Anna. What a delight it is to see you. And what a beautiful place you have. The fashion world treating you well, is it?"

I didn't know what to say, so stayed silent.

"That said, it's not that much of a safe house, is it?" he said, turning back to Danny. "Your muse is losing what I like to call her touch."

"Fuck off, Graham."

"Oh, you do disappoint me. That's an arrestable offence right there. Abusive behaviour. And do I detect the aroma of alcohol? Drunk and disorderly as well, while I'm at it. You're making this too easy for me."

He walked around the room, taking everything in, then ran his finger across the top of the TV, presumably testing for dust. The place was spotless. He looked at his finger, then shrugged.

"A little bird tells me you've been suspended, Danny. On full pay, which is unfortunate, but we can't have it all. Of course they won't find anything but I expect it'll make things very uncomfortable. Mud sticks, Danny, you know that. Luckily I've managed to wipe out the worst of your slurs by what I like to call exemplary policing, but I don't hold out much hope for your career. But you know, you can't say you weren't warned. Poke your nose in where it's not welcome and you're going to get into a lot of trouble."

"Why are you here?" asked Danny, refusing to be goaded.

"Just checking to see how you are. It's a dangerous world out there, you know. It's the sort of place where an innocent businessman settles down to watch the x-rated movies on his hotel TV, and then bang! Somebody shoots him. Cruel business. I'm telling you, you need to be careful."

"Are you here to arrest me?"

"Arrest you? I hate to disappoint, but good Lord, no, I'm having far too much fun. No, I'm not arresting you. Not yet anyway. I'll let you run for a bit and then when the moment is right, and the accolades are at their highest, I'll pick you up like a piece of litter. In the meantime, I just thought I'd come to see you.'

"Well, you've seen us, so can you now fuck off?"

"So hostile!" He walked back towards the door. "Actually, I'm sad to say I must be on my way. Criminals to catch and all of that. The murder rate seems to be going through the roof just lately. Goodbye, Anna. And if you'd like to see what a date is like with a real man, you know where to find me."

And with that he turned and walked back to the door, letting himself out. I don't think he saw my two-fingered gesture.

I expected Danny to be shaken, but he was standing there, legs slightly apart, looking the most grounded and strongest I've ever seen him. His expression had hardened, and he looked fearless and adorably resolute.

"That," he said, pointing back to the door, "will never happen again. He's going down. Whatever it takes and whatever I have to do. And it starts from now."

———————

We'd hardly had time to stop for breath before the door opened and Clare walked in.

"This doesn't look good," she said, when she saw our expressions. "What happened?"

"Did you see March out there?" asked Danny. "He was here about a minute ago. You must have passed him."

"Graham March?"

"How many other Marches are there?" Danny was clearly not in his most convivial mood. "What the hell is Graham March doing coming here? I though the entire point of coming to a safe house was to get away from the bastard."

Clare removed her leather jacket, and then sat next to me on the sofa.

"That's not good," she said.

"Well?"

"What do you mean 'well'?"

"I mean what's the bloody point of coming here?"

"Hold on, Danny. I'm doing my best. I didn't have to offer you this. I wasn't aware that Graham knew it existed."

"Well, he clearly does."

"Evidently. But he's never been before. Did he follow you?"

"Not as far as I know."

"But you can't be sure?"

Danny looked a little bit sheepish.

"No."

"I didn't see anyone following us," I added. "It doesn't mean he didn't, but we were careful. We were only at home for five minutes and then we came straight here."

Clare nodded, then bit her bottom lip, seemingly lost in thought.

"Did he give the impression he knew this was connected to me?" she said.

"He said something about it not being much of a safe house, and my muse having lost her touch. I expect he meant you."

"Christ. As bad as it could be then."

She sat back and sighed, looking to the ceiling.

"Well, so much for giving up the fags. Today's obviously not the day."

"Have you given up smoking?" I asked, shocked at the concept.

"Danny told me to."

He shrugged. Clare reached into her jacket pocket and withdrew a cellophane-wrapped pack of Silk Cut.

"I don't want to speak out of turn here," I said, once I'd got over the surprise of that one, "but if he knows this is your place and he knows you invited us, presumably he'd expect you to be meeting us. Wouldn't he? Shouldn't we be getting out and going somewhere miles away? He'll be waiting outside and then come and arrest you."

She turned to me, and put her hand on my leg, presumably for reassurance rather than a repeat of our club exploits.

"That's not out of turn. That's good thinking, but he won't."

"What?"

"He's not going to be arresting me. Not at the moment, anyway."

"What on earth are you talking about?" Then realisation dawned. "Wait. What are you not telling us?"

"Clare?" prompted Danny when she didn't answer.

She let go of my leg, then stood up, walked to the kitchen and returned with a glass of wine and the bottle, topping up my glass.

"It's nothing sinister," she said.

"That already sounds bloody sinister to me," said Danny. He really was getting quite feisty. "What is it?"

"Okay."

I braced myself for a revelation, but she stopped, then walked over to the window and closed the curtains. I think she was just buying time.

"It's complicated," she said at last.

"Christ. Is that your favourite word?" said Danny. "Everything you've told us since you rang on Friday has started with the assertion that it's complicated."

"Okay. Complex then. Better?"

"Not really."

"Sorry, Danny, but that's the way it is. We don't live in simple times. You remember last year, how we saved his life?"

"You did," I said. "We weren't able to move at the time."

She nodded.

"I suppose. Anyway, he came to see me after that. At my hotel in Sofia. The one where we met Georgi, actually. He'd arranged to have me executed."

"Jesus," said Danny.

"Don't worry, I knew what he was up to. He came up to me in the bar, told me some shit, and then looked the pinnacle of smugness as his four henchmen turned up, ready to take me away. That would have been it, game over. But what he didn't know was that Georgi knows pretty much everything going on in Sofia, and he'd given me advance warning. So I simply placed a higher bid, and when the hit squad turned up, they took Graham away, rather than me."

Danny looked suitably horrified.

"But they didn't kill him?"

"Evidently not. Not really my style." She said that without any sense of irony. Either she really had changed, or she'd forgotten who she was talking to. "No, they just took him away and gave him a warning. Admittedly it probably wasn't too friendly, but it's safe to say, I don't think he'd arrest me."

"That's a relief," I said, my mind conjuring up an image of four big Bulgarians giving March a well-deserved slap.

"It's not a hundred percent a relief," Clare continued. "I wouldn't put it past him to have another go at killing me."

That was not so good.

"But why?" asked Danny. "I mean, I know we were investigating him before you disappeared, but why would he want to kill you? You saved his life. Twice over, by the sound of things."

She sighed again.

"I'm sorry, I am going to need a cigarette for this." She walked over to the cabinet underneath the TV and removed an ashtray that she placed on the coffee table. "Sorry, Danny."

"That's okay. But go on."

"Well, where to begin. You know I've had some business dealings in Germany?"

"Uh-huh."

"Some of the people I've met over there haven't always exactly been on the straight and narrow. They're not bad, but they bend the rules a bit. But then there's a second group that I didn't ever deal with directly, and they're the bad ones."

"I already don't like the sound of this."

"Don't worry. It's not as bad as it sounds. Otto, who you're going to meet, is one of group A. He's okay, really. But some of the people he works with have tangible links with group B."

She lit a cigarette before continuing.

"March has done deals with group B. There's one called Stefan. He's kind of the ringleader, and he seemed very happy to have a man within the Met who could arrange to turn a blind eye. And when all that went down last year..." Her voice trailed off.

"Go on," said Danny at last.

"There's no easy way to say this, but when March got himself in a spot of bother, some of his group B friends went to my group A and asked for my help to keep him safe."

"They did what?" Danny's voice was getting louder. I'd never heard him lose his temper with Clare before, but it seemed to be heading that way. He sank to the floor, and sat propped against the wall.

"I didn't really have an option. It was for the greater good. The people we put away were doing far worse things. When I first bumped into you in Cologne, I thought March was running things, but then it became clear that he was way out of his depth. I traded information in exchange for promising to do my best to keep him safe. But that was the information we needed to stop the trafficking. Don't hate me, Danny."

"I don't hate you. I just wish you'd been honest with me. With us." He looked at me. It wasn't hard to read his expression.

"I've never lied to you," said Clare, barely audibly.

"That's not true."

"Well, maybe not told you the whole truth, but you've always known you can trust me."

"Trust you? You set me on the hunt for March, and we nearly get killed, and all the time you're his bodyguard?"

"That's not how it was."

The silence returned.

"Look, Danny," she said at last. "None of this is ideal. It's just a question of looking at the bigger picture. We will get March. We'll make sure he's stopped, and put away for good. But last year was about something bigger than just him. You saw those girls. You saw what was happening. If it meant holding fire on Graham in order to stop that, I thought it was a worthwhile sacrifice."

I thought back to the horror I'd witnessed. Danny was clearly battling with his thoughts, but then I turned to Clare and she looked more vulnerable than I would ever have thought possible. And then it dawned on me. Despite all of the bluster and mystery, she really was looking for our approval, and was deeply upset at the thought that she'd disappointed us. It was a truly staggering concept but explained so much. She stubbed out her cigarette.

"Can I make a suggestion?" I said. Danny looked up at me, and Clare turned in my direction. Were those tears in her eyes? I didn't wait for either of them to answer, but instead stood up. "Come here, the pair of you. Group hug."

Neither argued. Both came. I squeezed them as tightly as I could.

"Let's not fall out," I said. "You're right. It was a small price given the outcome. But now we're a united front, okay? I'd say we were like the three musketeers, or something, but frankly one of you is unemployed and the other is clearly dodgy, so I'll settle for me just being the voice of reason."

She laughed and squeezed me back. I wasn't far from crying either. Eventually we all let go.

Clare looked at Danny.

"Are you okay?" she asked.

He nodded.

"It was a shock. But yes, I do hear what you're saying."

"Thank you."

"Can you promise me there's no other agenda now?"

"I promise you, Danny."

The mood thawed slightly. Clare looked at her watch.

"Right, we've got an hour and a half before meeting Otto. I'll give you the address and meet you there." She wrote down an address in Farringdon.

"Bring your stuff. I don't think it's a good idea to stay here, so I'll find you somewhere else. I'll see you there at ten."

"Where are you going?" I asked.

"I've got things to prepare." The new spirit of openness clearly had its limits. This wasn't the time to push it.

When Clare left, Danny looked at me.

"Thank you," he said.

I gave him another hug, then pulled away.

"I've just had a very bad thought," I said.

"Oh God. What is it?"

"This is a rather lovely bottle of wine, but it does rather mean I'm going to have to let you drive my car."

He smiled.

"You mean you're going to finish it?"

"It seems an awful waste to leave it behind."

"You're as bad as she is."

"We all have our vices, Danny." But more than that, I had a strong feeling that alcohol would be the least I needed to get me through the evening.

Chapter 26

I KNOW I've been looking to replace it, but I'm still very fond of my Honda. We've been through a lot together. It felt unnerving to view the road from the passenger seat, and I kept pressing imaginary pedals when I wanted Danny to slow down. I couldn't really fault his driving, but it wasn't an experience I wanted to repeat. We parked on a side street just off Clerkenwell Road, then got out to walk to the address Clare had given us.

As we approached, Danny suddenly perked up.

"I know this place," he said.

"Really?"

"Clare brought me here last year when we were looking out for Aurelia. She said it belonged to a friend, but she was allowed to use it."

"That sounds about right."

I checked my watch as we reached the door. It was just before ten. Danny pressed the doorbell. A shadowy figure appeared behind the glass in the door, heading in our direction. But when the door was opened it wasn't Clare.

"Amy!" said Danny, clearly as surprised as I was.

She didn't speak but held the door so I could follow Danny inside. He led the way through a hallway and into a sparsely furnished front room. There was no sign of Clare. I didn't know whether to give Amy a hug as well, or just take a seat on the sofa, but decided on the latter. It seemed the least fraught option.

"Clare should be here any moment," she said.

That took me by surprise. Obviously I knew Clare was coming, but there was something about the way she said it that made me think she wasn't poised ready with handcuffs.

"What are you doing here?" asked Danny. "It's great to see you again, but I think we're now officially on the run from the police."

"You're on the run from March, but I'm not sure he qualifies."

Before she could elaborate, we heard movement at the front door. I looked at my watch again. As I did so, the minute hand flicked up to the hour.

Clare walked in looking typically and annoyingly immaculate, with no outward sign of our earlier upset. Not for the first time I felt slightly dowdy in her presence. Her dark hair was beautifully styled and her make-up was perfect. I was also jealous of the gorgeous grey coat but slightly nervous, as ever, of what she might be hiding in her inside pocket.

But she wasn't alone.

"Danny, Anna, meet Otto," she said, looking serious.

Otto stepped forward, offering his hand. He was well-built, probably in his mid-fifties, with a moustache that in another setting would have lent his serious expression an edge of comedy. Danny shook first and then I followed. His grip was painfully strong. Nothing really made sense to me. I couldn't fully understand why Amy wasn't immediately whisking Clare off in the back of a police car, but I knew when it was best not to ask questions.

Clare took the armchair opposite our sofa. Otto leaned against the windowsill. He seemed to occupy most of the space within the room.

"I'll organise the drinks," said Amy.

"I'll come and give you a hand," I said.

"Don't worry," said Clare. "We won't start without you. Tea for me. Otto?"

"Black coffee, *bitte.*"

While we were in the kitchen I took the opportunity to seek clarification.

"What's going on?"

"Some very dangerous people are playing some very dangerous games," she said.

"No, I don't mean that. I mean that's Clare, and you're the police and..."

"It's complicated."

"Don't let Danny hear you say that."

She gave me a strange look. There was also a sadness in her eyes, as though she knew things that she couldn't say. I don't often want to go running home to the security of my mum's house in Manchester, but the thought was beginning to occur.

"It's not even my investigation - I shouldn't be here. I'm supposed to be looking at a robbery at a petrol station."

"Don't take this the wrong way but I'm very pleased to see you."

"And likewise."

"Really? I'm just the token confused person who makes everyone else look clever."

She laughed.

"I don't think anyone's got a clue at the moment."

Her phone started ringing. She answered the call, and immediately a serious expression came over her face. I carried on making the drinks while she turned away. When the call ended, she pocketed the phone.

"I've got to go," she said. "It's typical. Will you be okay here?"

I didn't know if she meant okay in general, or specifically with the drinks. Either way, I didn't have much choice. I nodded.

"Take care," I said. "Hopefully we'll catch up soon."

"I'll be in touch. I'll just say goodbye to the others."

A few minutes later I took a tray of drinks through to the front room, and placed them on the table. There was no sign of Amy. Otto was still standing. Clare was still in the armchair. I rejoined Danny on the sofa. It was time to be enlightened.

The small talk stopped. Clare took a deep breath.

"Just so we're all on the same page," she began, "everything said in this room stays in this room. Understood?"

I looked around. It wasn't like I had anyone else to tell, but we all agreed anyway. She turned to Danny and me.

"Otto is a very good friend from Cologne. I'd trust him with my life, and actually have already done so. And Otto: Danny and Anna are my two best friends here in England. I'd just like everyone to know that there's no hidden agenda. No half-truths. Everything is in the open. Does anyone have any questions before we start?"

She looked around. None of us spoke.

"Okay, good. Otto is going to help us try to get to the bottom of all this. But first, I think we'd both really appreciate you bringing us up to speed on how you found Julian."

Danny spoke, explaining how we'd turned up at the hotel, seen Christian Fuller leaving, and then gone to the room and found Julian's body. Even as Otto was learning the horrific details about the loss of a valued colleague, his expression didn't change.

"Okay," said Clare. "So we've got Fuller at the scene, with a possible motive. And he could certainly have killed Tom and placed the evidence back at Emma's flat. You said he claimed not to know her very well?"

181

"He said they'd met socially but not much apart from that," said Danny.

"And yet he still went to visit her to pass on condolences. Was that genuine or just an excuse to leave evidence behind?"

"It depends," said Danny. "I think he had a motive to kill Julian if he thought he needed to be silenced. But the motive for killing Tom is vague at best, and there's no logical reason to frame Emma unless she was just an easy target. We haven't established any real link between Fuller and Miroslav."

"Good." She turned to Otto. "Any questions so far?"

"Not at this moment."

"Okay. Let's go back to the beginning. As we all know, I've been facilitating deals in Bulgaria, with the help of Georgi. Otto is my main contact in Germany who helps me over there. Otto knows of Georgi, I think that's fair to say?" She looked at Otto, who nodded. "But Georgi doesn't know about Otto. Everything comes through me. I first became aware of Miroslav a while ago when Georgi alerted me to him, and I had a conversation with Otto, who agreed that it could be a dangerous situation."

"Because of the threat of gun smuggling?" asked Danny.

"Because of that, but also because of his reputation. He's not the sort of person you can easily do business with, let's put it that way. The war seemed to be entering its final stages, so it looked like a good idea to keep an eye on him."

"You said no hidden agendas and no half-truths, yes?" asked Danny.

"I did."

"Is that really why you were interested? Or were you looking to see if there might be any opportunities for yourself?"

The temperature in the room lowered a notch. I wasn't quite sure what had got into Danny, but in fairness it hadn't been a good day. I tried to stifle a yawn, suddenly overcome with tiredness.

"I'm happy to answer that question," said Clare. "I think what you have to understand is that there's always some crossover. Part of my job, if that's what you want to call it, is brokering deals between buyers and sellers. But just as importantly, if not more so, is keeping well-informed so I can spot danger from a distance. It helps me stay alive."

"I just can't help asking myself if you've got some sort of agenda here," Danny persisted. "Something you're not telling me."

"I can understand why you say that, but I promise you I'm telling you everything. No, I wasn't looking for any opportunities as such, but there was a degree of self-interest in finding out about him and knowing what he was up to. Does that help explain it?"

"It does. Thank you."

"It was very much a question of his reputation going before him," added Otto, in surprisingly good English. "There have been lots of war crimes in Serbia and lots of people looking to exploit others on both sides of the conflict. We were never sure if he was genuine, a businessman, a gangster, or a warlord. Whether he was acting perfectly innocently or whether he was laundering money through London. Depending on what he was doing, there could have been a threat to our business."

Clare nodded, then took over.

"I know some of you may find this hard to believe but I do have a conscience. I know that some of things I've done in the past haven't always been completely without a degree of self-interest, I know people have been hurt in the process, but believe me, those days, as I think you found out last year, really are over."

"Is that why Amy isn't arresting you?" I asked, and then suddenly thought maybe I'd spoken out of turn.

"That's something I can discuss with you, but it's not something we need to worry about at the moment," she said, mysteriously. "Let's go back to Miroslav. So he was investing money through the bank in London but it seemed like there was possibly more to it than met the eye."

She paused to look up at us. She had our undivided attention.

"I was busy working with Georgi, so Otto said he'd make a few enquiries. I think it's fair to say that you've got contacts within the financial services industry," she said, turning to him.

"It is fair," he said. "The bank appeared to be investing the money in slightly unconventional ways but I wanted to find out more. If Miroslav was laundering money and if the rumours of gun smuggling were true, then I thought I might be able to use some of my influence in Germany to stop him. We knew about the logistics company and rumours of attempts to smuggle weapons out of Serbia, and I don't think you need me to explain why that would not be a good idea. Not just for London and the UK but for Germany, for France, for all other countries of Europe."

"Are you some sort of global policeman then?" I asked.

Otto looked at Clare. She raised her eyebrows as though giving him permission to continue.

"I have served in German intelligence," he said. "Like Clare, I am now freelance but the way we work is to make sure that we cooperate with those in influence, and sometimes that means doing the right thing, passing on information, and using our contacts and knowledge to supply information to those who appreciate it."

I was glad he was on our side.

"So, Otto started to get close to the bank," Clare continued. "We couldn't understand why of all the banks in all the world, Miroslav was using Gersbach and Haller in London. I mean, why not the head office in Switzerland? But then we had a breakthrough."

"Ah," said Danny. "So this is where it gets intriguing?"

"Kind of. We discovered the source of his initial introduction, and believe me, it was quite an eye-opener." She looked back to Otto.

"It came through an associate in Romania. You know Emma, Tom's wife, I believe?" Danny nodded. "Then you know she was working for a charity that was involved with Romanian orphanages. Through that she came into contact with Miroslav's associate."

"But we didn't know why," added Clare. "We didn't know if it was entirely benign and a chance meeting, and she just recommended Tom out of some sort of family loyalty. Or whether there was something more to it: a more elaborate plan, which could potentially involve channelling the charity's money into, ultimately, the smuggling of guns."

"So you started to investigate Emma too?" asked Danny.

"Only in the early stages. It soon became clear that she was innocent. She really had no idea about Miroslav and what he was doing or about the funds and the investments that Tom was handling through the bank. But at the same time we knew that there might be information in their house that would help us to understand more about Miroslav. Which is where Julian came in."

"So you got Julian to sleep with her?" asked Danny, looking from Clare to Otto.

Otto shook his head.

"No, of course, that was never in the plan. But Julian was, how can I say, a young man. He was foolish, he got carried away. Yes, absolutely he was supposed to get close to Emma. We heard Tom was a regular at the gay club, we knew Emma was unhappy, and we knew that she might be open to flattery, but I had no idea that Julian would take things quite as far as he did. You have to believe me."

"Just for the sake of clarity, I didn't realise any of this at the time," said Clare. "I knew Miroslav was of interest, I knew Otto was investigating, but the first I heard about Julian was after March arrested Emma."

I suddenly realised that I'd finished my tea, so placed the empty mug on the floor.

Otto continued.

"Julian was supposed to get access to the house, sedate Emma if necessary, and then look for the information. But, being a fool, he got carried away, and, well, I don't need to tell you what happened next."

"I don't think it would do any harm," said Danny. "Just so we all know we're at the same place."

The big German seemed to think for a moment, then acquiesced.

"Tom came home, discovered Julian in bed with Emma, and threw him out. I was waiting outside. Despite getting carried away, he'd managed to get the information that we were looking for."

"Which was?" asked Danny.

"A Zip disk with briefing notes and voice recordings of conversations between Miroslav and Tom, from meetings away from the bank. Tom recorded them. Miroslav had no idea as far as we know, which was a highly dangerous thing in itself. But the information gave us a real insight into his plans. And that came as a bit of a shock."

Chapter 27

"I CAN'T do it, Graham, I'm sorry."

"I'm not sure I understand."

"I mean I don't have the money."

"No, I get that. English is my first language. I'm not like some wide-eyed foreigner that you can baffle with your command of linguistics. What I mean is, I don't understand why you think that is in any way acceptable, and equally why you think it is my concern."

"Because I can't pay you back if I don't have the money."

March frowned. The woman opposite looked close to tears.

"You see, I still don't understand. You were happy to borrow the money. Yes? And it's in the small print that you subsequently need to pay it back. With a little bit of interest, naturally, in recognition of the favour granted."

DCI Graham March looked at her. It was pitiful, quite frankly. He couldn't abide weakness, but some people just seemed incapable of looking after themselves. It was bad enough that she'd got herself into this situation in the first place. That, in itself, was pathetic. But to come to him for financial help and then renege on the repayments? He couldn't disguise his contempt.

"I can pay you a bit today and then some more by the end of the week," she said. "I get paid on Friday, so I can give you that."

"I rather think you're missing the point, Amanda. The money is due today. I don't think I could offer any more clarity on the situation. We don't want to incur added interest and late payment charges by waiting till Friday, do we?"

"Please, it's just two more days. I've already paid twice what I borrowed, for God's sake."

"And if you can't settle the next instalment now, then by Friday it's going to double again, so I really don't see how that's going to help."

And now she was crying. Great wracking sobs. That was all he needed. He really didn't have the time or the patience.

"Oh come on, please," she said, reaching out to him, a look of fear and pleading in her eyes. "I'll do anything. Anything you want. Just two more days. I'm begging you."

"Don't flatter yourself, love. I'm a man of taste so please don't insult us both by suggesting I'd be interested in so much as a hand job from a skank like your good self."

He sat back in his chair and finished his brandy. The barman was looking over. She was creating a scene, and that wasn't good for his reputation, even if her desperation was actually quite arousing.

"What do you think my other clientele would say if they got to hear that I was offering preferential terms to some slapper who told me yesterday she'd be paying on time, and then backtracked and broke her promise, eh? They'd all start wanting the same, and then where would that get us? Mayhem, that's where."

"But I don't have the money!"

"Amanda, my dear, I think you know my opinion on that."

He rubbed his chin. It was getting late. He needed to sort this.

"I'll tell you what I'll do for you," he said.

He thought he detected a flicker of hope in her eyes. How curiously naive.

"I can't discuss it here, but my office is a two-minute walk away. Come with me and we'll sort it out there."

He stood, nodded to the barman, and then made his way to the door, glancing over his shoulder to check she was following. She looked unsteady, but at least she was making an effort. He liked it when they did as they were told.

A couple of minutes later he led her down some steps towards the basement of a run-down building near King's Cross. He put his key in the lock, and once inside, gripped her tightly by the arm, and then pulled her along the corridor until it opened into a dimly lit room. There was already a man in there, waiting, leaning on a baseball bat next to a chair.

"Customer for you, Jimmy," said March. "We need to give her a little lesson about the importance of punctuality."

Amanda suddenly looked terrified. She tried to get away, but March tightened his grip, his fingers biting hard into the flesh of her upper arm. She'd have a bruise, he expected, although it wouldn't be the only one.

She screamed, but that wasn't going to help either. He didn't like hitting women, at least not with their clothes on, but really, she was asking for the slap that momentarily silenced her.

Jimmy led her to the chair in the middle of the room, and then fastened the ties that would keep her there.

"The usual?" he asked.

March nodded and then left the room. He made his way back up steps, grateful again that the sounds from the basement couldn't be heard from the street.

"What do you mean, a shock?" asked Danny.

Otto looked at Clare, as though seeking approval. Instead she spoke for him.

"The details were vague, but they confirmed what we thought about the logistics company. There was discussion of shipments, which we took to be guns, although he was careful never to mention that expressly."

"It sounds like it's true then?" asked Danny.

"Certainly looks likely. It backs up what Georgi was telling me."

"Do you think that was why Tom was killed? That maybe Miroslav somehow heard about the recordings and lashed out? Or maybe even Tom was trying to blackmail him?"

"That could have been possible," said Otto. "That might explain why the account looked to be losing money. But attempting to blackmail somebody like Miroslav is not wise for long-term career development."

"Can I propose a theory?" I asked. Everybody looked at me and I suddenly felt self-conscious, as though I might be about to make a fool of myself. Nevertheless, I battled on. "From what you've said, it seems to all make sense. Maybe Tom mentioned the recordings to Christian, thinking that he was his friend. But then Christian went to Miroslav and dropped Tom in the shit, presumably for a reasonable amount of cash. That would give Miroslav a reason for wanting to get rid of Tom, and give Christian a reason for doing it. And then also a reason for him to track down Julian and kill him before he had a chance to speak to anyone."

There was a moment of silence in which I could feel I was starting to blush.

"Very plausible," said Clare, eventually, much to my relief. Otto was nodding too.

"Although that doesn't explain Aleksander and what on earth he was up to," I added. "Nor why March was so keen to buy into it all."

"No," she said. "And we still don't have any actual evidence. It's good progress, though."

"Has Georgi said any more about Aleksander?" asked Danny.

"No, not really. I asked him, obviously, but he was vague."

"And you're sure you can actually trust him?"

"Georgi? Truthfully, no. Not really. But he's never lied to me before."

"As far as you know."

"It's been very much in his interests not to. And if he's lying to me now, I'd have to reconsider more than just my ability to judge his character."

I was getting desperately tired. Much as it was all truly fascinating, I was longing for the moment when it would be over for the evening and I could go to bed, wherever that may be. Thankfully, Danny seemed to be fading too.

"Next steps then?" he asked.

"We keep trying to find out who is responsible," said Otto, rather stating the obvious.

Danny seemed happy with that as a concept. I expect he was getting tired too. Otto announced he had to leave, but would be in touch soon.

"It looks like Miroslav and Christian Fuller, working together," said Danny, once it was back to just the three of us. "I'm going to talk to Amy and tell her what we think, unless you've got an objection."

"No, that sounds good," said Clare. "Don't discount that it could be someone else, though. There's still a lot we don't know."

"Maybe if we can get her to apply some pressure to Fuller we might start to understand the links to March. Could it be as simple as March being on Miroslav's payroll?"

"It could, but we'd have to work hard to discover that."

A smile began to creep over Clare's face. It was one of those smiles that indicated she was up to something, and rather

191

pleased with herself in the process. She caught me looking at her. I raised an eyebrow, and she winked in return.

"I have got some other news, actually," she said, then paused for effect. We were both too sleepy to respond with anything other than veiled impatience, so she carried on. "Georgi has been busy. He's managed to find Miroslav's address in London."

"That's good," said Danny. "Is he spending lots of time here?"

"A fair bit."

"Do you want me to stake him out and take some pictures?" I asked.

"No, there's no need. That's the other bit of news. He's arranged for the three of us to go and meet him."

It took a moment for that to sink in.

"What?" I said, when it did. "I hate be the spoilsport here, but isn't that tantamount to agreeing to get shot?"

"I'll try to make sure it isn't."

I looked at Danny, expecting him to be horrified.

"That's fantastic news," he said. It appeared they'd both gone equally mad. "When?"

"Ten tomorrow morning."

In just over ten hours' time. My head was struggling to work out the implications.

"All three of us?"

"Yes, of course."

"Can I just point out, again, that I inhabit the world of fashion. I am neither an investigative journalist nor somebody who is particularly suicidal at this moment in time, and would rather stay in bed somewhere so I'm fully rested. I'll need all my strength to arrange a double funeral."

"Anna, you'll be fine. I won't let you come to any harm."

"That's very kind of you, but I can do that myself by the simple act of not actually going."

"But you'd hate to miss out."

"And don't tell me, let me guess. He's also a keen amateur photographer and you need me to talk f-stops."

She laughed.

"I have no idea what he's into. I don't expect he has much time for hobbies."

"Too busy shooting people?"

"I very much doubt he does that himself."

"You're really not helping. Where are we sleeping, by the way?"

"That's the spirit. You can stay here. I'll come and pick you up in the morning."

"I still haven't said I'm coming."

But I knew that I didn't really have a choice. Clare always got her own way eventually. And yet I couldn't shake a nagging feeling that one day her luck would run out.

Chapter 28

"I'M sorry it's so late," said Danny. "Is it a good time to call?"

"Don't worry, I'm always up late," said Amy. "Where are you?"

"Still at Clare's place in Farringdon. We're staying the night. Clare's gone, and Anna's heading to bed but I wanted to bring you up to speed on the meeting with Otto."

"That's good. You are being careful?"

"How do you mean?"

"You know what I mean."

"I'm being as careful as I can, but I think we're making progress."

"Okay, so what have you got for me?"

He gave her a summary of the conversation, and then mentioned the forthcoming meeting with Miroslav.

"I think that's very high risk," she said.

"It is, but needs must. Can I ask a question about forensics?"

"You can ask. I can't promise I'll answer."

"Okay. The bullets found in Emma's place. They definitely matched the one used to kill Tom?"

"They did."

"And were they any particular type? Could they be traced to the Balkans?"

"I'm not an expert and I haven't seen the full report, but my understanding is that yes, that's where they originated."

"That's good. Well, not good, but at least consistent. There's no word, I suppose, on how Julian was killed or what was used?"

"That's a live enquiry, Danny. There's not much I'm able to tell you there."

"Because you don't know or you're not able to?"

"Bits of both. No, I don't know, and no I wouldn't be able to tell you, even if I did."

"I thought not."

Danny got a glass of water and sat down heavily at the kitchen table. He propped his head up on his arm.

"What are you doing?" she asked.

"Just trying to stay awake."

"You should get to sleep. There's an eyewitness report of you at Julian's hotel. It's irrelevant what I think, but March will be using that to try to pin it on you. He just needs to persuade the CPS that you're guilty and you could be in serious trouble."

"God. Is there ever any good news?"

"No, but don't make it easy for him."

"Warning heeded."

Danny took a deep breath. The next bit wasn't going to be easy.

"Can I ask a favour?" he said.

"I'm probably not the best person to ask for favours."

"I know, but it's important. Will you be interviewing Christian Fuller?"

"In relation to?"

"Julian."

"Probably, but not me personally. Why?"

"Could you?"

"Interview him?"

"Yes. And can I come?"

"Danny, let me stop you there. Even if I did get assigned to the case, and even if I did end up interviewing him, there'd be another detective and solicitors and all sorts. I couldn't invite a journalist to an official police interview. You know that."

"So let's have an informal chat instead."

"No."

"Oh come on. You wouldn't even know about him if it wasn't for me."

"No."

"I'm not going to beg you. But this is all about cooperation."

"Danny, you're a wanted man. I'm not even supposed to know where you are. I can't have you walking around beside me and pretend not to have noticed."

"Okay, so arrest me if you think I'm guilty. If you think there's anything in this."

"That's not what I'm saying."

Danny sighed, then decided on a different approach.

"Look, Amy, I know it's unusual."

"It's not that it's unusual. It's that it's enough to get me fired."

"Can you just think about it? This is our route to March. If he is on the payroll, he's going to cover it up. Whatever evidence links Fuller to Julian will get buried forever and March will probably pocket a small fortune in the process."

"I'm sure there'll be a thorough investigation."

"And you said it yourself. He has friends in high places. I know Christian. I've met him. Between the two of us, we can put him on the spot in a way that no official interview ever would."

"And what do we tell him? We're running a separate enquiry? Oh, and by the way, the press are here to record it?"

"We don't tell him I'm from the press."

"What? You're suggesting I facilitate you impersonating a police officer? This is getting worse."

Danny sighed.

"No, we just don't tell him anything. I can be the work experience boy for all I care. But I definitely think he's the best route into all of this and if we don't do it ourselves, we'll lose him."

"Oh, Danny."

"Just think about it, please?"

"I'll think about it, but the answer will still be no."

"Thank you."

Danny cut the call, closed his eyes and started to think.

———

DCI Graham March congratulated himself on another excellent idea. Prompted by a phone call, it was even better than his original plan, and it had gone down very well upstairs.

It was beautiful in its simplicity, and would finally solve so many problems. He couldn't do it alone, but there were plenty in his debt that he could call upon. Nobody should be allowed to see the full picture. It was far better to keep them all apart, and call upon specialists when they could be best deployed. Of course, some were more helpful than others. Stefan would play his part, he was sure, but not everyone was so entrepreneurial.

He looked at the man sitting opposite him in a booth at the back of a basement bar, off Brewer Street in Soho, gauging his reaction to the plan. Or at least the part that he was being asked to assist with.

"You must really hate them," said his companion.

"It's payback time," said March.

"Yeah, well, I understand that. But even so it sounds a bit extreme."

"I'm not talking about payback for fucking Clare and Danny, you lowlife. I'm talking about you."

"Calm down. Okay, I'm listening."

"It's just as well for your sake that you are."

"Are you threatening me?"

"I shouldn't need to threaten you but I will if I have to. We both know where we stand. I want this ended for once and for all. Or do you want me to finish you with them?"

Chapter 29

W ITH just over two weeks to Christmas, I should have been out attempting to buy the least-inappropriate presents, avoiding godawful so-called music and working out whether or not tinsel was in this year. Instead I was trying to choose a presentable outfit from a mere handful of emergency clothes, all packed in a hurry, for a meeting with a Serbian gangster who would probably kill me. Season's greetings one and all.

Clare turned up just before nine, and frankly pissed me off, looking like she'd just stepped off a film set. I longed for the day I'd catch her in jeans and a sweatshirt, or better still, something with a stain down the front. My mood darkened further with the discovery that Danny was looking immaculate in a suit. Where on earth had that appeared from?

"Are we seriously going to do this?" I said, while making everyone a cup of tea. Thankfully the teabags were of a half-decent standard. I'd hate to sign off with a Typhoo.

"Stop worrying," said Danny. "Nobody is going to kill us."

"I'll remind you of that when Saint Peter turns us down, on the basis that our visit is self-inflicted."

Clare laughed, which was also annoying. Danny excused himself to finish getting ready.

"In all seriousness, you may hear things that must not be discussed with anyone, and you should try not to appear shocked," she said.

"What the hell does that mean? What sort of things?"

"Our mission is to scope him out and get close. Not necessarily to speak about Tom but to develop a level of trust."

"Can you, for once, actually answer a question?"

"I thought I had."

Maybe it was just me? I gave up.

"Presumably it would be a substantially bad idea for anyone to know about this meeting. What if March is still following us?"

"That's a valid point, Anna."

"So?"

"So what?"

"So what are we going to do about that?"

"We're going to make sure he doesn't."

"This is testing my patience."

"Are you okay?"

"What do you mean am I okay?"

"You sound tense."

"For fuck's sake. Is it any bloody wonder?"

"Everything will be fine. I'm going to drive off in a moment, heading in the wrong direction, and then make a few circuits to make sure nobody is following. You can take the Underground with Danny and then get off, get on a bus, go too far, and get another bus back. I'll meet you and we'll go in together. He can't follow us all."

Well, that was a red flag.

"The Underground?"

"Yes."

"You are actually telling me to get the Underground to my destiny with death? Oh, that is the absolute full house. Somehow you've managed to make getting shot look quite appealing."

"Do you have a problem with the Underground?"

"You know I bloody do. It's not natural."

"Would you rather come with me?"

That needed thinking about.

"And leave Danny on his own?"

"He's a big boy. I'm sure he'll manage."

"Have you got a gun?"

"Of course not."

"You haven't even got a gun?"

"Why would I need a gun?"

"To shoot people when they're about to kill us. It's what you do."

She laughed again. Why was nobody taking me seriously?

"No, I haven't got a gun. I won't need a gun. Nobody is going to shoot us."

Danny appeared at the kitchen door. Clare explained the revised plan, in which I was getting a lift in her car, not that I'd actually agreed to it.

"Perfect," he said, without even raising any of the thousand or so quite valid objections he could have done.

I didn't suggest a group hug. I really wasn't in the mood.

———

Being chauffeured by Clare took paranoia to a whole new level. When she was finally convinced that we'd lost our imaginary tail, she pulled up in a parking bay, close to Lancaster Gate station. A couple of minutes later, a bus stopped on the opposite side of the road. When it pulled away, I saw Danny standing alone, on the pavement, waiting for us. Clare edged forward, pausing to let Danny cross the road and climb in the back. A minute later we pulled into the driveway of a hugely expensive looking, white-rendered house and parked alongside a big black Mercedes.

The door opened as we approached. Two giant black-clad hard bastards stood either side of the hallway, making no attempt to hide their weaponry.

"Mr Nikolić is expecting you," said one of them.

He led us into an opulently furnished room that was more of a luxurious office than a living room. A man was sitting at a desk, looking every inch the tanned Bond villain. He even had a pair of sexy women, one on each side. He clicked his fingers and they glided out of the room, closing the door behind them. I turned as they did so, and was unnerved to see the hard bastards standing either side of the closed door, like heavily armed and humourless centurion bodybuilders. There was certainly no easy means of escape.

"Good morning, I am Miroslav," said the man behind the desk. "You have already met Luka and Goran. To what do I owe the pleasure of a visit by such beautiful ladies?"

He'd overlooked Danny completely, which seemed harsh, but he was clearly a man with an eye for female flesh. Which concerned me. I let Clare do the talking. Obviously. I was way out of my depth.

"A mutual acquaintance suggested I may be able to help you," said Clare, after doing the introductions. She outlined her credentials, with some eye-opening revelations about people she knew in London, Germany, Bulgaria, Switzerland and various other countries.

Miroslav seemed unmoved, as though he already knew exactly who he was dealing with.

"Would you care for a drink?" he asked, but didn't wait for an answer. "Goran, four glasses please."

One of the thugs poured us each a measure of some evil-looking spirit, then returned to his place by the door.

"And how did you hear about me?" Miroslav continued.

"A colleague in Bulgaria recommended you," said Clare.

"His name?"

"Georgi Stoyanov."

"I do not know this man."

"He seems to know you."

"I see."

Miroslav stood up and walked out from around his desk. He was smaller than I'd imagined. He examined an ornament on a shelf of his bookcase, and then turned back towards us.

"And you expect me to take you seriously? You turn up out of the blue? On the recommendation of someone I do not know?"

Suddenly the tone was less obviously flirtatious, which concerned me even more.

"Hardly."

"Meaning?"

"Meaning you wouldn't have agreed to see me if I was turning up out of the blue. Meaning you know about me. You know about what I can do."

"Meaning I know you can't be trusted."

Clare lit a cigarette.

"You don't mind if I smoke, I assume?" It was too late if he did. Knowing Clare's reluctance to rely on assumptions only added to the irony.

Miroslav clicked his fingers again and an ashtray appeared.

"I've heard of you. I don't know that you can be of help to me."

"Maybe not now. But I heard you were looking to invest in this country."

"And I heard you no longer lived here. In fact you were unable to visit due to previous difficulties with the authorities."

"Just because rumours get repeated, it doesn't make them true. I am here - look, you can touch me."

My stomach turned. Really? I didn't think making that kind of invitation was wise. Luckily Miroslav just smiled and didn't take her up on it.

"So why are you really here?"

Clare did the Clare thing of avoiding a direct question by changing the subject. She'd have made a great politician, albeit in a country where they take a more relaxed view of previous misdemeanours. She started to discuss the pros and cons of the Dayton Agreement, and asked for his opinion as a Serbian national.

"I am naturally glad that the war is over," he said, "but I think the accord was driven by the need to please the electorate in the USA. Will it last? I do not think so. It has created a disunited nation in Bosnia. But what do I know? I am not a politician. I am not a warrior. I am just a simple businessman."

"I heard you were making investments through Gersbach and Haller," said Clare. I held my breath. This was the moment where it could all go disastrously wrong.

"And so now we come to the truth of the meeting." I heard movement behind me and glanced round. The bodyguards seemed to be standing even straighter. "I should have known. Do you take me for a fool?"

"I ask without any agenda."

"And yet still you ask?"

"Okay, so maybe an agenda of sorts. It's just, if that's not working for you I may be able to make some introductions."

"And there is something in this for you?"

"There is an element of self-interest but maybe not purely financial. I am a very connected person, Miroslav. I see opportunities. If I bring those to the attention of others, I may not benefit materially, but my reputation is enhanced. And that is all I have to trade on."

"Your reputation is... how can I say... controversial."

"And again, we refer to rumours. There are plenty who will vouch for me."

"I've heard about some of your deal-making in Bulgaria."

"Exactly."

"Asset-stripping a nation for personal gain."

"I wouldn't put it quite like that. Those deals were necessary. They would have happened. I just made sure that they were done in the best interests of all concerned."

"For a fee."

"We all have overheads."

Miroslav laughed.

"And so now you come to asset-strip Serbia through me?"

"No."

"But you think you can help me?"

"I think there are maybe opportunities for us to help each other. I heard the tragic news about Tom Napier."

"And *now* we get to the truth. You want to know if I had anything to do with that."

"No, of course not. But I heard rumours that the bank had not made the most lucrative return for you."

"All investments carry a degree of risk."

"Of course. But we work to minimise those. Can I ask what happened with Tom?"

"No."

"But his death causes you problems?"

"It is a huge inconvenience, but you shouldn't be asking me about that. There are dark forces and it's a dangerous world. You should ask the Croatians or the Bosnians or indeed any of the other vermin who split from our country."

I was aware that neither Danny or I had uttered a word, but nobody seemed to notice. It was obvious who were the stars of the show.

"You think they were involved?" asked Clare.

"They have a different way of working to Serbia. A different moral code."

"Can you give me names?"

"Why should I give you names?"

"So I can ask them about what happened to Tom. In an appropriate way, obviously."

"I was being, what I think you call, rhetorical."

Clare stubbed out the cigarette.

"I understand that. But if we do end up working together, in any sense, however loosely, I would prefer that the same did not happen to me."

Miroslav retook his seat, and then fixed her with a glare.

"I know of no specific threat but there are Croatians in London who try to make things difficult for me. They are all corrupt. It could be any one of them. But I am a quiet man. As I said, I am trying to run a legitimate business. I have funds to manage and must do my part to rebuild our country."

"I understand."

He tapped something into his computer keyboard, then turned back towards us.

"It has been a pleasure to meet you, Ms Woodbrook," he said. "And your colleagues. Leave me your card and I will be in touch should an opportunity arise."

It was clear that the meeting was over. And we were still alive. For the first time I became conscious that I was breathing.

One of the thugs showed us back outside, and the big door closed behind us.

"Interesting," said Clare. "Get in the car and I'll drive you back to Farringdon."

Clare edged out into traffic before any of us spoke. We joined a queue of cars waiting for a traffic light to turn green.

"Well, I didn't know some of that," said Danny, eventually.

"Which bits?" asked Clare.

"Some of the things you'd been up to."

"I wouldn't worry. I said I'd always be honest with you, but I don't think that needs to extend to everyone."

She started to edge forward. The lane to our right was moving more quickly, but she didn't make an attempt to join it.

"Do you think he's guilty, then?" I asked, from the back seat. "I could be showing my naivety, but he seemed very well protected for a simple businessman."

"He's definitely guilty of something. I don't know, though."

"Have you got doubts?"

"I've always got doubts until I get absolute proof."

"It was interesting what he said about Croatians," added Danny. "Especially as we still don't know who Aleksander was, or what he was up to."

"I've got my doubts about him," said Clare. "I don't like not knowing. He was so brazen about trying to bluff us, he's got to be hiding something. And whatever it is, he'll be trying to make us guess it's something else. I think that's very dangerous."

I didn't want to hear that. A big 4x4 pulled alongside us in the adjacent lane as we started moving again. Just as I was about to comment on how scary it looked with its blacked-out windows, one of them started to slide down. It took a moment for my brain to process what my eyes were seeing, and the delay was almost fatal. Somebody had a gun and they were pointing it at us.

"Clare!" I shouted. But she'd seen it too. She floored the accelerator, but she couldn't go very far. There was a space of about six car lengths and then the traffic had stopped again. The lights in front were on red.

Chapter 30

I DUCKED. Danny did the same. At any moment I expected bullets to rip us to pieces. Clare kept her foot to the floor. Impact was inevitable. She should have been braking by now.

Then the car lurched, hard to the left.

"Hold on!" she shouted. I looked up through the gap between the two front seats just as a huge jolt rocked the car. She'd mounted the pavement, blasting her horn as pedestrians dived out of the way. She was getting faster and faster. I dared to look back, but as I did so, our rear window exploded in a shower of glass and noise.

I think I screamed, but everything was a blur. Seconds later she pulled hard left again, taking the junction on the pavement. The side of the car scraped against the traffic light, but with another huge jolt we rejoined the road, and she floored it again, before braking sharply to take the first turn on the left. As we turned, I caught a glimpse of the junction behind us. The 4x4 was still in the queue, indicating to turn towards us, but unable to fit through our gap.

Clare powered the car through several more turns until finally she slowed enough to take a breath. I don't think my heart had ever beat faster. I'd looked down the barrel of a gun before, but never been so convinced it was about to kill me.

"Sorry about that," she said. "Is everyone okay?"

I couldn't speak, but Danny looked back towards me. I nodded.

Clare started driving again and then turned into an underground car park. She pulled into a space in the furthest, darkest corner, then cut the engine and told us to get out and follow.

Hidden away behind a row of overflowing bins was the service lift. She pressed the button and the door opened, painfully slowly.

"Where are we now?" I asked.

"Take this to the top floor, and wait for me there."

"Are you not coming with us?"

"I'll be four minutes."

Four minutes was curiously precise. It was almost as if she'd done this before, whatever it was, and knew exactly how long it would take. There again, she probably had.

We waited outside the lift on the top floor, standing on bare concrete. The harsh fluorescent strip lights gave our skin a sickly glow. I didn't know what to expect next. I held onto Danny, still feeling waves of shock taking all the energy from my legs.

"I'm sorry," I said. "I'm going to have to sit down." I collapsed against the wall and sank to the floor. Danny joined me, and put an arm round my shoulders to hold me tight.

A moment later, Clare appeared from along the corridor. She knelt down beside us, her face conveying a look of concern. I didn't understand how she'd made it to the top floor without using the lift. Surely she hadn't run up the stairs? Where even were we?

She asked if we were okay to walk. When we said yes, she helped us up, and led us through a door. Suddenly there was carpet, and the lighting was more forgiving. It appeared to be the public part of a hotel. She pressed a plastic card against one of the room handles, and opened the door so we could pass through. It wasn't the most opulent decor, but it was certainly better than some I'd stayed in over the years.

I sat on the bed while she opened a cupboard beneath the TV and removed a tray containing a kettle, tea bags and little pots of milk. There were only two cups.

"Don't mind me," I said. "I'll start on the minibar." I meant it as a joke, which was brave, given the circumstances. I closed my eyes, only to open them a moment later to see Clare pouring me a small glass of white wine. She passed it over.

"So," she said. "Sorry about that."

"To think I'd been just about to make some comment about how we'd managed to get out of there without being shot," I said.

"Amazing driving," added Danny. "Where did you learn to do that?"

"Needs must, Danny. We'll be safe here for an hour or so, until we know we're not being searched for."

"Who was it in the car?" I asked.

"I think if we knew that, we'd know the answer to everything," she said.

"It must have been someone from Miroslav's personal army. What were they called? Luka and Goran. Did you see their faces? Who else knew about the meeting?" I looked at Danny.

"Only Amy and Otto." He paused, thinking. "Christ. And Georgi." All eyes were on Clare. "Come on," he continued, "this is too much of a coincidence. You've got to see that."

"I know how it looks, Danny, but let's think this through."

"What is there to think? You said yourself you couldn't trust him. It wasn't Amy. I don't think it was Otto. If Miroslav wanted to kill us, he had the perfect opportunity, so who else does that leave?"

The wine didn't last very long at all. And then there was a knock at the door.

"Who the fuck is that?" I hissed. And then it started to open and I knew I was about to die.

Chapter 31

DCI Graham March was at his desk when the call came through.

"A shooting?" he said.

"Apparently."

"How very unfortunate."

"No reports of casualties, but eyewitnesses spoke of a car having its back window blown out, and then mounting the pavement."

"That sounds rather dangerous. Did they get a description of the driver?"

"I can send that to you. If you really need it."

He chuckled.

"I think I could maybe write it myself. And you're absolutely sure nobody was injured?"

"A couple of pedestrians have bruises where they dived for cover, but none in the getaway car as far as we know."

"Hmm. That's a pity. It must have been quite scary for them, though. Where's the car now?"

"We're running CCTV. We should find it soon."

"Please let me know if you do. And the car with the gun?"

"Vanished into thin air apparently. It's weird how these things happen."

"It is indeed. I'll file the report, although there's not much we can do in the circumstances. But keep me informed if you hear anything."

"I will. Anything else you need?"

"There may be. I'll let you know. Excellent work in the meantime."

He replaced the handset. Things were coming along very well indeed.

———

I expected Clare to reach for a gun and start firing, but it was just as well she didn't. It was a room service porter, who apologised for interrupting us, then carried in a bottle of wine in an ice bucket and three glasses, which he said were with the compliments of the manager. He put them on the desk and then turned to leave.

"Thank you," said Clare. He nodded then closed the door behind him. Clare refilled my glass from the bottle and poured one for Danny, then helped herself to a Diet Coke from the minibar. I was tempted to steal one of her cigarettes to calm my nerves but decided that would just make my head go fuzzy, and I was quite happy to let the alcohol do that on its own.

"I think we need to take a step back," said Danny, once things had resumed a semblance of normality. "What if we're starting from the wrong place?"

"Go on," said Clare.

"Okay. So far we've been thinking that the war's ending. It's time to diversify. It's time to get money out of Serbia. Miroslav moves to London and gives his money to Gersbach and Haller.

213

The money may be from his haulage company, or maybe not. We've only got Georgi's word for that."

"Agreed. But you've got your doubts?"

"I know he's your friend, but who else knew about the meeting today - and why invite Aleksander in Sofia, whoever he is?"

"I wouldn't say 'friend' so much as someone I've done some work with."

"Right, so let's park that. We'll come back to it. Tom is investing money, but into what? We don't know. Maybe the funds are more creative than you'd expect, but presumably the scale of the investment buys a certain amount of expertise unavailable to the casual investor."

"Agreed."

"But then Tom loses money and gets killed, and Emma gets arrested, but the evidence is so ridiculous only an idiot like March would be taken in. Our starting point has been: who killed Tom and why, and who framed Emma and why? And we suspect the answer to the last bit is: to deflect attention from the person who really did it. And is March just an idiot or is he part of the cover-up?"

"Okay. And you think that's the wrong premise?"

"Maybe. Bear with me. What if Tom wasn't the victim? What if Emma was? What if this whole thing started as a set-up to get Emma arrested, and Tom was just an innocent pawn in some other game that we've never considered? Emma introduced Miroslav to the bank, remember? And if that's the case, who wanted Emma arrested and why? Miroslav? We're focusing on trying to find out if Tom had any enemies, but what if the only crime he committed was marrying the wrong person?"

Clare looked thoughtful.

"It's possible. What do we know about her?"

"On the face of it, she's a good person, if we don't dwell on the infidelity aspects. She's got money, obviously, but she seems to want to do good."

"You mean the charity thing?"

"Yeah, the orphanages. Fundraising and active involvement as far as I can tell. I wish I'd asked her more about that. I don't know enough about it really, except that the situation in Romania was horrific. Julian was sent in to investigate Emma but now he's dead. What if he was killed because he got too close to her? Not because he knew something about the murder of Tom. Our only evidence in any of this comes from Georgi again. Sorry."

"There's no need to apologise. If Georgi is up to something and trying to play me, he'll live to regret it."

"Or maybe not live to regret it," I said, as an attempt at a joke.

"Quite," said Clare, seemingly failing to appreciate my wit, and sounding like her old scary self.

Danny paused, looking thoughtful.

"I don't know," he said, eventually. "I say all that and then we still have the issue of Christian being at the hotel. I need to get Amy again and see if she's managed to speak to him, to see what his story is."

Clare stood up, and started to put her jacket on.

"We've got a lot more questions than answers," she said. "But most important of all, somebody doesn't seem to like the fact that we're investigating, judging by today. Whatever you do, be careful."

"Are you off?" I said.

"I'm just popping out for a moment," she said. "I've got a couple of calls to make. Back in a minute."

When she'd left the room, I lay back on the bed and closed my eyes.

"I'm so sorry about all this," said Danny.

"I'd like to say it was exciting," I said, "but I think I'm the most scared I've ever been."

.   .   .

After maybe ten minutes, Clare returned.

"Everything okay?" asked Danny.

"Nothing I can't sort out," she said. "I've extended the stay at Farringdon. I think you'll be safe there, now we can't use the Camden safe house."

"Are we heading back there now?"

"There's no immediate rush. Finish the wine and I'll arrange a taxi."

Danny excused himself and went to the bathroom. I took the opportunity to speak to Clare on her own.

"Is this what life is like for you?"

"No, not really," she said. "Believe it or not, I like a quiet life."

"I've never really had a chance to thank you properly for what you did for us last year."

"There's no need. And I may be undoing it if this all goes wrong."

It was the first time I'd heard her express doubts about anything.

"You're scaring me."

"Don't take me seriously, Anna. I just wish I knew who the enemy was. It's much easier when you know who you're dealing with and what they have to lose."

"That doesn't sound like living the quiet life."

"I didn't say I was very good at it."

"But couldn't you do that? Haven't you got enough money now? Couldn't you just disappear somewhere peaceful and invite us for holidays?"

She looked at me. It seemed like she wanted to say something. Wanted to trust me. But something was stopping her.

"Do you need a hug?" I asked, when she didn't speak. She thought about it and then nodded. I got off the bed and walked towards her. Her arms were open. It felt strange to hold her and equally as strange to be held by her. She had a way of making me feel special, and yet she was such a contradiction. So strong and yet so fragile.

"Hello," said Danny, as he emerged from the bathroom. We let go of each other and she winked at me. She had such a natural smile in her eyes. It made it all the more incomprehensible that her troubled mind lurked just beneath.

Clare's phone started ringing. She checked the number then answered the call.

"I'm going to call Amy," whispered Danny, to me.

I sat back on the bed while they both spoke on their phones. Both calls sounded lively, and then both ended almost simultaneously. It was fascinating to watch them in action.

"You first," said Danny.

"Okay. Good news. That was Otto. He's going to meet us at Farringdon later and take us to where Julian was living. Hopefully before the police find it, so we get first look. You?"

"That was Amy. She's going to interview Christian Fuller, but she wants to meet with me first."

"Excellent. That all sounds like progress. When are you meeting?"

"As soon as I can."

"You'll come back to Farringdon straight after?"

"Of course."

She turned to me.

"Are you happy to go back there now? I can't really use my car, but I can arrange a taxi."

"Actually," I said, "could I be cheeky and ask for one to my studio? I've got a few work things to sort out."

"With Diana? Will she be there?"

"How do you know about Diana?"

"I'm sure you mentioned her."

I was equally as sure I hadn't.

"Keep your phone handy in case you need to call me," she

continued. "I'm sure you'll be okay, but at the first sign of anything out of place, call me and I'll come and get you, okay?"

"Okay," I said. I'm sure she said it to try to reassure me, but as I headed off on my own, the words had had precisely the opposite effect.

Chapter 32

DANNY stood on the street and watched as a Ford Mondeo pulled up at the kerb. DS Amy Cranston reached across and opened the passenger door so he could climb in.

"You look pale," she said. "Is everything okay?"

"Don't even ask."

"Rumour has it there was a car chase."

"You've heard about that?"

"Just the basics. I thought I told you both to be careful. What happened?"

Danny gave a summary, both of the meeting with Miroslav and the subsequent events at the traffic lights.

"Did you see who it was?"

"No, I heard Anna scream and I ducked. I was on the other side of the car."

"Well, at least we know it wasn't Christian. He's been at his office all day."

"That's good. In one sense, anyway. You've managed to arrange an interview?"

"Not as such, but I thought we could catch him when he leaves the office, in the car park."

"*We?*"

"Danny, I have to warn you, do not take me for granted."

"I could kiss you."

"Yeah, well, don't do that either."

He laughed.

"Thank you so much. What made you change your mind?"

"Don't start questioning me or I'll change it back. This is way out on a limb. If he asks to see your warrant card we're buggered, to use a technical policing term. And this is all unofficial, okay? Background research. You don't record anything. You don't quote anyone. In fact, you don't even ask questions."

"Okay, understood."

"We've got to be careful with this. If March hears about it, he could make things very uncomfortable. This is not my investigation, Danny. Ready?"

"As I'll ever be."

They sat in their car, in the underground car park of Gersbach and Haller, facing Christian's Porsche and waiting for him to emerge.

"So this is where Tom was killed?" asked Danny.

"Over there." She pointed at a pillar, midway along the second row. "His secretary discovered him."

"It looks the kind of place. There's something inherently scary about underground car parks. I think I've seen too many films."

"I know what you mean."

They didn't have long to wait. Shortly after four, they saw him appear from the doorway at the far end of the car park, and start to walk in their direction.

"Action time," said Amy.

They got out of their car.

"Christian Fuller?" she asked. He looked up. "DS Amy

Cranston, Metropolitan Police." She flashed him her warrant card. "I just need to ask you a few questions."

"Me?"

"Yes, if you're Christian Fuller."

"In connection with what? I'm afraid I'm rather busy. If you would like to make an appointment with my secretary, she will see if she can fit you in."

"And I'm afraid I don't have that option. This won't take long. Unless you'd like to accompany me to the station and we can do it there."

He stopped walking, appearing to weigh up his options, and then noticed Danny for the first time.

"I'm sorry, I don't understand. Are you the guy that came in for the meeting about investments? Was that some sort of attempt at entrapment? Some illegal undercover sting?"

Amy put out her hand to stop Danny replying.

"It won't take us long, Mr Fuller."

"I'm not answering any questions without a solicitor."

"Which of course I can arrange for you, down at the station. But I was hoping we could keep this informal. Of course, if you would prefer to make it an official interview, I can take you down there now."

"Are you arresting me?"

"Why would I want to arrest you? Hopefully that won't be necessary. But I do need to talk to you, and I need to do it now. Follow me, please."

She wasn't going to be deterred. Danny was impressed by her cool efficiency. Christian Fuller looked hesitant but finally followed. She opened the passenger door and he climbed into her car. She walked round to the driver's side, while Danny got in the back.

"What is this about?" asked Christian. "If it's about Tom Napier, I've already been interviewed and told you everything I know. Not that I really know anything."

221

The scent of expensive aftershave began to fill the car.

"No, it's not about Tom. Where were you yesterday evening?"

"Yesterday? Why?"

"Just answer the question."

"I was at work, then I went home."

"Well, that's already bullshit, if you excuse the expression."

"I beg your pardon?"

"Mr Fuller - Christian - we know that is nonsense. You went to a hotel after work, did you not?"

"A hotel?"

"The Belgravia International. Does that ring a bell? You're not going to try to deny it, are you?"

"I... Well, yes, I may have done."

"May have done?"

"Yes, I think I did, now you mention it. I'm sorry, I'd forgotten. Every day merges into every other. What is this about?"

"It's about what you were doing at the hotel, Mr Fuller. I suggest you tell us everything."

"There's nothing to tell."

"Really? Because we're investigating the discovery of a body in one of the rooms and an eyewitness report of you leaving shortly after. It's not looking good for you, Christian."

"What? That's ridiculous."

"No, it's not ridiculous. So I'll mention it again: I can make this a formal interview, if you prefer, or we can keep it off the record and discuss it now. Either way, unless you're going to start talking, you're in a lot of trouble."

Chapter 33

THERE was a bead of sweat forming on Christian Fuller's upper lip. Danny was watching his body language carefully.

"Which would you prefer?" asked Amy.

"Okay, ask what you like, but I need to know what *he's* doing here." He indicated to Danny, sitting behind.

"I'm the one asking the questions. Starting with what were you doing at the hotel?"

"I went to meet a new client. He didn't show up."

"Right."

"It's true. I waited in reception. He didn't show. I gave it an extra half hour and then I left."

"Can anybody vouch for you?"

"The concierge, the receptionist, doorman. I don't know. Ask anyone you like."

"And you waited in reception all that time?"

"In the bar, but it's just off the reception. I had a Coke. I've got the receipt somewhere. I'll show you." He took his wallet from the inside pocket of his suit jacket, and started searching through it.

"That's not necessary," said Amy, halting him. "Who was the client?"

"I can't remember."

"That's useful," Amy said, ironically.

"I can't. It was Julian something, I think. I don't know. I meet lots of people. I can't remember all of them."

"Who made the appointment?"

"He did. I believe he phoned in. Check with the secretaries if you don't believe me. A girl called Lucy passed it to me."

"Tom's secretary?"

"Former. She's being reassigned. I'll call her now and she can confirm it for you."

He took his phone from his jacket pocket, then stopped.

"What is it?" asked Amy. "Worried she'll deny any knowledge of it?"

"No, she won't be there."

"Even better."

"She wasn't in today. I think she called in sick, probably with the stress of everything."

"That's highly convenient."

"Call her at home. Reception will give you her number."

"I'll do that."

Danny thought Amy's relentless focus was admirable.

"Seriously, I never met the guy," Christian continued. "I didn't even know who he was, so if anything happened to anyone at the hotel, I haven't got a clue what you're talking about."

Amy adjusted her position, to face him more directly.

"Okay, take us back a stage. What was Tom working on?"

"I thought you said this wasn't about Tom."

"It isn't but I'm interested. Humour me."

"I can't answer that."

"You don't have any option."

"For God's sake. Investments."

"For?"

"Clients."

"Oh, come on, Christian. Listen, so here's the deal. This is off the record. I'll check out your story. If it stacks up, you've got an alibi. So you've got no reason to be defensive. But I need you to answer questions."

"I've already answered questions."

"Bullshit."

"I did, when Emma was arrested."

"Right. And you think she did it?"

"The police think so."

"And you?"

"Presumably."

Danny was desperate to join in, but with an effort, he held himself back. Amy was doing a great job. Christian looked rattled.

"Who are you protecting, Christian?" she continued.

"What?"

"It's a simple question."

"Nobody. Why would I be protecting anybody?"

"And again, bullshit."

He took a deep breath. Then reached for the door handle.

"You're not going anywhere," said Amy.

"I'm not sitting here listening to this shit."

"I said you weren't going anywhere. So again, who are you protecting?"

"Nobody. I told you."

"Okay. Talk to me about Tom. Plain sailing, was it? Everything going well?"

"Not exactly. He was under pressure."

"From?"

"The compliance department."

"Why?"

"He'd lost a lot of money. Some deals went bad."

"For which client?"

225

"I can't discuss clients."

"Which client?"

"A Serbian guy."

"Miroslav Nikolić?"

Christian's shoulder's slumped as some of the fight went out of him. "Yes."

"Good. That wasn't too hard was it? What was he doing for him?"

"I don't know. Just investments."

"Really?"

"Maybe."

"What does maybe mean?"

"Sometimes it's best not to ask. Look, the country's been at war. I know it's over now, but they don't mess about. Know what I mean? And they want the kind of return that takes a certain amount of creativity."

"Laundering?"

"No."

"This is off the record, remember."

He thought for a moment.

"Look, I don't know the details, but no we don't launder money."

"What then?"

"I don't know."

"Not good enough. It's not sticking it in a high-interest savings account, is it? So what kind of investments?"

"It could be anything. Shares, commodities, futures, bonds, currencies. Nothing illegal. But probably something fairly imaginative."

"Insider trading?"

"No, definitely not."

"Definitely?"

"Yeah, definitely. He wouldn't have done that."

Danny thought he was beginning to relax, now the subject had changed to more comfortable territory.

"So why were the compliance department interested?" asked Amy.

"I told you, he made big losses."

"And that's unusual?"

"Not unheard of but it's never good. There's a heightened state of due diligence at the moment, with the whole Nick Leeson thing."

"I can imagine. Do you think Tom was doing something similar?"

"No, of course not. He was just unlucky. It happens."

"Oh, he was definitely unlucky. I've seen his corpse. Was anyone else asking questions?"

"No."

"And you didn't think to mention the compliance department in the original investigation?"

"No."

"Because?"

"Because it was all wrapped up, wasn't it? They arrested his wife. They found the evidence. Call me old-fashioned but I care about my job. I don't want to do anything to embarrass the bank."

He was back to looking on edge, fidgety.

"Do you think she did it?" Amy continued.

"I was surprised but the reports said the evidence was fairly damning."

"Did you ever meet her?"

"Emma? Yes, of course."

"Where?"

"Tom was a friend. We'd have dinner parties. Work functions. Golf days. Ascot. Henley. Occasionally Emma would come along. Again, I'm sorry. I thought you said this wasn't about Tom?"

Amy ignored the objection.

"And what did you make of her?"

"You don't give up, do you? She seemed like a good person. She had a heart. She did a lot of charity work."

"She didn't strike you as someone capable of murder?"

He thought for a moment.

"No. But you never know, do you? What goes on behind closed doors."

"Were you aware Tom was gay?"

"Not until it came up in the investigation, no."

"Really? And yet you said you were the best of friends. Wouldn't best friends tell each other something like that? It's not easy to hide."

"I didn't say we were best friends. Does anyone have a best friend as an adult?" In the rear seat, Danny suddenly had a vision of Anna. "He was a colleague. We got on. We saw each other outside the office occasionally, but it was normally something work-related."

It was time for a different approach. To throw him off guard.

"Are you married?"

"What's that got to do with anything?"

"Maybe nothing, maybe something. So are you?"

"No. But I'm not gay either if that's what you're thinking."

"I'm not thinking anything, Christian. I've got an open mind. What did you think when you heard Emma had been having an affair?

"I was shocked by that as well."

"Really? It never occurred to you? You never got close on one of your away days?"

"What? For heaven's sake. No. Of course not."

And now he seemed to be losing his temper. This was fascinating.

"Did Tom have any enemies?" asked Amy.

"Not that I knew of."

"Oh, come on. You work in investment banking. Even I know

that's a high-pressure, competitive kind of job. You're bound to have rivals from other firms. Maybe even from within your own."

"What are you asking?"

"Just trying to get a picture. It seems odd. I asked if he had any enemies and you immediately said no. I'd be much more inclined to believe you if you told the truth."

"I am telling the truth. I said none that I knew of. Rivals, yes, lots of those, but that's not how I'd define an enemy."

"Are you hiding something, Christian?"

"No, for heaven's sake. What is this?"

"It's a murder enquiry. I thought you knew that."

"For the guy in the hotel? Or Tom. Make your bloody mind up. Jesus."

His hand moved to the door handle again.

"The man in the hotel," said Amy. "Who you correctly identified as Julian."

"Well, if that's who got killed I'm terribly sorry, but I told you. He was a potential client. I never met him. I only turned up for a meeting and he didn't show. I told you all that."

"You did. Let's focus on the other murder. Personally, I'm not convinced that Emma killed Tom."

"What? Well, your colleagues are."

"One of them does, but I'm just checking to make sure he's right. Tell me more about Emma."

"What do you want to know? I hardly knew her."

"You haven't got any opinions to share?"

"I haven't given it any thought."

"Hold on. Your friend is murdered. His wife, another friend, gets charged with killing him. And you didn't give it any thought?"

"No, that's not what I meant. Obviously I thought about it, but I didn't try to work out who'd done it or whether she was guilty. I just assumed she was."

Amy turned to look at Danny, who nodded in recognition.

"Okay, so maybe we're getting there," she continued. "Here's your opportunity to think about it now. Who do you think helped her?"

"Why would anyone have helped her?"

"An accomplice? Maybe someone she worked with?"

"In her day job? Seriously, I've got no idea. She worked for a charity."

"And she didn't have a sideline in industrial espionage? Gave no indication of being an assassin?"

"No, of course not."

"And yet you still think she did it?"

Christian let out an exasperated sigh.

"I don't know what I think."

"But you think it's possible she didn't do it?"

"I don't know. Maybe. Maybe not. I'm not the police. You are. I only know what I've seen in the press."

"That's not strictly true, though, is it. You knew both the victim and the accused. They were your friends. You met them socially and you spent the working day with one of them, so probably at least eight hours every weekday."

"That's not how it works. We're not traders. We have our own offices."

"Even so, you know a bit more than you've read in the papers. You must do. I'm just interested in who you think killed Tom."

"Aside from Emma, I have no idea."

"Where were you that night?"

"I was in Zürich."

"Can anyone vouch for that?"

"Anyone. I was in meetings all day, the day before, and the day after. I was in a hotel that night, I ate at the restaurant, I had late-night room service. Interview the hotel staff, interview anybody who works at the bank in Zürich. Ask the airline. They'll tell you when I flew."

"Okay. And who do you think killed Julian?"

"Absolutely no idea. I'd never met the guy."

"Would it surprise you to learn that Julian was the person Emma had the affair with?"

"*What*?" The colour seemed to drain from his face.

"One and the same. So you see, there's definitely a connection. And this time it definitely wasn't Emma, as she's currently under secure lock and key."

"I just... I don't know what to say."

"Okay."

Amy stopped speaking and stared at him.

"What now?" he said, flustered. "I'm way out of my depth here."

"Interesting turn of phrase."

"It doesn't mean anything. I just mean I have no idea. I didn't know him. I didn't know he was the guy who had the affair with Emma. I don't know anything about any of this. I seriously suggest you stop talking to me and get out there looking for whoever's doing it."

"Who would you suggest we should speak to?"

"Not the first idea."

"There was nobody else at the bank who knew both Tom and Julian?"

"I don't know. Maybe Lucy. She made the appointment."

"Okay. We'll give her a call. Do you know Miroslav Nikolić?"

"No."

"Really? You haven't taken over the account?"

"No, I bloody haven't. Is there anything else? I really do need to be getting somewhere."

Amy took her warrant card from her inside pocket and removed a business card. She placed it on the dashboard in front of him.

"I'll leave you this. If anything does occur, make sure you call me."

Christian turned it round to look at it properly, but didn't immediately pick it up.

"And be careful, Christian. Somebody out there is killing people very close to you. I don't want you to be next."

"For heaven's sake. Are you trying to scare me?"

"No, I'm just trying to tell you to be careful. Because unless it's actually you pulling the trigger, you've been fairly close to the person who is."

"I'm not even going to respond to that."

"Okay." Amy nodded then looked at Danny. "Thank you for your time. Remember to call me. Don't forget the card."

He looked at it again, and this time picked it up and placed it in his wallet."

"Are we finished?"

"For now."

"Thank you."

With that, he got out, slamming the car door unnecessarily hard. Danny didn't move until Christian had fired the Porsche's engine and roared away. Then Amy turned to him.

"Well done for not joining in," she said. "I hope you think that was useful?"

"Very."

"But if his alibi for Zürich stacks up, there's no way he could have killed Tom."

"Just what I was thinking."

She started her engine.

"I'll give you a lift back to Farringdon, and we can discuss it on the way."

Chapter 34

IANA had a pile of paperwork for me at the studio. Before I opened the place, I'd never realised that running a business would be so complicated. I thought I'd be free, all day, to take beautiful pictures for well-heeled clients, and spend the rest of my time creating art, not dealing with lease agreements, public liability insurance, invoices and tax returns.

After I'd worked through some of it, I told her I'd return, hopefully tomorrow, to finish the rest. I was keen to get to the sanctuary of Farringdon and the relative security of being with Clare and Danny.

They were both there when I arrived, along with Amy and Otto, presumably ahead of the trip to Julian's apartment. Bizarrely, Amy still showed no inclination to arrest Clare.

Amy and Danny were in the process of recapping the details of their meeting with Christian Fuller. Now we knew a lot more but equally we were no further forward. I felt like an imposter even being included in these conversations, doubting that there was anything that I could add of any value. The spheres of industrial espionage, high finance, and hostilities in the Balkans were a world away from my existence.

When they'd finished, Clare stood up and moved to the window, next to where Otto was standing. She edged the net curtain to one side and gazed down the street as though looking for someone, or some threat that she'd yet to mention.

"Can I just point out," said Amy, regardless, "but it really, really pisses me off when people come to my city and start killing each other. I don't know what we're saying here. Do you still think it's Miroslav or some group of unknown Croatians? Do you have any leads you're not sharing with me?"

Clare turned back towards us.

"What we are saying is: Miroslav is a gangster, no question, but I'm beginning to doubt he's to blame for everything," she said. "He mentioned Croatians in London causing problems for him, but we're no further forward in identifying them. Aleksander was apparently Croatian, but we don't know if that's true or if he's linked to anyone in London. And we don't have any Croatian links with Tom or Julian. We don't know who shot at us in the car, either, or why."

"It also doesn't explain why March is so keen to stop us investigating," said Danny. "What is it that he's hiding? Is he just trying to protect his reputation because he arrested the wrong person? Or is he covering for somebody? Amy, whose investigation is this?"

"Which part?"

"Every part. All these things even being linked?"

"March and DC Lisa Miller took on Emma, and the last I heard he was jostling for Julian, but as for what happened with you leaving Miroslav's, I have no idea."

"DC Lisa Miller?" said Clare. She couldn't stop a grin appearing. I don't know if she spotted me watching her. Amy spotted it too.

Clare stood up and walked towards the door.

"Back in a moment."

I reached out to Danny and held his hand, giving it a squeeze more for my own comfort than for his. We were facing danger from unknown sources, and I still wasn't confident that we could walk down the street without a significant risk of being murdered. Danny turned to Otto.

"How well do you know Georgi?" he asked, taking advantage of Clare's absence. "Do you think he can be trusted?"

Otto started to laugh, but it was the kind of hollow, humourless laugh that made me think there was nothing in the slightest bit funny.

"Georgi is his own man," he said. "I only know him by reputation, but presumably he knows better than to get on the wrong side of Clare."

I could relate to that, having seen the way she operated.

"Bulgaria is a country in transition," he continued. "There is a lot of corruption, the economy is a mess and things are getting worse. Can you really trust anybody there? Personally I don't think so. But Georgi has benefited hugely from his association with Clare, and if he is jeopardising that then I can only assume he's either very brave, very stupid or had a very large offer from somewhere else."

"Well, I know he's not stupid," said Clare, coming back into the room, catching Danny in the act. I don't know what she'd been up to, but she seemed edgy. She sat back down. Everybody looked to her as though she'd know all the answers, and make everything okay. It was disconcerting to realise she was human and as much in the dark as the rest of us.

Though it was only afternoon, it seemed like the dead of night outside. We all squeezed into a taxi for the short trip to Julian's flat. It was on the ground floor in a terraced block near the Angel station in Islington. Otto had a key and he opened up for us, then flicked on the lights.

Amy produced a set of latex gloves for everyone, and we all started searching. I didn't know what we were looking for, but I tried to make myself useful. There wasn't much there. No books, not many clothes, and not much food in the cupboards or fridge. To my untutored eye, it looked like he hadn't spent much time there.

Amy and Danny opened Julian's notebook computer but were then stuck at a password screen. Clare was riffling through a pile of paperwork on his desk. Otto stood silently, not really helping, but not really getting in the way. I was aware that in all of this, he'd lost a friend and colleague. It must have been strange for him, to see the flat being picked apart.

The desk drawer was locked, but Clare levered it open. It contained a large pile of photographs, some tapes and a collection of Zip disks.

"Now we're getting somewhere," she said. She started to spread the pictures across the desk.

"Does anyone look familiar?" asked Amy.

There were lots of pictures. Mainly men, some women. Clare shook her head.

"They could be anyone. Maybe Croatian, maybe Serbian." She carried on examining them, then stopped. "I recognise those two. That's Goran and Luka."

"And they are?"

"Miroslav's bodyguards."

She put the picture to one side, then continued to go through the pile.

"Hold on," I said. "I've seen that before." It was a close-up picture of a ring, with an ornate design. "I've no idea where, but that looks familiar."

"Really?"

"I can't think where I've seen it, but I've seen it before. Not the ring but the design."

"Are you sure?"

"Definitely. It could have been in a magazine or something though." I tried to remember but nothing would come. "Sorry." Clare put the picture to one side.

Then suddenly we all saw somebody who looked very familiar indeed. It was Graham March, standing outside the Smoking Gun.

"Hello," said Clare. "Oh Graham, something you're not telling us?"

"Where's that?" asked Amy.

"It's a gay club. The one Tom was at the night he died."

"Presumably he went there to make enquiries."

Clare shook her head, lining up several prints of him, side by side.

"Look," she said, pointing to two in turn. "These have been taken on different days. He's wearing different clothes." She turned one of the pictures over. There was writing on the back. "And here's a date. When did Tom die?"

"November 14th," said Danny.

"So why was March at the club in October? If we believe these dates are true. And look, there's a poster behind him."

We all crowded round, trying to read the tiny writing.

"It's advertising an event. Look at the date. I can't read the number, but it definitely says October."

Clare stood back.

"Well, I wasn't expecting that," she said.

"What is Graham March doing at a gay club?" asked Danny. "Unless..."

He didn't need to finish the sentence. I'm pretty sure we were all thinking the same. Nobody spoke for a moment, while we all tried to process the revelation.

"Is anybody any good with passwords?" asked Amy, looking

back at the computer. Otto sat at the desk and tapped in a few attempts. Eventually the screen sprang to life, showing the Windows 95 desktop.

"I won't ask how you did that," she said.

"It was easy," he said, then rose from the chair so she could take his place. She nudged the TrackPoint to move the cursor to the My Computer icon and started to browse the contents of the hard disk. I still hadn't upgraded my computer to Windows 95 so it all looked a bit unfamiliar. A couple of clicks later she had a folder of documents. She started to open them, with Danny and Clare kneeling beside her to read them as she did so. It took a while before any of them spoke, but eventually Danny broke the silence.

"I think we've had everything wrong," he said.

"What is it?" I asked.

"Look."

I wasn't sure what I was looking at.

"I'm sorry, but you're going to have to explain."

"Some of them are about Miroslav. It looks like transcripts of recordings. But these..." He indicated a couple at the right of the screen. "They're about loan sharks, and blackmail scams. What on earth was Julian investigating?"

"Are you saying Miroslav was blackmailing people and lending money?"

"No. But somebody has been."

"It's like there are two distinct sets of files," added Amy. "And look at this one."

"TN Shortlist" was written in bold at the top. There was a list of names below, but all had been struck through apart from one. The only name remaining was Ljubica.

"Who on earth is Ljubica?" I asked.

"I don't know," said Amy. "But if TN stands for Tom Napier, it looks like Ljubica killed him."

In a black Mercedes, two men sat watching the door of a bar popular with London's Croatian community, keeping surveillance on known troublemakers, waiting to see who emerged. The inside of the car was momentarily illuminated by the glow of a mobile phone display.

The driver looked over to his front seat passenger, who pressed a button to connect the call.

"Luka," he said into the mouthpiece. Then paused. Listening.

Within a minute, the driver floored the accelerator and raced away.

Chapter 35

DANNY found a carrier bag in the kitchen, and loaded everything we'd found into it. All of the disks, the pictures, the tapes, and even the notebook computer itself. I could see it made Amy uncomfortable. We were removing evidence that could help the police with their enquiries, but as Danny pointed out, if March started investigating and came across the things we'd found, they'd disappear for ever.

Danny and I returned to the flat in Farringdon, but the other three disappeared into the night. I'd given up wondering where Clare was staying. We took refuge in our shared bedroom, but I didn't think I'd be able to sleep. There was too much going on, I was missing home, and the picture of the ring was haunting me.

When Danny headed to the bathroom, I moved to the window, looking out at the unfamiliar street, my mind lost, trying to fathom the intricacies of a world that I knew nothing about. It was hopeless. I was struck by my naivety and innocence. How dangerous the world could be. How little I knew of a country and region of Europe so ravaged by a brutal conflict, and how that must have shaped so many lives. Parents with children, with hopes and dreams, living in fear, facing tragedy, and the uncertain terror of living in a war zone. From my leafy London street it all seemed so very far away, and yet today we'd come face to face with the tiniest part of it.

The street was quiet. Eventually Danny came to join me. I felt safer when he put his arm around me. Unaware of the drama unfolding elsewhere in London, we went to bed, and prepared for another early start.

Graham March sat back in the plush leather armchair as the front door burst open. Seconds later, Goran and Luka rushed into the room, weapons at the ready.

Miroslav rose from behind his desk, hand raised to halt their progress. The two bodyguards stopped and looked at March, who stood, hand extended, as Miroslav made the introductions.

"Tell them what you told me," he said, once he'd finished.

March sat back down.

"I am merely here in an unofficial capacity, to give you a friendly warning," he said. "My only interest is to pass on information that has come to my attention."

"Tell them the information."

"Well." He crossed his legs, choosing his moment, delighted at the way things were going. It was even easier than he'd planned. "As you know, Miroslav and I know each other from the investigation at the bank. I told him he could always call on me if he ever needed any assistance."

He paused, but when nobody acknowledged him, he carried on.

"Miroslav called me late yesterday and told me that you were expecting three visitors this morning. A woman called Clare Woodbrook and two of her colleagues."

"I knew of her name, of course," added Miroslav, by way of explanation, "but she has a reputation. I asked Mr March to find out any background that might help me be prepared. To discover her agenda."

"Exactly. So I said I would check them out. I'd heard of them too. All three are well known to the authorities over here, although obviously Clare is the ringleader. I said I'd do some digging." It was all so effortless, he almost laughed. He turned to Miroslav. "What did they tell you when they arrived? What reason did they give for the meeting?"

"She was offering to help me," said Miroslav, looking furious.

"I see." He turned back to the others, getting into his flow. "Well, as I was just explaining, I discovered the real reason they were here. They are, in fact, guns for hire. All three of them. They work together, and, it transpires they've been retained by a Croatian gang from east London to come here, to gain your confidence, and then - not to beat around the old bush - ultimately to kill you. All of you, Miroslav included."

That got their attention.

"Of course, I cannot reveal my sources, but I can tell you that it is a serious and credible threat. Ms Woodbrook, as you're aware, is a known killer. I'm sure that you don't need me to remind you of her reputation. Last weekend all three of them were in Bulgaria, where I believe the plot was finalised. I have a still from the CCTV at the airport to show you." He handed it over. Goran looked at it, then passed it to Luka. Their expressions were deadly serious.

"And today I also discovered that it was Clare, in fact, who killed Tom Napier," March continued. "Firstly to destabilise Miroslav financially, but also to prove her worth to her Croatian friends."

He paused, to assess their reactions, but was met with a stone-faced silence.

"Now obviously this is very embarrassing for me personally, as I have to acknowledge the fact that I arrested the wrong person," he continued, "but it highlights that the woman is a devious and lethal enemy. And she needs to be stopped."

He withdrew another piece of paper from his jacket pocket.

"I have managed to identify her accomplices. The man was Danny Churchill. The girl was Anna Burgin. I don't know much about them, except that they are dangerous, and under Clare's command. They are currently residing in Camden. All of the details are here. And again, let me assure you, I am not doing this for any kind of recompense. I am merely here as the conduit to justice. I am not asking for payment. My interest is only in protecting law-abiding citizens and ensuring they have a right to go about their business without being, what I like to call, massacred."

He handed over the A4 sheet.

"Obviously, I cannot condone warfare on the streets of London, but I cannot overstress the danger that all three pose to you."

Miroslav turned to his bodyguards.

"Lying to me is the most severe form of treachery, and I expect it to be dealt with appropriately," he said.

Both nodded.

"Far be it for me to guide you on what form of action you may wish to take, but I can make sure a blind eye is turned," March continued. "We're all men. I think we understand each other. You can choose to ignore the warning, of course, or you could act to nullify the threat while you have the element of surprise."

He stood up.

"I will keep in touch if I hear any more, but in the meantime, I hope you take this advice in the spirit of international goodwill with which it was intended. And with that, gentlemen, I wish you a pleasant evening."

March was shown to the door. When he was back behind the wheel of his car, he could barely contain his excitement. Why had he never thought of this before? It was late, but he was in the mood to celebrate. And there was a new Lithuanian girl who would be a suitable beneficiary. He edged out into the late-night traffic, and started planning exactly what he'd do to her.

———

I was having an atrocious night. There was so much on my mind, and the unfamiliar surroundings were playing havoc with my ability to switch off and go to sleep.

It wasn't that I minded sharing a bed with Danny. Clearly, to Clare, it was a running joke, and hence why she kept putting us up in rooms with just the one double bed. But secretly that was the only positive aspect of all these shenanigans. I didn't like being shot at. I didn't appreciate feeling like a prisoner, being kept away from my own home. And I didn't like living out of a suitcase. Whatever else happened, I needed to pop back to Rochester Square, just to swap clothes, for the sake of my sanity.

The image of the ring kept flitting across my mind, along with the image of the shattered glass in the rear of Clare's hire car. I thought of the poor people back in Bosnia who'd been victims of so much torture and inhumanity. And then I thought of Graham March, seemingly being a regular at a gay swingers' club. It didn't make sense.

I knew lots of gay people and had a dozen gay friends. I couldn't see him as a part of that world. I'd borne the brunt of his sexism on many occasions. He acted as if all women were disposable, to be treated with contempt. I knew of his reputation as a frequent visitor to prostitutes and massage parlours. I was fairly sure, therefore, that his attendance at the Smoking Gun was nothing to do with sexuality. He was simply an evil, self-centred bastard, and one who was up to something. But what?

And then the cycle started again, and the image of the ring reappeared. Where had I seen it? I turned in the bed, flipped my pillow to make it cold, but nothing helped. Danny stirred, and I was aware I was disturbing him, but my mind just wouldn't switch off.

Eventually, at just past two, I decided enough was enough, and went to the kitchen to make a cup of tea. It wouldn't help me get to sleep, but at least it would make being awake infinitely more enjoyable. I took it through to the front room and curled up on the sofa. The heating had long gone off, and I didn't know how to fix it, so I put my jacket on to stay warm.

I thought back over the events of the week. Devon felt like so long ago, and had we really been to Bulgaria? It all seemed like a different lifetime. I thought about Julian, and the horror of finding his body. The sense that Clare's new spirit of openness and honesty clearly didn't stop her from always being up to something. Maybe she didn't realise she was doing it. I thought back to our first visit to Gersbach and Haller, and approaching Tom's secretary in the queue at Pret. I still wasn't happy that she had taken a shine to Danny, and I'd definitely need to keep those two apart, once this was all over. Assuming we lived that long.

And then, as the whole process started again, and just as I was about to set off in search of a biscuit, the realisation hit me. I knew exactly where I'd seen the ring.

Chapter 36

Friday, December 8th, 1995

I WAS desperate to wake Danny, but he needed to sleep. So I spent the next few hours wading through the bag of evidence we'd taken from Julian's flat, and then borrowed Danny's computer. I searched through CompuServe and then, when I'd exhausted that, I called up AltaVista in Netscape and started on the rest of the world wide web.

Everything made sense. I couldn't believe the ingenuity of it all. There were some things that still needed to be explained, but I knew who had killed Tom Napier. I knew how and I knew exactly why.

At six I couldn't wait any longer. If I was right, there was a busy day ahead. I made fresh tea and a plate of toast, then went back to the bedroom.

"Wakey wakey," I said, and gave Danny a nudge. Eventually he opened an eye, asked what time it was, then groaned and closed it again when I told him.

"I've made you tea and toast," I said, finding it hard to keep the excitement from my voice. "Oh, and I've solved the mystery."

"What are you talking about?" he murmured.

"Tea, toast and who killed Tom. Wake up and I'll tell you." I reached over and turned on his bedside light to force the issue. Suddenly Danny looked wide awake.

"What do you mean, 'who killed Tom'?"

I put the tea on the bedside table, then jumped on the bed, squashing his legs.

"What do you want to know first? Who did it? Or why or how? Or how I worked it out?"

I think the jumping thing was an error. He looked in pain, so I moved. He sat up, looking quite adorable, with hair all over the place.

"Okay. Start with who."

"Lucy."

"What?"

"Lucy. His secretary."

"What do you mean, Lucy?"

"Lucy killed him. Now do you want to know why or how? Or would you rather I explained my deductive powers?"

"Why?"

"Because her real name isn't Lucy. It's Ljubica. Lucy is the anglicised form. She's originally from Croatia. Miroslav killed her family. She was so disgusted with Tom working for the enemy, she took her revenge. Next?"

"Are you being serious?"

"Deadly, if you excuse the pun."

"How?"

"Here's the clever thing. She found the body, yes? But why? Because she knew that it was there to be discovered. My guess - well actually Julian's guess, but I kind of finished it for him - was that Tom didn't make a phone call at all."

"But we know he did."

"No, we thought he did. But we know Tom taped his meetings. Lucy was his secretary. Maybe she transcribed them, who knows? But on one of the tapes there's apparently a conversation between two people and during it Tom says 'Emma, no!'. Nothing to do with the murder and nothing to do with that particular evening, but it seems to have given her the idea. So she shoots Tom, takes his phone, calls her own number, and then plays that bit of the tape into the mouthpiece. It's genius."

"Shit." He was wide awake now.

"So, after the shooting, she went to see Emma with flowers from the office and planted the gun and phone. Then, my guess is that Julian was onto her, so she arranged to meet him in the hotel and killed him. But she couldn't do that without having someone to pin it on, so she made up a fictitious meeting for Christian to put him in the right place at very much the wrong time."

"Bloody hell."

"Are you going to ask me how I worked it out?"

"I can't get my head round this. Go on."

"It was her necklace. Remember after the meeting, when you went to the toilet and I went to talk to her? She wasn't exactly forthcoming, so I tried to make small talk. I noticed her necklace and complimented her on it. It was the same pattern as the ring in the picture. It's some Croatian religious symbol. As soon as I realised that, and I worked out her name, the rest just kind of made sense. I've been on the internet. The Croatians are big on religious symbols apparently. They normally tattoo them, but she had the same thing as a pendant."

"But who was shooting at us?" he asked.

"I don't know, but if she's Croatian then presumably some of her Croatian friends. Possibly Aleksander?"

"Oh, come here."

I leaned forward and he gave me a huge hug.

"You are a genius," he said.

"And you need to clean your teeth. Do you want to call Clare? Or Amy?"

I helped myself to a slice of toast.

Danny called Clare but it went to voicemail. Then he tried Amy. I don't think she was happy at being woken up, but she seemed very excited when Danny relayed my story.

"Remember Christian said she'd called in sick?" he said. "I suspect she may be doing a runner. You need to find out where she lives and get there quickly."

"I'm on it," said Amy, who ended the call.

I felt genuinely euphoric. I hadn't slept but I was full of energy. I knew it would catch up with me eventually, but the sheer joy of solving the case and not needing to worry about being shot once Amy arrested everyone was intoxicating.

Danny got up, had a shower and got dressed, then I did the same. He tried Clare again, but it kept going to voicemall.

"What do we do now?" I asked.

"We wait here. Let's see if Amy gets to her before we go anywhere. And we need to speak to Clare."

Amy called us at just past nine. She'd made an arrest. Apparently Lucy was all packed up, ready to flee the country, but broke down in tears when she was confronted. It was a quick call before they returned to the station for official questioning, but it looked very much like we'd nailed it.

Eventually Clare called back and Danny relayed the story again.

"She wants to meet for coffee," he said when he ended the call.

"Well, if it's all the same with you, I'll let you do that on your own."

"Are you sure?"

"You can take the glory. I've still got some things to do at the studio, and I want to get back to Camden to get some clean clothes. I'll meet you back here later, though."

"Perfect," he said. "Good plan."

I was excited to be getting my life back. But as it transpired, it was about the worst plan I could possibly have come up with.

249

C LARE had changed her hair again. Danny would have walked straight past her, had she not reached out for his arm.

"Wow," he said. "Have you had a perm?"

"I thought I'd give Anna a run for her money on the mad hair stakes," she replied, grinning.

"How did you manage that? Have you got an all-night hairdresser on call?"

"Something like that." But the grin faded as she changed the subject. "So Anna solved the case?"

"Yes, and Amy's made an arrest."

"That's good news. You should be pleased."

"I am. We all should be. It was a great team effort."

"Mmm."

The waitress arrived with their order. When she left, Danny spoke.

"You don't look as happy as I thought you would. What's up?"

"I think you've done a great job. You both did."

"But?"

"But I don't think we've tied up all the loose ends."

"In what way?"

"There are still things that I'm not happy about."

"I gathered that, but what?"

"Lucy killed Tom, I get that. But who killed Julian?"

"She did, obviously. She made the appointment to frame Christian."

"And your evidence for that is?"

Danny stopped, trying to think of an appropriate answer.

"Let me tell you," Clare continued. "At the moment, guesswork at best."

"It makes sense though."

"Nothing makes sense, Danny. As soon as one human being takes the life of another, traditional values and logic go out of the window."

"And you'd know all about that."

Clare's expression hardened.

"I know enough never to make assumptions without evidence. You do too. Come on, it's basic."

"Okay, but I'm sure we'll find evidence, or she'll confess."

"Maybe, but who shot at us when we left Miroslav's house? Was that Lucy in the 4x4? And if it was, can you explain how she was driving a car at the same time as poking a gun out of the passenger's window?"

"No." Danny's mood of celebration was fast running out of fizz. "We thought she must have some Croatian friends."

Clare laughed.

"Really? Oh, come on, Danny, you're better than that. Who? We've spent a week working on this and can you name one of them?"

"Only Aleksander. But Miroslav mentioned some."

"Which he failed to name. Can I remind you about two lorries making their way through Romania as we speak, possibly loaded with weapons? Can I remind you about Graham March visiting a gay club and ask how come we still don't know why that was of interest to Julian? Nor why March was so keen to arrest Emma rather than doing his job? Should I go on?"

"All right, you've made your point."

"I haven't even started, Danny, because I'm about to drop a bombshell. There are no lorries full of guns."

"What?" Danny's expression was pure confusion. "But I thought that was the whole thing that started this! You mentioned the lorries. You told us where they were."

"And unlike you, who's willing to rely on guesswork, I've actually been making enquiries. I spoke to Georgi who put me in touch with some of his security friends. It transpires that the borders out of Serbia are heavily guarded by NATO, Danny, precisely to make sure that kind of thing doesn't happen. Containers are sealed and signed for. It would be impossible."

"But..." Danny stopped, momentarily lost for words. This was all a bit much.

"The word from Bulgaria is that Miroslav is genuine."

"*What*? In what way?"

"In that he was just looking to take money out of Serbia to build a business. You have to remember that the general consensus is that Serbia is the bad guy in all of this, but he was actually looking to rebuild his country."

"By taking money out?"

"Georgi now thinks he acquired the trucks to shift raw materials into Serbia from outside. He was going to use the profits from the investments in the UK to help rebuild some of the broken communities in Serbia. Don't get me wrong, he's not a saint and he's very much still a gangster. But rather than seeking to smuggle things out of the country, he was looking to legitimately bring things in."

Danny put his head in his hands, needing a moment to let this sink in.

"But none of that explains what Julian was working on. We've got no idea about the blackmail or loan sharking he was apparently looking into," Clare continued. "And in case you've forgotten, March has still got a vendetta against you. You're still wanted for the hit and run. You're still suspended. He'll still be looking to put you away for Julian's murder, given that you were at the hotel, and witnesses will testify. In short Danny, it's brilliant that you got Lucy. But don't think that this is the end of the investigation. Not by a very long way."

———

Once we'd finished the paperwork at the studio, I gave Diana the rest of the day off. We were winding down for Christmas, and everything was in order, so I suggested she could take the afternoon to go present shopping. I was tempted to go with her, but the lure of home was too strong.

I made the mistake, however, of lying down on the studio sofa. It was blissful to rest my eyes as the mayhem of the last few days faded to a peaceful silence. For the first time in a week I could think happy thoughts, still glowing from the sense of making a tangible difference.

I woke up in gathering darkness. It was time to head back to Farringdon to meet the others, but I wanted to have a shower first, and a change of clothes. I locked up the studio and set out to make the short drive home.

———

Miroslav's briefing left no room for misunderstanding. Luka and Goran knew exactly what they were expected to do. The element of surprise would play to their advantage. There would be no need to ask questions. It was far better to kill than be killed.

They took a professional pride, however, in making sure that everything ran smoothly. Yes, March had promised that he would turn a blind eye, but nonetheless they needed a strategy, and a plan to make a getaway with the minimum of fuss.

It was agreed that they would strike just after dark. It was the perfect time. The noise of traffic in the evening rush hour would mask any sounds of conflict. March had given them the target address, so they spent part of the day looking at an A-Z, familiarising themselves with the streets of Camden, planning their best route of escape.

As the afternoon wore on, it was time to make their move. They each took two Zastava CZ99 handguns from Miroslav's private arsenal, and made sure they were all fully loaded. Then they made the journey from Lancaster Gate, through Camden Town. After a slow drive-by past the address, they parked just around the corner. Their final approach would be on foot, so they could head in different directions before meeting back at their car. And then they counted down the minutes until it was time to strike.

I parked up and let myself into the flat. It felt strange to be back home, but it was only a fleeting visit. I headed straight for the shower, and quickly stripped. The warm water revived me, and I allowed myself the indulgence of washing my hair, despite the time risk. It would take a concerted effort with the hairdryer to knock it into any semblance of acceptability, but the sensation of overall cleanliness was worth it. I would just have to be quick.

I wasn't sure what time we were supposed to be meeting, and the drying wasn't going particularly well, so in the end I just tied my hair back, and got dressed in clean jeans and my favourite fluffy jumper. With a touch of make-up I was ready. The whole process had taken less than half an hour, which I considered a big success.

Annoyingly, however, I couldn't remember what I'd done with

my car keys. Normally I hang them up just inside the door, but they weren't there, so I went back to my bedroom to search through the pockets of my discarded clothes. And then, to add an extra layer of frustration, somebody started ringing my doorbell. Well, they'd have to wait, whoever it was. It was not like I was expecting anyone.

Luka pressed the bell, while Goran stood ready with a gun. Whoever opened the door would be met with a hail of bullets. But nobody came to answer. They looked at each other, then Luka decided to take matters into his own hands, and launched himself at the door. The frame gave with a screech of protest, and immediately they were inside, triggers ready to end the first sign of life.

Chapter 38

DANNY sat at the kitchen table of the Farringdon flat, looking through the piles of evidence taken from Julian's flat. What had Julian discovered that cost him his life?

He'd spent the afternoon thinking about what Clare had said. She was right, of course, and he was furious with himself for assuming that everything was over when there were so many questions still outstanding. Never make assumptions. When they'd worked together as investigative journalists, that had been the first thing she'd taught him.

Clare had turned up to join him about twenty minutes previously, but she'd almost immediately taken a phone call. She'd moved to the front room and closed the door. He was tempted to stand outside and listen, to see if he could discover any more about her secret life - but that would be a massive breach of trust.

Eventually she came back to the kitchen. For the first time he thought she looked on the edge of losing her cool.

"I don't like this. I don't like this at all," she said, taking a seat and lighting a cigarette.

"What's happened?"

"That was Georgi. This is not good news, Danny."

"You're worrying me."

"And with bloody good reason. He's been speaking to Miroslav."

"I thought Miroslav was okay? And I didn't realise they knew each other?"

"Everyone knows everyone in that world. The bigger issue is that he mentioned we'd been to Bulgaria."

"Is that a problem?"

"Yes. Because for some reason Miroslav has got it into his head that we're plotting to kill him. He'd heard we'd been out there to meet some Croatians to seal the deal. Georgi confirmed the trip but before he had a chance to say what we were really doing, Miroslav apparently went off on one, and slammed down the phone."

"Oh shit."

"Shit indeed. Danny, he's a bloody gangster with a private army, armed to the teeth. We don't want to get on the wrong side of the bastard."

"Oh Jesus. But that's ridiculous."

"It's ridiculous to us, but these are paranoid people. They don't tend to give the benefit of the doubt."

Danny felt his temper snap.

"It's always fucking Georgi," he said. "The only thing he's done is to introduce us to Aleksander, who is quite possibly a Croatian hitman. And just in case it's not quite enough to have the one Balkan assassin on your case, he pisses off the Serbians so they're now trying to kill us too. I mean, for fuck's sake."

Clare laughed.

"What's fucking funny?"

"Oh, Danny, nothing. You just used to be so calm and respectful. It's nice that you're swearing at me."

"Can you blame me?"

"No, given the circumstances."

He stood up, and walked round the table, as the realisation sank in.

"I hate to raise a thorny issue," he said, "but you're a lot more experienced with gunmen and professional hits than I am. Any bright ideas?"

"I'm working on one."

"Brilliant. And in the meantime?"

"In the meantime we have to be careful. These are battle-hardened people. They don't ask questions. We need to be extremely careful."

"I need to get Anna."

"Where is she?"

"I don't know. She was popping up to her studio but I haven't spoken to her since this morning."

"Try her now."

He tried. The phone rang, but nobody answered.

"Try the phone I gave you."

Danny reached for the second handset but the result was the same. He tried the studio and the flat in Rochester Square, but none of the calls was answered."

"Maybe she's driving," said Danny, trying to convince himself that everything was okay, but feeling a rising sense of panic.

"Try them all again."

He did so. Nothing.

"I'm sure she'll be okay," said Clare.

"Don't, just don't, okay? I don't want to hear fucking platitudes. I want to know she's safe. There's at least one, possibly two armed fucking hit squads roaming London looking for us and ... Jesus, if anything's happened to her..."

"I know."

Then Clare's phone rang again. She answered the call, but immediately Danny sensed something was seriously wrong. This time there was no mistake. She looked very worried indeed.

Goran rang his boss.

"There's nobody here," he said.

"Are you at the right address?"

"Flat thirty-two. There's no sign anyone's been living here."

"Right."

Miroslav thought for a moment.

"Okay. Abort and come back. I will speak to March."

Miroslav ended the call. Clearly they were on the move. March would need to find out where they'd gone to, or there'd be serious repercussions.

Clare ended the call and looked ashen.

"What's up now? asked Danny.

"That was the security from the safe house. The first one I took you to in Camden. Two big bastards just smashed the door down. They've left but they're out there somewhere."

"You think Miroslav sent them?"

"Apparently they sounded eastern European and fitted the description of Goran and Luka."

"Shit."

She stood up.

"Come on, we've got to move. And keep trying Anna."

"All right," I shouted. "I'm coming." The doorbell was ringing for a third time. I gave up looking for my keys and went to see who it was.

"Delivery for Anna Burgin," said the man in a UPS uniform, when I finally opened the door.

"That's me," I said. I examined the package and then had a jolt of excitement when I realised what it was. An American magazine had published some of my photography, and the picture editor promised she would send copies. I never tire of the thrill of seeing my work in print, although it would have to wait for the moment.

I signed for the package and then closed the door, and resumed the key search. I couldn't remember going to the kitchen, but maybe I had, and maybe that's where I'd left them. This was getting annoying. I could have spent longer trying to sort my hair out.

I opened the door and flicked on the light. There was a man sitting at my kitchen table, pointing a gun at me, and holding my keys on the end of his finger.

"Looking for these?" he said.

Chapter 39

"HOW on earth did they get to know about the safe house?" asked Danny, as Clare drove. He hadn't asked where they were going. "I'm not being funny, but it's not particularly safe, is it? First March, now them."

She hit the brakes.

"That's it!" she said

"What?"

"March must have given them the address. He showed his hand when he visited. Nobody else could have known about it."

"Fuck. But if he did that, he must have known what he was doing. The devious bastard. What is he playing at?"

"I'm sorry, Danny."

"It's not your fault."

"I feel responsible, though. I brought you into this."

"March has hated me for a lot longer than just the last week."

"I know, that's what I meant. If I'd never given you a job you'd never have met him."

Danny looked at her, then reached across and touched her arm.

"Don't ever apologise again. I owe you the world."

She reached across and gave his hand a squeeze in return.

"We make a good team." She put the car back into gear, and pulled out to join the traffic. "The bigger issue is where they'll look next. Rochester Square? He knows you're not there at the moment, but he may have given them that address anyway."

"Jesus. We've got to go there, now."

"We could be walking into a bloodbath, Danny."

"Do I look like I care? If Anna's not answering her phone, I'm not taking the risk of leaving her."

Clare turned right onto Farringdon Road and hit the accelerator.

All I could hear was the sound of phones ringing, but I couldn't get close to answering them. Whoever was calling seemed very determined. But there again, so did the man sitting opposite me, holding the gun.

"Who are you?" I asked, my voice cracking in fear. I tried to process what I was seeing, but none of it made sense. Why was a man in my kitchen? How did he get there? Why did he have a German accent? And was he about to kill me?

"You're coming with me," he said. And it didn't look like I had any option.

Clare pulled into Rochester Square. Danny's door was open before the car stopped moving, and he sprinted up the stairs to the front door. Everything looked normal, and her car was parked on the street. Maybe she was inside, sleeping, or listening to music on headphones.

Danny opened the door and rushed inside. Clare wasn't far behind. He called out but there was no answer. They went from room to room, but there was no sign of Anna.

"She's definitely been here," said Clare. "Look." She pointed to a pile of clothes on the bedroom floor. "That's what she was wearing." She reached out to a towel hanging over a radiator in the bathroom. "Still damp."

"So, where is she?"

"I don't know. Could she have gone to a shop?"

"Possibly, but only to the garage over the road. Anywhere else she'd have taken the car."

"Let's go and check."

They crossed Camden Road and ran to the petrol station on the other side of the street. The assistant said he'd not seen Anna for several days, and he'd been there all afternoon.

"I'll call Amy," said Danny, when they got back to the flat. "See if she's heard anything, or at the very least tell her what's happening."

He made the call. Clare stood, listening for a moment, and then made one of her own.

When they'd both finished, he gave an update.

"Amy hasn't heard from her, but she sounded worried," said Danny. "She's coming to meet me. She's not far away."

"I don't think it's wise to stay here a minute longer than we need to."

"Agreed. She said the same. I'm meeting her down by the canal."

"Good plan. Leave a note in case Anna comes back and then let's get out of here. I'm going to head back to Farringdon in case she turns up there, and make some enquiries, but I'll call you, okay?"

Danny nodded.

"Call me the minute you have news."

Ten minutes later Danny was standing at the bottom of the steps that led to the Regent's Canal towpath on the corner of Baynes Street, waiting for DS Amy Cranston. But when she turned up she wasn't alone.

Chapter 40

"DANNY, meet DC Lisa Miller," said Amy.

"Please, call me Lisa," said the DC.

"I'm so pleased to meet you at last," said Danny. As he took in Lisa's red hair, he was struck by how different she looked to the other DC Lisa Miller - the imposter he'd followed for so long while trying to find Clare a couple of years before. Lisa looked slightly puzzled by his greeting, but he reached out to shake her hand, wondering, as he did so, why she was there. He led them both along the towpath and then stopped under cover of a bridge, in near complete darkness.

"DC Miller isn't here officially," said Amy. "But there again, neither am I."

"I'm pleased to see you though, both of you." He didn't know quite where to start. Amy filled the gap.

"Tell us again what happened. When did you last see Anna, and why are you worried about her?"

Danny launched into the story, explaining about Miroslav being tipped off and how he'd sent his bodyguards to find them. How they'd been to the safe house, and how only March could have given him that address. And how they could be turning up at Rochester Square at any minute - which is where Anna was headed.

"It all boils down to March," he concluded, looking at Amy as his eyes adjusted to the dark. "He's so got it in for me, but he's playing with fire now. If this is some sort of elaborate joke, he's gone mental. So, anything you can do to help me find her would be massively appreciated."

"What do you think?" Amy asked, turning to Lisa.

"Truthfully?" She kicked a stone into the canal. "I hate to say this, but I don't think this is a joke."

"You think he knows what he's doing?"

She nodded.

"Shit."

Amy let out an exasperated sigh.

"Look, Danny, I'll level with you," she said. "This is all off the record, okay?"

"Forget about the paper. I'm suspended anyway. Trust me, the last thing I'm looking for here is a story. I just want to get going and find Anna."

"I know, but Lisa came to see me a few nights ago. This is important. Actually, I'll let her explain."

Lisa took over.

"I worked with March on the Tom Napier case."

"I heard that," said Danny, with a rising sense of impatience.

"I know. I've not long been back from maternity leave and that was the first time I'd worked a case with him, although I knew his reputation, obviously. Anyway, I'll give you the details later, because we've got bigger priorities right now, but I knew it wasn't Emma. Then he tried to make a pass at me. So I went to see Amy because I knew she'd been there before."

"Lucy's confessed by the way," added Amy. "She claims no knowledge of Julian though, which is a worry."

"God," said Danny. "You know what, though, it doesn't surprise me. I got a bollocking for assuming that she'd done it without any evidence to back it up. I don't know how March gets away with it."

"I've told you. Friends in high places," said Amy. "We're going to fix that, but cracking that little cabal is going to take everything we have and more."

"But Anna first," said Lisa.

"Cheers," said Danny.

The problem was that they didn't have a clue where to start.

"You've checked her studio, your flat?" asked Lisa.

"Yeah and she's not at either. And she's not answering her phone, anywhere."

"Could she have gone off shopping? Maybe she's on the Tube. That would explain the phone if there's no signal."

"Anna doesn't use the Tube. She hates it. I'll try again now."

He dialled her number, the glow of the screen temporarily lighting his face, then switched to the Clare phone and tried that too. There was still no reply.

"There's nowhere else she could have gone?" asked Lisa. "Meeting friends? Maybe a work thing?"

"Her car's at home."

"She could have got a taxi if she's gone for a drink. Maybe she's in a noisy bar, and can't hear her phone. It's nearly Christmas. It's the party season."

Danny thought for a moment, trying to picture Anna with a group of friends, ploughing through bottles of Sauvignon Blanc, oblivious to his rising sense of dread. But he couldn't make it seem realistic, no matter how hard he tried.

"Maybe," he said.

"But you don't think so?"

"She would have said. She was supposed to be meeting us back in Farringdon this afternoon."

"Maybe she's there then."

"No, Clare's there. She said she'd call if Anna showed."

Lisa looked towards Amy and then turned to Danny.

"Clare?"

And now Danny felt a fresh wave of panic.

I had no idea where I was, but my mind was racing. I kept picturing Otto, wondering what I'd missed. He was the only German I'd come across in the last few days. Surely this couldn't be a coincidence, could it? But why would Otto send one of his henchmen to kidnap me? He was supposed to be on our side, unless he'd been playing us all along. Unless there was some grand and elaborate betrayal. And if so, what was happening to Clare and Danny? Where were they? Were they safe? And if they were, how long before they missed me?

"Who are you?" I asked the man pacing around the room. The man who'd brought me here, and tied me to a chair. The man with the gun and the German accent who kept asking me questions and looked like he was wired and becoming increasingly unstable.

"You will answer the questions, not ask them," he said.

"I only want to know your name so I know what to call you." I hoped that sounded braver than I felt. I was terrified.

"You can call me Stefan," he said. "What do you know about Serbia?"

"Serbia? What do you want to know about Serbia? I know it's been having a war, but it's over now. That's about it."

"I don't believe you."

"I don't know what you want me to say."

"You have been meeting with a Serbian criminal."

"What? Miroslav?"

"So now you do know more about Serbia."

"I really don't." I was completely flummoxed. "I went to a meeting but that was it. I don't think I said a word the entire time I was there."

"But you are working for the Serbians, yes?"

"No, I'm not. Really. I'm a photographer. You know, pictures of outfits. I'm not working with anyone from Serbia. I have no idea who you think I am or what I'm supposed to know, but really I think you've got the wrong person."

"And again, I do not believe you. Do not make me force it out of you. That would be very painful."

"But I don't know what you want me to say. Were you the one who shot at us as we left?"

And then he slapped me across the face. Not hard enough to break the skin, but certainly hard enough to sting.

"You have been seen at the bank that invests Serbian money but next you will claim no knowledge of that. I am not a fool. Where is Danny? Where is Clare?"

That gave me hope that at least they were still alive.

"I don't know."

"Do I have to hit you again? The second time is harder."

"I don't know where they are. Seriously. I haven't seen Clare since yesterday and I left Danny first thing this morning. They could be anywhere."

"Would they come if you asked them? If your life depended on it?"

"I... I don't know."

"Let us put that to the test."

He walked over to a table, and picked up a phone.

"Tell me the number and we will call them."

"Would that be the famous Clare I've heard so much about?" Lisa continued.

"It's all right, Danny. Lisa's on the team," said Amy. "I've given her the background."

"Jesus. Everything?"

"As far as I know."

And then, for the first time in a long time, Danny smiled.

"You know what I've just realised? The last time I was standing in exactly this spot was with Clare two years ago, also in the dark. And she was pretending to be you." He looked to Lisa.

"Me?"

"Yeah."

"Why was she pretending to be me? Especially two years ago. I was just a PC. How did she even know me? Are you sure it was me?"

"Oh yes, very definitely you. I'll tell you over a drink when we've found Anna. She'll have something to say on the subject as well."

"You didn't tell me about that," said Lisa, turning to Amy.

But before she had a chance to respond, Danny's phone started ringing. He pressed the button to connect the call, and then stood stock still as the blood drained from his face.

Chapter 41

MY'S phone started ringing too. She connected the call, while Danny stood silently with his own phone to his ear, looking increasingly worried.

"No, I haven't seen him," she said. "Shit. Okay. Really? Okay. I'll keep a lookout. Yes, you'll be the first to know. Yes, she's here. Okay I'll tell her."

She pocketed the phone, then waited as Danny ended his call.

"Are you okay?" she said, when he didn't move.

"That was Anna."

"Oh, thank God. Is she okay?"

"No." He turned towards his two companions. "No, she's very much not okay. Shit, shit, shit."

"What's up?"

"She's been abducted. She didn't say much but she's going to phone back in half an hour with instructions. She needs me to turn up or... Well, I don't need to elaborate."

Amy reached out to hold his arm.

"Jesus, Danny, what are you mixed up in?"

"I really don't know."

"What are you going to do?"

"I'm going to have to go. I've got no choice, have I? If anything happens to Anna I couldn't live with myself."

"Right, well, don't panic. I'll organise SO19 and get an armed response."

Danny's mind was calculating every possible scenario.

"They said no police involvement."

"They always do."

"I just need to think about this."

"Danny..." She stopped and paused for a moment. When he didn't speak, she continued.

"Look, I don't want to add to your troubles, but that was work on the phone. There's a warrant out for your arrest. Everyone's looking for you. And Lisa, they need you back there immediately."

"I can't go now," she said.

"No, you should. You may be more help there anyway if I need someone to coordinate things. Get going and I'll be in touch."

"Okay."

Lisa reached out and put her arm round Danny's shoulders.

"We'll do everything we can," she said. "We'll get her back, I promise you."

But Danny knew that the promise was as hollow as the feeling in his stomach.

They walked back along the towpath and then Danny and Amy watched Lisa climb the steps in the dim glow of a street lamp. When she disappeared from view, Amy spoke again, in a soft voice.

"Did you hear what I said about the warrant?"

"Yes. Sorry. What does that mean?"

"It means the Metropolitan Police is looking for you."

"I know that, but why?"

"Hit and run, potential murder, phone tapping. Those as normal. But now they've also got you on CCTV flying to Bulgaria on a fake passport. I'm not even going to ask."

"Fuck!" Danny felt like his head was about to implode. "It's not what you think."

"I'm trying not to think anything. But we probably should have a chat when this is all over."

"Understood. I'm sorry."

"And in the meantime, I haven't seen you and I have no idea where you are, so just watch your back, okay?"

"Amy." He shook his head and looked to the ground. "Thank you."

"We'd better disappear. Separate directions and as much distance as we can. And turn your phone off as soon as you've heard from Anna, in case you're being tracked. I'll speak to Clare and try to coordinate there."

Danny thought for a moment. It was time to take a risk.

"I'll do that, but look - can I trust you, completely?"

"You know you can. What is it?"

"I'll turn my main phone off, but I've got another number. Nobody knows it apart from Anna and Clare."

Amy raised her eyebrows.

"I wondered why you had two phones."

"Exactly. But listen, I'm under strict instruction not to call anyone apart from Clare and Anna and not to give the number to anyone. Strictest of the strict. And if I go against that, I'm risking everything, but this could be a question of life or death. Actually, there's no 'could be'. It is. If I ring you, or give you the number, I have to plead with you that it goes no further."

"You cannot ask me to bury evidence in a police investigation."

"I know. I won't do that."

She shook her head.

"That's not how it works, Danny. Irrespective of what I do, the minute you call me, it's logged on my phone. That's trackable by anyone who's looking. So even if I promise you I won't say a word, it's a leak waiting to happen. Much as I appreciate what you're saying, it's not under my control."

Danny sighed.

"However, I can give you a number you can call."

Realisation began to dawn.

"Has she given you one too?"

Amy smiled.

"It's just the four of us, Danny. Clare and I have an understanding, for the moment at least. And just so you know, just to put your mind at rest, I already have your number. I'll call you on it now, so you'll also have mine."

Danny and Amy split at the top of the stairs. Danny set off back in the direction of Camden High Street, unsure of what to do for the best while waiting for Anna's call. His heart was racing, and his legs felt weak. A police car approached so he quickly turned into a side street until it passed.

He tried to call Clare, but there was no answer. A moment later, she returned the call.

"Thank God," he said, "I'm so pleased I've caught you. Anna's in trouble."

"A little bird tells me you considered giving out this number, Danny. That would not have been wise."

"I'm sorry but it's serious. Anna's been abducted."

"That is serious. But trust between us is absolutely paramount and that is a major red flag, Danny."

"Are you listening? Anna's been kidnapped. So yeah, feel free to give me another bollocking, but maybe some time when I give a fuck, okay?"

"Danny, calm down."

"For fuck's sake. Don't bloody patronise me."

"I'm not. I'm being serious. You're not going to be rational if you're panicking. Tell me about Anna."

"Where are you?"

"About four paces behind you."

Danny turned, not in the mood for games.

"Do you always have to do that?"

"I clearly need to keep an eye on you. Come on, follow me."

Clare led the way into a shop and then past the counter and out through a rear exit. She grabbed Danny's hand and ran to a car. They both got in and she started driving.

"Where are we going?" he asked.

"We're going to get Anna."

"We don't even know where she is. We don't even know who's got her."

"No, we don't."

"And if it's the fucking Serbians, we're going to walk into a room and come out full of bullets."

"As I said, we don't know."

"What exactly are we doing then? Where are we actually going?"

"I hesitate to bring up the thorny issue of logical semantics, Danny."

"*What?*"

"*We* don't know. That doesn't mean I don't."

"For God's sake. This is beginning to do my head in. You're saying you do know?"

"And again, that's you making an assumption, and what have I always told you about those?"

"Piss off! Stop messing about. Do you, or don't you? This is bloody serious."

"Danny, I'll say it again. Calm down. Please?"

He'd had enough.

"Stop the car. Seriously. I don't need to be lectured by you. I've got enough on my mind just at this moment. If you're going to twat about I'll do this on my own."

Clare pulled over and stopped the car.

"Off you go then."

Danny took a deep breath and closed his eyes, but didn't make a move to undo his seatbelt.

"I'm sorry," he said, after a moment. Clare rested her hand on his leg. In a previous life, at another time, the effect would have been intoxicating.

"Go on then," he said. "What's the theory?"

"You're not leaving?"

"You know I'm not."

"That's good. Following you is a pain in the arse."

Danny smiled, despite everything.

"Well, let's face facts," Clare continued. "It's not the Serbians."

"Okay. And why? We know they've been to the safe house. We know Anna was at home and we think they had that address as well, so that seems most logical to me."

"We know because she phoned you. I told you, they shoot first and ask questions later. Actually, they're not even that hot on asking questions even then. If it was them, Anna would be dead already."

Danny exhaled.

"Okay. So who?"

"My guess is the Croatians."

"Brilliant. They've still got guns then."

"They have but they're probably less trigger happy. They'll be more interested in information than killing anyone. At least until they get it. Meanwhile, Amy says there's a warrant out for your arrest, so we have to be careful."

She stopped at a red traffic light.

"I know. It's ridiculous. I'm hiding from bloody Serbian bastards, we've got Aleksander and his chums shooting at us and wanting me to go to get Anna, and possibly get killed in the process, and then March raises a warrant for just about everything. There'll be a prize for whoever gets me first."

"Life as a fugitive has its perks, Danny."

"*Really?* I don't have your money, Clare. And I think the bit you're missing is that I don't want to be a fugitive. I was writing a story about bent footballers, for heaven's sake. I want to file that, move on to the next one. Maybe get married one day. Have a family. I don't want to be either shot by Serbians, shot by Croatians or incarcerated by bloody Graham March."

"Well, we may not have to wait much longer to find out who gets the trophy."

"What do you mean now?"

She indicated behind.

"March and a colleague seem to be right behind us and as we passed that street lamp I could see him smiling at me."

Chapter 42

"OH, for fuck's sake," said Danny. "What now? I don't have time for this. I've got to get Anna."

"I can try to lose them."

"Right. A good old-school car chase. Have you seen the traffic?"

Clare shrugged, then dropped a gear, turned the wheel and blasted up a side street. Danny looked behind. March's Mondeo was turning into the street behind them, gathering speed.

"Well, that didn't work," said Clare.

"I think you've given me whiplash."

"There's more to follow if you don't start trusting me." And with that she slammed the brakes, stopping in the middle of the street, waiting for the Mondeo to catch up.

"What are you doing?"

"Watch and learn."

Behind them the Mondeo stopped. A moment later the doors opened. March got out from the passenger seat, his sidekick from the driver's side. They started approaching the car. As they arrived, Clare looked across to Danny.

"Hold on," she whispered, before dropping the clutch, wheels squealing in protest as the car lurched forward, straight towards a crossroads, straight towards another red light. It changed, and Clare floored the accelerator. Danny could see March and his colleague back in their car, giving chase, but the lights changed back. It didn't stop them. Horns blared as they shot across the junction in hot pursuit. Clare took a right, then an almost immediate left, turning the wrong way up a one-way street. An oncoming cyclist shouted abuse and stuck up two fingers.

The end of the street approached, and she turned into a bus lane, undertaking a line of slow-moving traffic. In the door mirror, Danny could see March approaching, lights flashing. Clare turned again, this time into a slightly wider road. Traffic was on their side. Until a squad car pulled up, across the junction, blocking their exit.

Clare accelerated towards it until, at the last minute, she pulled the handbrake and expertly turned the car ninety degrees, heading down the street the squad car had just left. But traffic was heavier again. She tried to weave through it, but it was hopeless. Behind, March was gaining all the time. Five cars behind. Then four. Then three.

Clare hit the handbrake again, then turned sharp right. Then immediately slammed the brakes again. She turned into the entrance of a multistorey car park. Up, spiralling, floor after floor.

"Okay, Danny, I'm going to stop. Get out and run. I'll catch up with you."

Danny reached for the door handle.

"Good luck," he said.

"You too. If he catches you, don't fight back."

"What?"

"Do as I say. Don't put up any resistance."

And with that he made a dash for it, just as March's Mondeo came into view a floor below. The staircase was in the corner. He sprinted towards it. From somewhere he heard the sound of tyres squealing. And then voices shouting. Danny paused to catch his breath. Up or down? Up to hide or down to escape? The cars were going up. He headed down. Flight after flight, getting dizzy, sprinting, feeling the lactic acid in his newly energised legs, glad of the hours spent building endurance in the gym.

At last he came to the ground floor. He pushed open the door, looked both ways trying to find the exit to the street. Disorientated. He decided on a direction and started to run. Anna's life depended on it.

He turned a corner, past a concrete pillar, and came face to face with DCI Graham March standing legs apart, arms folded, an evil sneer forming on his haggard face.

"Going somewhere, Danny old son?" he said, with a cold smile. "That wasn't a question, by the way. More of a statement. We're going to take a little trip together. It's time to start paying the price for what I like to call your misdemeanours."

"Seriously, Graham. Not now. Anna needs me."

What was it Clare said? Don't put up resistance? It didn't make any sense. He had to get away.

"I hesitate to agree with you there, Danny. She needs a man, I'll give you that, but probably one with a bit more of a future, if you catch my drift. She'll have no shortage, don't you worry. I could even be tempted myself."

"Will you just stop being a twat? Have your little joke another day but she's in serious trouble. I'll come in, honestly, just not now, okay?"

"She might be in trouble, but I suspect nowhere near as much as you. It's not the time for deals, Danny. Unless you want to add resisting arrest to your already lengthy list of charges."

All was calm. There was the sound of traffic, a distant siren. But time was motionless.

"Seriously. I'm pleading with you. Have some humanity for Christ's sake."

"Danny, put out your arms, and my good colleague will apply

the handcuffs. I'll ask him not to be too rough with you. How does that sound."

Suddenly, from behind March there was movement. The policeman didn't have time to react before a leg appeared between his own, rising upward at speed, connecting with vicious force to his groin. He gasped, looked pale and fell to the ground. And as he did so, Danny saw Clare standing in the space previously obscured by his bulk. She didn't need to speak.

Then March's colleague appeared with a gun, pointing it at Clare.

"Run, Danny," she shouted. He didn't have time to think. He started to sprint, but then looked back to see Clare in handcuffs, being shoved into the back of a police car, her time as a fugitive coming to an ignominious end.

Chapter 43

OVERCOME with fatigue, Danny stopped running, and was suddenly consumed by an overwhelming sense of futility. Who was he kidding? There was safety in numbers, but now he was on his own. Clare, his mentor, and for so long his guardian angel, was on her way to a police cell from which she would never return. March would make sure of that. The game had changed. And without her protection, what hope did he have?

And yet despite everything she'd done for him, he'd thanked her by losing his temper in their last ever conversation. Danny felt sick with fear, and sick at the injustice. Despite all her faults, Clare had made the ultimate sacrifice to save him. She could have run herself, but she'd given herself up so that he could escape. Escape arrest for crimes that were in any case entirely fictitious. After everything she'd done, and everything they'd been through, it seemed like a tragic and pointless waste.

He couldn't go home, he couldn't go to the safe house, and even Farringdon was probably a risk. He was suspended from work and hiding from the combined might of the Metropolitan Police. And yet the only thing that mattered was that Anna was still being held captive. He took a deep breath. No matter how bad things seemed, nothing was more pressing than that.

He was just deciding whether or not to call Amy when his phone started ringing. It was Anna.

"Anna, thank God. How are you?"

"I've got instructions," she said. Why was she not answering the question? "There's a taxi rank at King's Cross, on the York Way side. Wait there and someone will collect you in thirty minutes."

"What do they want from you? Who are they?"

"Remember, no police, Danny. Promise me."

"I promise. Are they treating you okay? Don't worry, Anna, I'm coming to get you."

But it was pointless. The line went dead.

"My man will pick him up," said Stefan. "For your sake, he had better be alone."

"I told him not to contact the police," I said. "He won't."

I felt terrible making the call. Despite all my protestations, pretending to myself that I'd given up on any thoughts of romance, I bloody loved Danny. I always had, since the very first time he came to my rescue as a naive student, way out of my depth in the big alien environment of the capital, and every day since, no matter what nonsense I said to myself and others. The thought that I might be putting him in danger was unbearable.

The only saving grace was that I knew he still had Clare on his side. She'd rescued us before. She possessed magical powers. I didn't know how she'd do it, but she'd find a way, somehow. Maybe she'd follow, unseen by Danny's driver, and then sneak in, take out whoever she needed to, and lead us away to a glorious sunset. She'd never let us down before and I had every faith that she'd pull off a miracle again. She was indestructible. A genius, and yes, maybe she had a couple of character flaws, but when it came down to it, I bloody loved her too.

In the meantime, I was determined to find out everything I could.

"What do you actually want with me?" I said, emboldened by thoughts that rescue might not be too far away.

"What do we want with you? We want to know what you know."

"I don't know anything."

"I hardly think that's true."

"Of course it's true, for God's sake. I've told you. I'm just a photographer."

"Who are you working for?"

"What?"

"Who are you working for?"

"I heard the question. I just didn't understand it."

"Who. Are you. Working. For?"

"Most recently a fashion brand called Mistresse, if you really want to know but I'm freelance."

I earned another slap across the face for that. And yes, the second was much harder.

"You will wait here in silence until your friend arrives."

Danny thought back to the first time he'd ever been to King's Cross, on his first ever trip to London as a twelve-year-old boy. He'd stepped off the train from his native north-east holding his mother's hand, and breathed his first lungful of London air. It seemed so big, so noisy, so busy, so vibrant. Only in later years had he learned about the darker side of the area: the pimps and pushers preying on the vulnerable, and the prostitutes who made it their place of business.

He waited by the taxi rank on York Way and watched as two

buses parked up in turn, passengers disembarking, and disappearing into the night.

And then he saw the car. The driver flashed its lights as it approached, and then stopped a little way further up the street. The back door opened, but nobody got out. Tentatively he walked towards it.

"Get in," said a voice from the back seat. He did as he was told. It was pointless to try anything else. A blindfold appeared and was wrapped around his eyes. That, at least, was something. If he was going to be killed they wouldn't need to stop him seeing where they were taking him.

It was hard to keep track of time, but after perhaps twenty minutes of silence, other than the noise of the car and traffic, the driver stopped and cut the engine.

Danny's door was opened and he was dragged out of the car. He stood, aware of his own defencelessness, while beside him the door slammed shut.

The blindfold was removed. Danny blinked, temporarily dazzled by the fluorescent strip lights. It looked like another underground car park, but there wasn't a single other car.

There were two men, both holding guns. Neither spoke. One grabbed his arm, and led him to the side of the car park, and then through a door. A corridor led to a room at the end. Sitting in an armchair was a man Danny had never seen before.

"Danny, so good of you to come and see me. Please, have a drink."

He passed him a glass of something that looked like whisky. Danny picked up the glass but didn't take a sip, wary of the contents.

"I didn't have any choice. Where's Anna?"

"She'll be along in a moment. But first we need to have a little discussion."

"I'm not discussing anything until I know she's safe."

"May I remind you, you're in no position to lay down conditions."

"And can I remind you that I'm not discussing anything until I know she's safe."

The man paused for a moment as though trying to assess the new arrival. Then finally he clicked his fingers.

"Very well," he said. A side door opened and one of the bodyguards returned. The man in the chair said something in a language that sounded like German. The guard nodded and left the room. A couple of minutes later the door opened again, and he returned, holding Anna by the arm.

I wanted to run to Danny immediately and give him a hug, but a big bastard with a gun had a very tight grip on my arm. Instead I looked into his eyes for reassurance, for some indication that Clare and the cavalry were right behind, but he just looked terribly tired and worried.

We were each given a chair. We weren't tied up this time, but in reality it would have been pointless showmanship. We weren't going anywhere.

"So," said Stefan, looking at both of us in turn.

"Who are you?" asked Danny. It was lovely to hear his voice.

"He's Stefan," I answered, and then saw the glare of death I received from our German captor, and decided I should probably be more careful.

"Stefan," said Danny. "Can you please tell me why we're here."

"It's simple," he replied. "I want to know who you're working for."

"The Daily Echo," he said. Inwardly I winced, expecting Danny to get a whack too.

"And what is this?"

"What? The Echo? It's a newspaper."

"Ah, very good. Inventive."

Danny looked at me. I shrugged and shook my head.

"Can I ask who you think we're working for? I have no idea what's going on. I'm sure there's some misunderstanding."

The big German laughed.

"Yes, very good indeed." The laughter stopped abruptly. "But unless you tell me what I want to know willingly, I will be forced to extract the information from you. And let me just reassure you, that won't be pleasant, as your friend is well aware."

Danny sighed.

"Look, I don't know who you are. I don't know what you want. But I'll tell you everything I'm working on and if you think I'm hiding anything, please stop me."

Stefan seemed to think for a moment. Finally he spoke.

"Go ahead."

And so, Danny began, explaining about his investigation into Premier League footballers, how he'd seen Graham March at a press conference, and decided to investigate because he had severe doubts about Emma's guilt. About the visit to the bank, the Serbians, Bulgaria. The fake charges and police campaign against him. Even about now being targeted by a Serbian hit squad, which was news to me, and utterly terrifying, as though I wasn't already scared enough. When he'd finished, the silence hung in the air like the smoke in a particularly crowded pub. Eventually, Stefan stood up.

"You'll wait here," he said, presumably to both of us. And then he left us with just the armed guards for company.

DCI Graham March was exceptionally pleased with his evening's work. The elusive Clare Woodbrook was finally in captivity, and Danny was right where he wanted him. Of course, there was much more to come. The denouement would be quite spectacular, and he was going to savour every moment, and every inch of the resulting newsprint. The irony was tantalising.

His phone rang. He connected the call.

"Stefan," he said, recognising the number.

"I've got the two of them here. There's no sign of the third one."

"You don't need to worry about that. I've got the delectable Ms Woodbrook under lock and key."

"What do you want me to do with them?"

"How do they seem?"

"Terrified."

"That's good. Keep scaring them."

"Do you want me to hurt them?"

"Haha, tempting though that is, I'm not an animal, Stefan. There's no need to make their final moments too painful. Let's just say not to make things too comfortable."

He sat back, and put his feet up on the desk.

"Anna is a pretty girl," said Stefan.

"I can read your mind, you dirty sod. No."

"Oh, come on, there has to be some perk."

"The perk is I turn a blind eye to your more nefarious activities."

"My what?"

"Learn the bloody language, can't you?"

Sometimes he wondered if he would ever meet someone on his level.

"How long should I keep them?" asked the German.

"Not long. I feel for Anna, poor girl, but nobody will miss Danny. Listen carefully and I will tell you how to dispose of them."

Chapter 44

W HEN he judged enough time had passed, Graham
March unlocked the door and stepped into the
room. Clare was firmly attached to a chair with a
combination of tape and cable ties, pulled just tight enough that
they were biting into her skin.

"Sorry about that my dear, just a bit of business to attend to,"
he said.

"Nice of you to put me up somewhere so salubrious,
Graham."

"No expense spent, my lovely. I could hardly take you to a
police station like a common criminal."

"I appreciate the gesture. Would you care to enlighten me as
to the workings of your addled mind? I could do with something
to lighten the mood."

March laughed.

"Funny to the end. I shall miss you, you know. Albeit in the
same way that I'd miss a verruca."

He took a chair, facing her.

"Well, the hour is late," he continued, "but my offer still stands if you'd like to test my reputation as a lover of repute. Although I'd rather have to insist on you taking a shower. You're looking somewhat dishevelled."

"Cleary I'm going to have to kick you slightly harder next time. I thought I'd done enough to put you out of action for a few days, saving some poor prostitute somewhere a miserable five minutes."

"Very droll. Let me assure you that ladies of my acquaintance enjoy the experience as much, if not more, than me. You should have taken advantage while you had the chance."

"Ah, Graham." She laughed. "Putting your delusions to one side, would you care to tell me what you're up to? I'm sure you're dying to tell me how clever you've been."

March took a packet of cigarettes from his jacket pocket, and took one out, sniffing along its length.

"Mmm, the aroma of freedom. Would you care for a last one? No? It's a moot point anyway as I only brought them here to tease you."

Clare didn't rise to the provocation.

"You've had a busy week," he said.

She didn't respond. Her mind was preoccupied, calculating, looking for escape. But the ties were biting harder every time she tried to move.

"I could make some statement, read a prepared speech, like a grand theatrical monologue, but I hardly think it's worth it, do you? I've warned you about interfering and you chose to ignore the warnings. So really, there's nobody to blame but yourself. It's too late now to beg for forgiveness, I'm afraid. I really have had enough of you."

"Well, if it helps, the feeling's mutual."

"We could have worked together, you know. But I never would have been able to trust you. That's your problem. You think you're clever, you think your actions are never going to catch up with you. That you'll always be able to dodge the bullet like some slutty female version of James Bond. But you can't always rely on somebody shooting to miss."

Clare blinked, calmly assessing the situation. But the assessment was bleak.

"I knew it was you," she said.

"You knew what was me?"

"Arranging someone to have a pop at us from the 4x4."

"You worked that out? I'm impressed."

"Of course. If it was some mythical Croatian hit squad, I don't think they'd have been inept enough to just blow my window out."

"Indeed. Although they weren't supposed to hit you. Just give you a fright."

"I don't scare easily."

"We'll see about that."

March looked at his watch.

"You know the problem?" he said. "Now I've got you here, I am actually rather enjoying it. I know you must be full of questions, but I just want to sit here watching you, looking at your eyes. It's strangely arousing to know that the last thing you'll ever see is me."

"It's not quite how I envisaged things, I'll give you that, you fat fuck."

"Your language, my dear. It really is quite atrocious."

He stood up and walked behind her. Clare tried to turn, but pain shot through her wrists. It felt like they were bleeding.

"I do have some good news for you, though," he said. "Your wayward friend Danny came to the rescue of the lovely young Anna."

"That's good."

"Well, kind of. I'm afraid it's a hollow victory for the boy. You see, he thought he was doing the valiant thing, but actually now he's there he's proving rather a liability. I'm disappointed to report that both will very soon cease to - what I like to call - exist."

At first we sat in silence, but when Stefan didn't return, Danny and I tried to swap messages by looking at each other, and mouthing words that neither of us really understood. Eventually he moved tentatively towards me, and when the guards didn't react, I rushed into his arms.

"What happened to your face?" he whispered, looking beyond me, presumably to the man with the gun who was sitting on a stool at the back of the room.

"It's fine, don't worry. I'm so pleased to see you."

I wanted to ask him about Clare. Surely she'd burst through the door at any moment, but I didn't want to spoil the surprise.

For his part, Danny held me tightly. It was enough just to feel the grip of his arms.

But it didn't last long, and things soon took a dramatic turn for the worse. The door opened, and Stefan appeared, holding a roll of duct tape and two blindfolds. We were gagged and had our eyes covered, our arms pinned behind our backs. There was no point trying to resist.

After that, I wasn't sure if Danny was still with me. I was led from the room, sightless and disorientated, along possibly a corridor, and then suddenly the temperature dropped. It felt like I was outside.

"Danny?" I tried to call, feeling a rising sense of panic, my voice heavily muffled through the gag.

I heard a grunt in response, then the sound of impact and a groan as presumably somebody punched him, hard. I braced for the same, but it didn't come.

There were low voices, speaking in German, but I didn't understand the words. Someone coughed. Then there was a click, followed by a creak. It sounded like a car door being opened. Somebody grabbed my arm, and pulled me. I stumbled, then cried out in pain as my shin came into contact with something hard.

"Step up," said a voice.

I reached out a leg, and then somebody pushed me. It seemed like I was being loaded into the back of a van. My head was pushed down, and then my shoulders. I found myself falling, until somebody dragged me again. And then I was seated on a cold metal floor. My other senses were on high alert. I could smell diesel fumes. This is it, I thought. This isn't going to end well. Where was Clare? She was leaving it a bit late.

But Clare didn't come. The engine started, sending vibrations through my body, and we lurched forward. I fell backwards until my head hit something solid. Was it the back door? It was painful, whatever it was. I felt tears of fear, frustration, and the onset of a greater panic, but I was powerless to do anything. I started to feel physically sick, with rising nausea making the panic even worse. The van rocked. I fell again, this time colliding with something soft. I think it was Danny. And then I was lying on the floor, unable to see, the nausea getting worse, the sounds getting louder, the motion more violent, the speed picking up.

Eventually we slowed down, but the jolts were worse. It felt like we were driving over rough ground, the van lurching from side to side. And then suddenly we stopped. A moment later the driver killed the engine. The only sound was the blood pumping in my ears.

The door opened, and a blast of icy air came as a welcome relief to the nausea, but the relief was short-lived. Somebody grabbed my arm, and I was dragged from the back of the van, and then dropped on the ground. A rock, or something like it, sent a shooting pain through my ribs.

"Kneel," said a voice. But with my arms tied behind me, I was powerless to comply. Then I felt somebody, maybe two people, grab me beneath my arms until I was kneeling on the hard ground. It was wet. I felt icy moisture seeping through my jeans.

Our blindfolds were removed. I felt disorientated but it didn't take long for my eyes to adjust. A cold light from the moon gave everything a deathly luminescence. I looked to my left. Danny was kneeling beside me. There were two men in front. One was leaning on a shovel. The other was holding a gun.

We seemed to be miles from anywhere. There were sodium street lamps, far in the distance, but waste ground stretched out before us. I didn't know our location, but I knew exactly where we were. The perfect place for a double execution.

Chapter 45

"WHAT do you mean, cease to exist?"

"Ah, Clare, I remember the days when you thought you knew everything. Although I always thought you underestimated me."

"Stop playing games."

"I have no games to play. I shall miss the boy."

"Graham. For once in your life, stop being a twat."

"And Clare, for once in your life, acknowledge when you're beaten. The great Ms Woodbrook, losing control. I've seen it before, of course."

He walked back in front of her and retook his seat.

"What do you mean?" asked Clare.

"You forget I've followed your career. From the lowly hack ploughing the furrow most recently inhabited by the late Danny Churchill, to international fugitive, via various misdemeanours involving lesser men who didn't know how to deal with you. Do you have daddy issues, Clare?"

"*What?*"

"Neglected by your father? Maybe even a little bit of excess discipline, if you catch my drift?"

"I'd appreciate you leaving him out of your delusions."

March laughed.

"Oh, now we're getting there. Touched a nerve, have we? What is it? The need to prove yourself after the heartbreak of rejection, or the need to take revenge after one beating too many?"

"Neither."

"Maybe he was a bit rough with old Mother W, is that it? You had to watch as he rolled home from the pub every night after too many pints of wife-beater and then gave your frail old mother a lesson in how it got its nickname?"

"Graham, shut up."

"Kiddy-fiddler then? Reputation amongst the kids at school for taking too keen an interest in sports day? Turning up to watch you run the egg and spoon but secretly he's trying to catch a glimpse of virginal white schoolgirl knickers?"

"I'm warning you."

March leaned forward.

"You're in no position to warn me, I'm afraid. But was it the boys, then? Even better. Well, that explains your curious lack of interest in all things sexual. Can't be easy having a boyfriend at a tender age, knowing your own father wants to split him asunder."

"Oh, for God's sake. Fuck. Off." Clare fixed her eyes on the man in front of her. It wasn't possible to hate anybody any more.

"Now I think we're getting there," he continued. "It starts to explain your failings as a member of society. I don't know why it never occurred to me before. Daddy was a child-raping, wife-beating monster, and the young Clare is so damaged by the trauma she decides to take it out on the world by shooting people. You could have used that to lessen your term. Maybe got you sectioned to Broadmoor rather than seeing out your days in one of Her Majesty's less hospitable guesthouses."

She took a deep breath. She hated the thought of humouring him, but every minute was a minute more of the most precious commodity of all.

"Do you really want to know?" she asked.

"Oh, here we go. Come on then, enlighten me."

"I don't even know why I'm entertaining this."

"I'm all ears."

"Hardly all ears. You're mainly stomach, Graham. And bad breath and ill-fitting dentures."

"Very droll. Anyway, confession time. I won't take pleasure in knowing I'm right."

"You couldn't be more wrong."

"Oh my God. He was a common burglar with a sideline in Thai ladyboys. I should have guessed."

She paused, thinking.

"What time is it?"

"Nearly time to make you suffer, my dear."

"Oh, please grow up. The actual time?"

"Why?"

"It's important. I don't want to even talk to you, but if you want me to explain about my dad I need to know the time."

"What difference does it make?"

"I hate being interrupted."

"We've got all night if need be."

"Just tell me the fucking time."

"And again, not particularly ladylike."

Clare stopped, took a deep breath and then decided to continue.

"It's okay," she said. "You can try to be as unhelpful as you can, but I've seen your watch, so I already know. Ten to two. Do you want to know the truth then?"

"I doubt you know the meaning of the word, but attempt to amaze me."

"Okay, so shut up and listen. I'll say this once, but only because I have a few minutes to kill and hopefully it'll stop you from talking nonsense for a moment."

He leaned back.

"I can't wait."

She ignored the interruption.

"My dad was the most brilliant man I've ever met. He worked hard and then went to night classes to work harder still, learning new things so he could apply for better jobs to provide security and a better home for his family. He didn't beat me, didn't beat my mum, just worked every waking hour to try to give us a better life. He fought for us. Worked hard for us. Sacrificed his free time for us."

She paused to see if there was a reaction. There wasn't.

"And do you know what happened, Graham? Just as he was getting the qualifications he'd worked so hard to achieve, he developed cancer. I had to help nurse him through the final year of his life, watching this great man steadily lose his mind to the pain and morphine, until finally, one night, the ambulance came to take him away and he never came home. I was eleven. So no, no daddy issues, as you so insensitively put it. Just unending respect for a wonderful person who I still think about with every day that passes."

Still March seemed unmoved.

"Is that why you smoke then? To get reunited as quickly as possible?" he said at last.

"God, you're pathetic. I smoke because I have other issues, not that they're any business of yours."

"Fair enough. Not that it matters because I'll be able to speed up the reunion for you, anyway."

"Will you now?"

"It seems the very least I can do. I expect you'll thank me. You'll be able to introduce him to your good friends Danny and Anna. Quite the party."

"What the fuck have you done to them?"

"It's not what *I've* done. I was keeping them safe, but they seemed to want to leave the security of my babysitting service. It's ironic really. Danny rescues Anna, thinking he's leading her to safety, and instead he leads her quite literally into the firing line. But there again he always did get the wrong end of the story."

———

The men walked behind us. I looked at Danny for one final time, and then closed my eyes. Waiting for the bullet to the back of the head. I didn't know what I'd done wrong, but it was too late to start worrying now. It was too late for anything.

Behind me I heard the sound of the van door closing, and then the engine started, spewing out a cloud of diesel fumes. I coughed. And then I heard the crunch of gravel as tyres started moving. I didn't understand what was going on. Why didn't they just get it over with?

But the engine noise started to move further away. I looked at Danny and then we both turned, watching the retreating lights on the back of the van as it rumbled away over the waste ground. It was moving slowly, rocking from side to side over the uneven landscape. But then it slowed further, and turned, and rejoined the road. We watched as it disappeared into the distance.

I didn't know what to think. My mind was lost in a mess, part relief and part sheer confusion. Why bring us all this way? Why leave us? What on earth was going on?

Danny levered himself up and then came towards me. Neither of us could speak, but he gestured with his eyes. Suddenly I understood. He had limited movement in his hands, but he managed to grip the edge of the duct tape around my wrists. He pulled. The edge started to give. He gripped more and pulled again. It stung, like removing the biggest and most painful sticking plaster ever, but after significant effort my hands were free.

I gripped the tape across my mouth and pulled, and that hurt even more, but the pain was inconsequential. I breathed great lungfuls of air as I set to work on Danny, removing the tape first from his wrists and then his face. We were free. I fell into his arms, feeling tears of relief, still unable to quite comprehend what was happening. My legs nearly gave way.

"I thought that was it," I gasped through the sobs, as much to myself as anyone. He gripped me tighter. I never wanted him to let go.

Eventually, though, he had to. We needed to get out of there. We needed to get to safety.

"Danny," I said. "What the fuck is going on?"

He looked at me, his beautiful eyes as confused as my own.

"I don't know any more."

"Where's Clare? Traditionally she turns up to save us at this point." It was said as a joke, but I could see from Danny's expression that it wasn't one of my funniest. I wasn't laughing either.

"She's not coming. March arrested her."

"She's what? Oh shit."

And then he explained about the car chase, and how she'd sacrificed herself to save him. Any sense of anguish about her non-appearance was replaced by even greater respect.

But without Clare we were on our own. In the middle of nowhere. I looked to where the van had joined the road. I could see cars passing. If we could get there we could maybe catch a night bus. It didn't matter to where. Anywhere was better than here.

I could see Danny thinking the same. He reached out for my hand.

"Can you walk?" he asked. I nodded.

But then in the distance we saw a car turn off the road. Its headlights were dazzling as the driver came straight in our direction.

Chapter 46

CLARE found it hard to comprehend what she was hearing. It was like he was pleased with himself. Had he finally lost his mind?

"You see, my good friend Stefan was keeping them safe. Apparently there's a rather violent Serbian nutcase who seems to think all three of you are trying to kill him. But, no, you know Danny, he'd have wanted to be the hero. So Stefan suggested dropping them off somewhere, right in the middle of nowhere, so they could fend for themselves."

She knew there was a "but" coming.

"But the only problem is, the aforementioned Serbian is very familiar with the place. That's my fault, actually. I accidentally mentioned it." He shrugged his shoulders. "But what are a couple more casualties after a war that killed thousands?"

"You'd better be bullshitting me."

"Or what?"

"Or you'll discover what you'd probably like to call my less charitable side."

March laughed.

"You're not in a position to show me anything, my dear."

Clare thought of Danny and Anna. She wanted to go to them, to save them, but she was powerless. But a few more minutes had passed. At least she was still alive. All she had to do was prolong that for as long as possible.

"Explain to me," she said, changing the subject, giving him a chance to show off. "You knew Lucy killed Tom."

"Of course."

"But you still arrested Emma."

"I did."

"Why?"

"Because it took some of the pressure off the bank."

"And you care about corporate PR all of a sudden?"

March seemed to find that hilarious.

"Oh, you haven't got a clue, have you?"

"Enlighten me."

"Why would I do that?"

"Because you're a smug bastard and you seem ever so pleased with yourself."

He tutted.

"Okay, so tell me why you killed Julian, instead?" she continued.

That took him by surprise. He looked as though he was going to deny it, but then he shrugged and started speaking.

"I knew Julian. I knew he was working for Otto. And I know Otto, of course, I know his reputation. We each have our groups of German friends."

"Except Otto is straight up, and you mix with the sewer rats?"

March ignored the jibe.

"I came across Julian when he started investigating the bank's relationship with Miroslav," he continued, "but then when Tom was killed, he started to ask too many questions. It got to the point where it wasn't tenable."

"What are you talking about?"

"It's obvious, isn't it? Because, my dear, it was only going to be a matter of time before he realised Tom wasn't gay."

———————

The headlights got brighter still as the car got closer. We both held our hands over our eyes to shield us from the glare. Then the car stopped, although the driver left the engine running.

We should have run, but we were rooted to the spot. Neither of us could make sense of anything any more.

But then the rear doors opened. Two people got out, one on either side. They started to walk towards us, turning into silhouettes as they walked in front of the car and got caught in the beam of the headlights. Danny reached out to hold me. I expect he'd also noticed that they were both carrying guns.

———————

"What do you mean he wasn't gay?" asked Clare.

"And that, you see, is beautiful. Because you try to pretend you're all-knowing and yet you made an assumption based on the fact he was a regular at a gay club."

"As were you, apparently."

"Indeed, but strictly in a business capacity. Tom, you see, may have seemed like the upstanding banker, but he had a little problem with the white stuff."

"Cocaine?"

"Quite. That's how I first got to know him. I was going to do him for possession, but then when we got chatting, I realised he was actually a very naughty boy indeed. He'd got himself into some fairly serious money trouble, but he developed a lucrative sideline to get out of it."

"Which was?"

"This is the 1990s. I know we're supposed to be enlightened, and tolerate poofs, and whatnot, but sadly, there are still those who haven't moved with the times. Tom got taken to the Smoking Gun by an extrovert client, and then spotted a business opportunity. He realised that there was a chance some of the clientele really shouldn't have been there. He was quite enterprising, was Tom, so he popped back on another day and gathered a little bit of photographic evidence. A small exchange of cash later, and the subject could walk away with the negatives. Everyone's a winner."

"Jesus. It's almost like you actually believe that."

March was on a roll.

"But he was also a banker, and understood a bit about the lending of money, and making investments that were hard to trace. Once he'd made a bit of capital, he branched out into financial services on a freelance business. At an appropriate rate of interest, of course."

"Loan sharking?"

"I call it more of a public service. Of course, once I found out about that, he realised he couldn't do it on his own, and he asked me to help him out on the legal side of his enterprise."

"So, to clarify, you were running a blackmail, extortion and loan sharking racket with Tom."

"If you want to be so coarse. So, when Lucy killed Tom in a familial temper tantrum, I really didn't think it would do any good to have things looked at too closely. But luckily Lucy, bless her, had already decided to frame the lovely Emma, because she was an easy target, and because she blamed Emma for putting Miroslav in touch with Tom in the first place. All I had to do was see it through."

"And Julian?"

"His trouble was that he didn't stop. He arranged to meet Christian from the bank, because he wanted to ask a few inappropriate questions about my former business partner. Well, I couldn't let that happen, obviously."

"So you killed him?"

"He rather brought it on himself. And of course, it didn't help having yourself and Danny looking too closely, either, but we've sorted that one out as well now. All is well that ends well. And talking of which, I'm very pleased to announce that your time to say goodbye has come."

He walked to the back of the room, and took a picture from the wall, revealing a safe hidden behind. After a few taps on the keypad, the door sprang open.

"You know, I'm tired of your voice. Tired of your face. Tired of even being in the same room as you. I think it's time to get this over with, don't you?"

He took a handgun from the safe, then loaded it while Clare watched him dispassionately.

"Say hello to your passport to daddy," he said, as he turned to walk towards her.

Chapter 47

AS the men got closer, I realised that I knew who one of them was. It was Otto. Him again. My head was spinning.

"Are you okay?" he shouted, above the noise of the engine. "We need to get moving."

It took a moment for realisation to hit. If Clare couldn't come to rescue us, this was the next best thing. We ran towards him, grasping the need for urgency.

"What's happening?" Danny asked him.

"I need to get you somewhere safe. But we need to be quick," he said. "Get in the car."

"What's with the guns?"

But before he had the chance to answer, a shot rang out, and the window in front of us shattered. I instinctively ducked. Danny did the same as another shot pinged off the metalwork of the car. It was like the first drops of rain in a particularly violent thunderstorm. Otto crouched down with surprising agility, and returned fire, but I didn't know where the shooting had come from. I don't think he did, either. Somewhere, in the dark, from the cover of the waste ground, someone was trying to kill us.

And then another shot came in from the other side. The rear side window this time. A fourth whistled past me, connecting with the door just as I was about to open it. Otto and his colleague shot back, but it was impossible to see the enemy. All we knew was that there was more than one of them.

"Keep your heads down," he shouted as Danny and I scrambled into the back of the car. I tried to squeeze across the footwell, with Danny piled on top of me.

Otto's colleague screamed in pain as a round ripped through his arm. A few inches to the right and it would have been fatal. He collapsed across the rear seat while Otto returned one last volley from the passenger side. And then, as another window shattered, he managed to get far enough inside that the driver could floor the throttle and get us the hell out of there. I could hardly see a thing, just a small sliver in the gap between the front seats, but it was enough to scare me senseless.

Otto's door swung open as the driver pulled hard to the left. I thought he was going to fall, but the driver reached out and grabbed him just in time. But in so doing, he lost control of the steering. All I could hear was gunfire and the screaming of an engine being revved to the limit. Otto managed to pull himself back inside, and hold on to the grab handle above the door, giving the driver a chance to regain control. And then he flicked through the gears, lurching us hard across the rough terrain, but picking up speed as he did so. I felt warm blood from the man lying on the seat above us dripping onto my face, but somehow, miraculously, we were all still alive. I had no idea where we were going.

***

"You're a bastard, Graham," said Clare, looking from the advancing barrel of the gun up to his cold, heartless eyes.

"I recoil at your animosity. Of course, there's a possibility

Danny may survive the night, but even then, the prognosis isn't good. As you may know, he's been a naughty boy. Hit and run, phone tapping. Possibly even a little bit of murder."

"All of which is complete bollocks, if you excuse the technical terminology."

"That's for others to decide, once they've seen the evidence."

"Which you fabricated."

"Well, maybe polished to make it easier for a jury to appreciate. Anyway, the point is, he's got other things to be concerned about rather than poking his nose into police investigations, especially when they've been undertaken by yours truly."

"Even though you arrested an innocent woman?"

"She's hardly that. I mean yes, she's a lovely lady, but she's shown a shocking disregard for the sanctity of her marital vows."

"Oh, that's outstanding coming from you. But when you've stopped talking shit, could you at least let me know why you're doing this to me?"

March stood in front of Clare, legs slightly apart, holding the gun with both hands, as his right index finger closed in on the trigger. She was powerless to move. The more she strained at the cable ties, the harder they bit.

"Well, I think there are some scores to be settled, don't you?" he said. "Last time we had some time to ourselves, in sunny Sofia, you arranged for four of your friends to give me the opposite of what I like to call a friendly reception."

Despite the gravity of the situation, Clare couldn't suppress a final, ironic smile.

"Graham, has the syphilis finally claimed your remaining brain cell? As you very well know, the four friends you refer to had been hired by you to take me somewhere to be executed. Luckily for me, I knew what you were up to and managed to outbid you. So if they gave you a lesson in manners, which I very much hope they did, it was entirely of your own making."

"Not good enough, Clare. Admittedly I chose badly but you could have stopped them. You'll notice I haven't made the same mistake this time."

If nothing else, she could try one last attempt to appeal to any remaining shred of humanity.

"Can I just point out, this was just a few months after I saved your life in a warehouse? And you repay me by arranging to have me killed? You've got a funny way of showing gratitude."

"Business is business, my dear."

"Yeah, and how is business? Still managing to run your little financial services enterprise without your partner? I'm surprised you didn't kill him yourself, so you didn't have to split the profits."

"The thought did cross my mind."

"According to Otto, the Germans have disowned you."

"Otto is an ageing fool."

"He says you're a has-been. Arguably a never-was. A mere pretender, out of his depth, led by his genitals without the wherewithal to be of any lasting value to anyone. And those are just your best bits."

March let go of the gun with his right hand and slapped her across the face.

"Oh, and now the big man thinks it's clever to hit women? Is that what you do to your prostitutes, Graham?"

"I can hit you harder if you'd like."

"I'm sure you could. But where would it get you? And where is the colleague you arrested me with? Surely he's expecting me at the station?"

"He does as he's told. He's learning fast."

"Oh God."

"So you see, I've had to make a decision. Do I take you in, and see you locked up for life in the relative comfort of Holloway? Seems a bit too luxurious if you don't mind me saying. Or maybe I should have let you go running to Danny's rescue and watched as you got taken in the crossfire. Endless possibilities. All of them intriguing."

"And you don't think I could rescue them without putting myself in danger?"

"Well, that was the risk, of course. So finally, I decided I should make sure the job's done properly by doing it myself. You know the saying."

"And what happens if Danny and Anna get killed by the Serbians? Or whoever you think may be about to shoot them?"

"We'll arrest the killers, obviously, but not until they've had their bit of fun. Too late for you by that stage of course."

Clare stopped. And then this time the smile was genuine.

"Oh, Graham, you do make me laugh. I do sometimes wonder. You've really got no idea, have you?"

"Meaning?"

"Meaning you haven't got the faintest clue."

And at that moment the door caved in.

311

Chapter 48

AHEAD of me, the two men with guns burst through a door. There were shouts of 'Drop your weapon!' and I heard a metallic clunk. Otto waved us into the room, and there, much to my surprise, I saw Graham March, hands in the air, with an expression of utter shock on his face.

Otto took a penknife from his pocket and started to cut Clare's bindings as one of the men punched Graham hard in the stomach. He fell to the floor, gasping for air, the force of the blow knocking all of the air from his lungs.

March looked terrified. I'm not a vindictive person, but it was a wonderful sight.

"You're going to have to try harder than this, Graham," said Clare, standing above him, rubbing her wrists.

He looked up with fear in his eyes as she picked up his gun and aimed it at him.

"Should I kill you? Is that what you want? Or should I ask my friend Otto to do it for me? Your choice."

She looked over her shoulder at the big German.

"You know that wouldn't be wise," he said. "We've always got on. We understand each other."

"I understand you're a duplicitous self-centred bastard. Give me one reason why I shouldn't end it now."

"We have our disagreements, but you know you need me."

"Do I?"

"Our friends in Germany wouldn't be happy."

"*Our* friends in Germany? Graham, look around you! Who do you think just smashed your door down? You've got no idea about the scale of the network. You may have persuaded Stefan to give little Anna a scare. But you've very much outlived your usefulness where the big boys are concerned. And that puts you in a very delicate position."

"Bollocks." He tried to snatch the gun, but it was a futile gesture. Clare was one step ahead. She stood on his hand as it touched the floor, causing him to wince.

"In fact, I'd go so far as to say you've become a liability," she said.

"But I saved you." He was sounding ever more desperate. "You could have been locked up now, looking at a life sentence."

"You really think that? You really think this is the only safety net I have?"

And then she fired the gun. Instinctively I closed my eyes. It was incredibly loud. When I reopened them, I saw that the bullet had missed his leg by inches, shooting up shards and splinters of floorboard.

"Just checking it was loaded," said Clare.

"Jesus, you mad bitch. Okay, I'll let you walk free."

"You'll do what?"

"You can go. Call it quits."

"God, you're pathetic. I'll tell you what you're going to do. You're going to phone your office now, while I listen in. And you're going to tell them that all the made-up shit you tried to pin on Danny was the product of your addled mind."

"You know I can't do that."

Clare wasn't in the mood for negotiation. A second bullet

exploded through his trouser leg, missing his knee by millimetres, but still close enough to burn.

"Jesus fuck!"

"It's not even a skin graze, you cry-baby. The only reason I didn't shoot you in the cock was because I didn't want to risk getting hit by the debris of the thing. I'm not going to ask you again."

"Get me a fucking ambulance."

She smashed him across the face with the butt of the gun. Blood erupted from his mouth.

"Last chance, Graham."

"I'm fucking bleeding to death here," he said, his voice distorted by the gaps where his teeth had been.

"I've not even shot you yet. But I can. Make the call."

"Oh, for fuck's sake."

Otto passed him a phone. The look in March's eyes was pure hatred, as he dialled a number. As soon as the call connected, Clare grabbed the phone and put it on speaker, so we could all listen in.

"Who is this?" she said.

"DC Lisa Miller. Who's that?"

"It doesn't matter. I was just checking he'd rung the right number. Can you record this?"

"I can."

"Perfect. Let me know when you've started, and I'll pass you back."

And then we watched as DCI Graham March confessed his sins. He admitted running a campaign of intimidation against Danny, and fabricating evidence of the hit and run. He admitted the accusations of phone tapping were groundless. He explained Danny had a watertight alibi for the shooting of Julian and then said something about travelling on a fake passport that I must have previously missed out on.

When he'd finished, Clare took the phone again.

"Lisa, did you get all that?"

"I did."

"Perfect. Anything else you need?"

"No, I don't think so. Is that Clare?"

"Never heard of her," said Clare. "But tell Amy I said hello."

There was a great sense of calm once the call was finished. March was still sitting on the floor, looking bloodied and beaten. Clare and two of Otto's men were still pointing their weapons at him. He couldn't go anywhere.

Then Clare put her gun in her pocket.

"Listen to me," she said. "I'm going to let you live, because I'm a nice person. And because putting you out of your misery would deny the world the privilege of watching you suffer. But let me tell you this: it ends here, okay?"

March closed his eyes. He seemed to be listening, but his face was contorted in pain.

"In the highly unlikely event that your friends in the upper echelons of the Force, or wherever the scumbags reside, manage to get you off the hook on this one, there's one thing above all others that you need to understand. If you ever, *ever*, try to come after me again, or lift so much as a finger in the direction of Danny, or Anna, I'll make sure you die in so much pain you'll hate me for not simply having ended it now. But you know what? I won't actually care. Because you're an evil bastard, Graham. You're a selfish, deluded, psychopathic fuck."

She turned to Otto's henchmen and gave them a signal. Both men lowered their guns.

"We'll lock the door on our way out but I'm sure you'll find a way of opening it. Just know that I'm not joking. I don't want to see you ever again, okay?"

March just nodded, eyes clenched.

But then with astonishing agility, he made a desperate lunge at one of Otto's men, grabbed his gun, and went racing out of the door.

315

Chapter 49

THERE was mayhem. Everyone surged past me through the door. But March had summoned an amazing turn of pace for someone so portly. I looked out just in time to see a door bang at the far end of the corridor. Otto's men ran towards it, with Danny and the man himself in close pursuit. Clare stopped briefly, only to ask me if I was okay, and then went racing after them.

There was a lot of shouting, and then yet more gunfire. I'd heard enough in one night to last a lifetime. I tentatively made my way to the far door, and pulled it slightly open. There was a staircase behind. March had clearly run upwards to have the benefit of height. Bullets were whizzing in both directions. There was a cacophony of voices, interspersed with guns being fired, and the sound of bullets pinging off railings. I saw Clare telling Danny to stay back, but they seemed to be making progress, a flight at a time, sometimes quickly, sometimes slowly, but always rising.

And then, it all fell silent. I followed as quickly as I could, desperate to make sure everyone was okay.

An icy breeze was flowing down the staircase. When I reached the final flight I understood why. There was an open door, which looked like it led out onto the rooftop. Everybody else had disappeared so I followed, going as carefully as I could while still trying to get there quickly.

I reached the door and looked out. I don't know how high we were, but there was a splendid panorama of the city at night. There were lights in the distance, of tower blocks and bridges, but the roof was only illuminated by the same weak moonlight that we'd had on the waste ground.

I could just about make out the shape of Otto's men standing on the far side, then Clare to my right. Otto and Danny were midway between, crouching behind an air conditioning unit. I couldn't see March. Had he jumped? Was he hiding? Clare ran across to Danny and Otto, gun raised, while one of the others covered her. I tried to signal across to them, but their attention was elsewhere, and they probably couldn't have seen me anyway.

I wanted to join them, but I didn't know if it was safe. I took a small step forward to get a better view of the rest of the roof.

And that's when March grabbed me.

I screamed, and tried to fight, but I was no match for someone over twice my size. Especially when he had me in a bear-like grip, with the barrel of a gun pointing at my temple.

"Let her go, Graham," shouted Clare. She started walking towards us, gun extended. One of Otto's guards approached from the other direction. There were three weapons, all pointed directly at me, and nobody seemed particularly stable.

"I said to let her go," she repeated.

"Or what? You'll kill both of us?" said March. "Put down your weapons, or I'll shoot."

"You won't do that," said Clare.

I wasn't sure. From the corner of my eye I could see his finger on the trigger. It was trembling. His whole body was shaking, whether from adrenaline or fatigue, I couldn't be sure. There was a terrible smell of stale sweat.

He started walking backwards, pulling me with him, never once loosening his grip.

"Stop where you are and put the gun down," warned Clare. But March didn't stop. And the others kept advancing.

"Is this what you wanted?" he shouted, his voice laced with bitterness. "The amazing Clare, with yet more blood on her hands? Is it? Is this what gets you off? Is that what does it for you?"

He kept dragging me back, further and further across the roof, further and further away from the staircase. And all the time the others were advancing, fanning out to cover him from all angles.

And then we couldn't go any further. I dared to look back, and my heart nearly stopped. All that was between us and perhaps a ten-storey drop was a concrete wall that only reached halfway up my thighs.

"I told you to put your guns down," he shouted. "I'm going to count to three."

"Graham, don't be stupid," shouted Clare. My spirits leapt when I noticed reinforcements gathering behind her. Four police marksmen appeared, all with weapons raised. Standing in the middle was Amy. But my optimism vanished as quickly as it came. It didn't matter how many guns were aimed at Graham. The one that would kill me had its cold barrel digging into my flesh.

"One," he shouted.

"Let Anna go. She's never done anything to hurt you."

"Two."

"Graham…" Her voice was getting louder. The guns were raised. At any minute we'd both be blown away. And if the bullets didn't get me, the fall to certain death would.

"Final chance, Clare."

He paused. My heart nearly did the job for all of them.

"Put your gun down, Graham."

"Two and a half."

And then Danny stepped out, and started walking towards us.

"Graham, you haven't got a problem with Anna," he said, his voice conveying a calmness and certainty that I'd never heard before. "She's never done anything to you. I know why you've got a problem with Clare and I know why you've got a problem with me, but Anna is nothing to do with any of this."

"Stop there, Danny boy."

But he didn't stop. He kept walking towards us, slowly and calmly, his eyes fixed on the man standing behind me.

"I'm not armed," he said, holding his arms aloft. "Look." He removed his jacket and dropped it on the floor. "See? Just me. I understand why you want to take somebody, but take me, Graham. You don't want to leave me free to write about you, do you? To tell the world about everything you've been up to? I'm the one you want, Graham. Let go of Anna and take me."

"I told you to stop walking, you - you worthless prick."

Danny stopped. He was about two thirds of the way towards us.

"You can shoot me if you want. You can throw me off the roof. Your choice. But I'm the one you hate, Graham. I'm the one who's been pursuing you. I'm the one who got you suspended and now I'm the one who's going to tell the world all about you. Let go of Anna. Take me."

Time seemed to stop. Danny stood in front of us, his white shirt billowing in the breeze. He took another step forward.

"I'm warning you, Danny. One more step."

Danny stopped.

"Come on, Graham, do the sensible thing. Look around you. You've got an audience. You're the centre of attention. It's what you always wanted. But there's no escape. Not this time. Either put down the gun and take the consequences, or keep it and kill me. For once in your miserable life, try to be a man."

"Three."

With that, everything happened at once. I felt March loosen

319

his grip, just a fraction, and I dived for my life. As I fell, I saw him raise his gun, pointing it straight at Danny, who was no more than a few feet away. And then I heard the guns.

Bullets ripped into March from all directions, but not before he'd offloaded his own weapon into Danny. I screamed, then watched as the force of the assault swept March backwards, and over the wall. I saw Danny fall to the floor, his white shirt turning red in the dim light of the moon. My last thought was that the story would never be written. That I'd never again see his beautiful eyes. And then everything went black.

Chapter 50

Three months later: Friday, March 8th, 1996

T HE door to the balcony was fastened open, the net curtains pulled back, but moving gently in the breeze. From outside I could hear distant voices and the gentle splash of water as gondolas and Vaporetto waterbuses plied their trade on Venice's Grand Canal.

I lay on my bed, propped up on pillows, succumbing to the calm. But my eyes were sore and my head felt tender. I couldn't remember when I'd last slept through without a nightmare, assuming I'd managed to drift off in the first place. Miroslav and his minders had been arrested. Graham March was dead. Word had come from Bulgaria, via Amy, that Aleksander, far from being a Croatian hitman, was actually working as a spy for NATO, keeping an eye on whatever we'd been up to. But every time I closed my eyes, my brain flashed images that would haunt me forever. I picked up my book, but my mind, as always, was elsewhere.

"It's Torcello tomorrow, isn't it?"

"What?"

"You're going to Torcello, aren't you?"

The voice brought me out of my daydream. I looked up as Clare walked back into the room, her cigarette safely extinguished. She came over and sat on the end of the bed.

"Book good?" she asked.

"Not really."

"What is it?"

I looked at the cover, then put it aside.

"I've got no idea. I must have read a hundred pages and I don't think I've taken in a word."

I knew that she understood, that no further explanation was necessary. She sighed, then went over to the sink and washed her hands.

"Cup of tea?" she asked.

"Hmmm. If you can concoct one." I had little enthusiasm. There were tiny bags of a generic so-called English Breakfast tea, and a supply of long-life milk in individual plastic pots. I hadn't had much tea over the last three months. Part of the ritual was having somebody to make it for, and seeing a single cup on the counter was yet another reminder that I was now living on my own. That Danny was no longer with me. That he'd taken a bullet to save me. And that my life would never be the same again.

"What are you doing in Torcello?" Clare asked, as she attempted to make the best of limited resources.

"It's just an ad for a hat company."

"A hat company?"

"Yes. No idea why Torcello, but it's what the art director wanted."

"It's good that you're back working. And you get to spend a few days in Venice."

"I suppose."

She put the tea on my bedside table. It looked a passable colour, but it was only a tiny cup.

"Thank you," I said.

She sat back on the end of the bed.

"I hope you didn't mind me popping in. I heard you were here and... Well, I just thought it would be good to see you. I didn't know if you'd want to see me, though."

"You just happened to be in Venice?"

She smiled and started to play with her ring, which was a sure sign she was up to something.

"You know me too well," she said.

"Ha."

I propped myself up on the bed.

"Okay, I had a couple of free days. I knew you were here, and I knew you were on your own and..." She looked towards the balcony. "I don't know, I just thought I should come to see you. I understand if you want me to go again, and disappear forever this time."

I sighed.

"Oh, Clare. I don't blame you. Really, I don't. I'm just... Sorry, I'm not used to talking about it."

She nodded and reached out for my hand.

"I understand."

"It's good to see you, though," I said. "Honestly. Where are you staying?"

"Room 103 on the floor below."

That got my attention. She caught me looking at her, and appeared worried.

"I'm sorry," she said, "that probably sounds awful, like I'm stalking you. I'm really not. I'll keep out of your way. It's just that I've stayed here before and it's lovely."

"It's not that," I said, starting to smile. "It's just that in all the time I've known you, you've never, ever told me where you were staying."

"Really?'

"You've always drifted in and out, all mysterious and

323

intriguing, never telling me, just disappearing off and returning the next day, as if from nowhere."

The look of concern turned into a frown.

"Do I really do that? I don't mean to."

I laughed.

"That is the most ridiculous thing I've ever heard. Of course you know you do that. You must do."

"No, honestly. I just never liked to feel I was imposing on you, or getting in the way of you and Danny..." Her voice faded to silence as she realised she'd mentioned his name. Just the sound of the word played havoc with my emotions.

"I'm sorry," she said.

"How are you?" I asked, changing the subject.

"I'm okay."

"Sure?"

She thought for a moment.

"It's hard, you know?" she said eventually. "But you know what we should do? We ought to go out for an amazing lunch, my treat, and have as many bottles of the finest wine as we can get through, right up to the point where we have no idea how to find our way back."

"It's easy to get lost in Venice."

"It is. We shall take a map, though. And when we do get back, I promise that you can ask me any question you like, and I will give you an honest answer."

That really did make me laugh.

"*Any* question?"

"Any question at all."

"Even about boyfriends, and where you live, and what you actually do all day?"

"Even that."

"Wow. I'll put my shoes on."

She lay down beside me on the bed, then propped herself up on one elbow, looking at me.

"There's only one tiny little condition," she said, making a shape with her fingers.

"Oh, here we go. Which is?"

"You don't tell anyone else."

"And you get me so drunk I'll have forgotten it all by the time I wake up with a storming hangover?"

"And again, you know me too well."

I smiled.

"Come here," I said, then reached out and gave her a hug. As ever, it felt special to spend a moment in her presence.

"If Danny could see us now he'd be green with envy," I said, after a moment.

"I know." It was touching to see that the thought of him, and the way that it ended, brought moisture to her all-knowing hazel eyes.

"I do miss him, you know," she said, eventually. "I can't imagine what it must be like for you."

I let go of her and sat up on the bed, then sighed with an overwhelming sadness. The image of that night still robbed me of all my energy, leaving me with a hollow feeling of utter injustice.

"I miss him terribly. Every day. Every morning when I wake up, assuming I've been to sleep. I miss his smile. I miss the fact he's not there to talk to. I even miss the things I used to find really annoying."

"I understand that."

"But... "

"I know what you're about to say."

"Do you?"

"I think so. But say it anyway."

"Okay." I paused, trying to find the words. "But, you know what? When they finally let him come home, and he wants me to look after him, and he keeps suggesting I wear that bloody nurse's uniform, a tiny little part of me will want to give him a slap."

325

Clare laughed.

"I mean, for God's sake. That's the second time I've seen him get shot in front of me, and he doesn't half like to make a meal of it."

"But he's on the mend, though?"

"Fingers crossed he's finally home by next weekend."

"That's fantastic news."

"Admittedly this time it was a bit more serious, but I'll still tell him it was just a graze and to get over himself."

Clare reached over, put her arm round my shoulders, and pulled me towards her.

"He's very, very lucky to have you," she said.

"I shall make sure he knows that."

She let go of me, then moved to edge of the bed and stood up.

"So, lunch?"

I nodded.

"That would be lovely. Thank you. And you're sure I can ask you absolutely any question?"

I couldn't quite read her expression, but it looked suitably mysterious.

"I think I may regret having said that," she said.

But she was as good as her word. And three bottles of wonderful wine later, she'd told me an awful lot of things that she regretted even more.

The End.

33238/UK0001B/316/P
UKHW040633151118
Milton Keynes UK
Lightning Source UK Ltd.

Also available: **Out Of the Red** - book 2 in the Anna Burgin series

The gripping, twist-filled sequel to Cold Press.

Investigative journalist Danny Churchill is hot on the trail of Graham March - the disgraced former police DCI. The investigation takes him to Germany where he soon starts to uncover dark secrets and new depths of depravity.

Back in London, and aided by his flatmate - fashion photographer Anna Burgin - Danny's investigation intensifies, but as he gets closer to the truth, the body count starts to rise.

Help is offered from the most unlikely of sources, but if Danny accepts, is he doing a deal with the devil herself?

If you enjoyed Fade To Silence, you should read **Cold Press** - book 1 in the Anna Burgin series.

London. 1993. Investigative journalist Clare Woodbrook goes missing on the brink of unveiling her biggest-ever story. Is it kidnap? Murder?

Worse still, the police investigation into her disappearance is being headed up by a corrupt DCI - himself the subject of one of Clare's current investigations.

Clare's researcher Danny Churchill sets out to find her, and enlists the help of his flatmate - feisty fashion photographer Anna Burgin. But they soon realise that nobody can be trusted. And as the search becomes ever more desperate, suddenly their own lives are very much on the line.

Packed with intrigue, twists, conspiracies, and dark humour, Cold Press is a hugely entertaining British thriller, with a sting in the tail.

SPECIAL THANKS...

Fade To Silence was a lot of fun to write, partly on location in Bulgaria and Devon, but mainly snuggled up at home with candles.

Huge thanks to Jeff King, Peggy Holland, Jonathan Killin, Barbara Woods, Luna Tune and everyone else who reviewed the previous books on Amazon and Goodreads. Your feedback and encouragement is a huge help and motivation.

It was a pleasure to meet the amazing Clare Davidson during the writing process - and fellow Actors Studio students Lea, Rachel, Natasha, Vicky, John, Oriana, Alexa, Diana and Shayla. Pinewood was a blast and Torcello is for you. :-)

And, as ever, huge thanks to my editor, Carrie O'Grady, for vision, clarity, and making me smile.

FEEL FREE TO SAY HELLO... :-)

If you enjoyed the book, have any queries, or just want to say hello, I'd love to hear from you via www.davidbradwell.com.

While you're there, you can also download a FREE copy of the series prequel - In The Frame:

Photography student Anna Burgin didn't expect to be arrested, but she's the only suspect for a series of crimes, and the Police have found damning evidence in her room. But Anna has no recollection of doing anything wrong. Was it a moment of madness? Or is somebody setting out to destroy her? And is the stranger in the bar really trying to help, or just part of an evil conspiracy?

You can also follow me on Twitter: @dbshq - or see what Anna is up to: @AnnaBurginNW1